Confessions of a Reformed Tom Cat

DAISY PRESCOTT

ebook ISBN: 978-0-9864177-9-5

Paperback ISBN: 978-1-7329580-1-2

Cover Design by ©Julianne Burke at Heart to Cover

Editing: Melissa Ringsted at There for You Editing

Proofreading: Marla Esposito at Proofing with Style

Formatting: Jennifer Beach

For my readers, who asked me to reform Tom

PROLOGUE

W hen she walked toward me, I was ninety-percent certain she wanted to slap me. I spread my stance and tensed for the impact. Sadly, she wouldn't be the first woman to smack me or attempt it. Good thing I was pretty fast at dodging and weaving.

I held her gaze as she got closer. Part of me wanted to close my eyes and turn the other cheek ... literally. Or back down the hall and hide in the men's room. Ah, the men's bathroom. A place no woman dared to go unless absolutely necessary. Urinals freaked them out.

I took a big step backward and then another until the darkness of the hall to the back room enveloped me. I wasn't running. Far from it. I moved slowly and kept my eyes on my assailant stalking toward me.

I probably should have asked myself why she wanted to slap me. Had I stopped to think, I might have realized unlike most women with the same expression on their face, I hadn't actually given her a reason to be mad at me. At least none I knew about.

Her eyes narrowed and she cut the distance between us in half with two long strides. To my left was the door to the bathroom and potential salvation. Further behind me stood the backdoor and freedom. While I debated hiding or fleeing, she made the decision for me by grabbing the front of my shirt.

"Hey, what's up?" Always act innocent. In this case, I didn't have to act.

"I've been looking all over for you tonight."

I raised an eyebrow. "You have?"

She stared at my mouth and pressed her lips together. "I have. Why is a good man hard to find when you need him?"

Her words rearranged themselves in my head after she'd spoken them. "Don't you mean a hard man is good to find when you need him?"

She snorted out a laugh. "Exactly. You read my mind." Her hand not clutching my shirt touched the bared skin above my belt.

"Hey, whoa, where you going with that hand?" I jerked my hips back to escape her wandering fingers.

"I need a good man. And since I don't know any good men, I decided I needed a hard man tonight."

"Okay." I grabbed her hands in mine to protect myself from her assault. "Can I ask you one thing?"

"Sssure."

The subtle slur answered my question, but I asked it anyway. "Have you been drinking?"

"Tommm, don't be mean. You sleep with everyone on the island. I need you to sleep with me. Now." The slight rasp to her voice had strengthened into a sultry purr.

Definitely not sober. "What happened to your own man? Have sex with him."

She pressed a finger to my lips. "No talking, more sex."

"More implies there's some sex to begin with." I couldn't figure out why I bothered to argue. Sex without strings was my thing.

But could I have stringless sex with her? I had rules.

While I was lost in some sort of moral debate, she kissed me.

Worse, my body responded, and I liked it. A lot.

She was an amazing kisser—even buzzed and with grabby hands, her lips and tongue teased mine with a balance of aggression and skill.

When she bit my bottom lip, I did the smart thing. I kissed her back.

ONE

Confession:
I don't do the dating thing.

I headed toward open water with the outbound current. Going with the flow, motor puttering a small wake as I steered the *Master Baiter* out of Langley Harbor in the late summer afternoon, nothing could have been easier. Saratoga Passage lay smooth and deep blue ahead of my bow. Not a care in the world. That was me.

Summer was winding down. Labor Day meant the end to the official summer season. Tourists would dwindle to drabs, and that meant my pickings for hook-ups were about to decline. I frowned at the thought of the summer fun ending. Now that I'd lost my wingman, John, to his better-looking better-half, more than summer was over. Not to be sentimental, but it felt like the end of an era.

I glanced behind me at my best friend and his girlfriend sitting in the sun, the wind tangling through Diane's long brown hair. She didn't seem to notice. Her head was thrown back in laughter at something the big oaf had said. I'd known John since childhood and we'd been each other's partners in crime ever since. Borrowing a truck at fourteen, stealing beers at seventeen, and breaking hearts along the way, he was the brother I never had and I was the family he needed when his fell apart. Despite myself, I smiled at their happiness. He would marry that girl someday.

And what did that mean for me?

Nothing.

Tom Cats aren't the marrying kind.

The best I could hope for was one of Diane's bridesmaids would be hot. And single. Or not.

Tan arms draped across my shoulders and blonde hair blew in a sweet, girly cloud around my face.

Right.

Kiersti, the girl of the moment.

Or was it Kristi?

"Babe, I can't see through all your hair." Babe always seemed to work with the girls I hung around; calling it dating made it sound too formal.

Female laughter rang in my ears. The hand moving into the waistband of my shorts didn't solve the problem of blindness from blonde hair that wasn't my own.

"I can't steer if I can't see."

"I'll help you steer. I'll hold the throttle," she purred into my ear.

"That's not the throttle," I removed her hand from the front of my shorts, "and you steer with the wheel. Throttle makes us go fast." Sometimes I pretended chicks were toddlers. Easier than explaining the big words.

"Fine." She flopped into the seat next to mine and extended her long, tan legs toward the front of my shorts. Amazing how nimble her toes could be.

I stared over my shoulder, willing Diane to entertain my guest. This outing had been her idea. Being on my boat meant I'd be busy steering and getting us up the island to Coupeville in one piece. Not receiving hand-and-foot-jobs in the middle of open water.

Wait.

That wasn't necessarily a bad thing.

Boats and sex went hand in hand—no pun intended—and had since I was a teenager, when my dad let me take his boat out with "friends" to go "fishing" or pull traps. As long as I showed up with a story about the one that got away or a few crabs, my parents believed me. Or ignored the hickeys peeking out from the collar of my T-shirts.

However, there was no way I'd get off in front of an audience.

Kiersti/Kristi's foot moved dangerously close to my crotch. A few choppy waves from another wake, and I'd end up with bruised balls. Something needed to be done.

"Hey, Diane," I called over my shoulder. "You should tell the story about Dave's mounted deer head." It wasn't even a great story, but my pointed look caught Diane's attention. When she saw the location of K's foot, she laughed and rolled her eyes at me. I stood up and the offending foot dropped.

"Kiersti, come sit and I'll tell you the fascinating story about a stuffed deer head in my old cabin."

Kiersti.

John stood and gave up his spot, taking the recently abandoned seat near me. "Smooth move, Donnely. By the way, I'm not rubbing you with my foot."

I groaned.

"She seems," he paused, "nice. Where'd you find her?"

"Over in Seattle. She's not much of a talker."

"I can see that. Looks like she prefers to communicate with body language." His sunglasses covered his eyes, but through his thick, dark beard I saw him fighting a smile.

"It explains why we're taking the boat up to Tobey's. Trying to impress the town girl?"

I shrugged. "It was your girlfriend's idea, but it's a gorgeous day, and I figured it'd be nice to be out on the water."

"And?"

He knew me well. "It's difficult to have a conversation going full speed on the water," I shouted as I opened up the engine and pushed to cruising speed.

The girls yelped when the spray wet the seats, causing them to move from the stern to the little table inside the cockpit, bringing with them the scent of salty water and sunscreen.

I smirked at John.

Who needed conversation anyway?

———

Turned out, Kiersti was allergic to shellfish and didn't like any seafood. She regaled us about her hives and swelling while she picked at a plate of grilled cheese and fries. How could you be from Washington and not eat any fish? Allergies I understood, but salmon was lifeblood. She wrinkled her nose at the idea of fried salmon and chips. I put her on the "nice knowing you list" after she stole both pieces of garlic bread that came with my mussels.

Sipping my pint of beer, I stared out the window while she explained her goal of becoming a cupcake empire.

"Oh, so you like baking?" Diane asked. Thank God for Diane. She appeared to be listening and asked questions at the right time. John kept coughing, but behind each cough was a laugh he tried to cover-up.

This was why I didn't date.

"I don't bake. Or cook," Kiersti replied. "I really love cupcakes. They're so small and pretty. Like little puffy hearts of cake."

Puffy hearts?

No way.

I tapped my knuckles on the table twice like a fighter

tapping out from a match. John caught my meaning and offered to go up to the bar for another round of drinks. I went with him.

While we waited, I stared at the moose head above the entrance to the bathrooms. Lucky bastard had glass eyes and stuffing between his ears. Didn't have to put up with yammering about puffy hearts of cake. Then again, he was dead.

"Hi, Tom."

I turned toward the familiar voice. Long red curls framed a pretty face.

"Hi, Ashley." I smiled down at her

Ashley Curtis was a repeater. Someone I could hang out with, have occasional sex with, and she never clung or demanded... or refused to eat seafood.

"You remember John, right?"

She smiled at him and he nodded.

"What've you been up to?" I asked, knowing it had been at least since April since I'd last seen her.

"Oh, you know. Summer."

Ashley was easy. Not in a trashy way, not at all. Easy because she knew what she wanted and knew me enough to not ask for anything more than what she saw.

"We should hang out soon."

She leaned around me to glance at the table. "Your date doesn't appear too happy about you talking to me."

I glanced over my shoulder where Kiersti glowered at me. Sheesh. I was only talking to someone. Yeah, that someone was a hot redhead, but Ashley could be anyone. Like my sister or even worse, one of my sisters' friends.

"Don't worry about her. Let's hang out this weekend."

She scanned my face and I gave her a wink, then flashed my signature dimpled grin.

"Sure. I'm around."

"Great. I'm looking forward to it."

John cleared his throat and held up our round of drinks. "Nice seeing you again, Ashley."

"You too." She gave us a little wave.

"Nicely played there," he said on our way back to the table.

"Always good to have a back-up plan." I slid into the booth.

"Back up plan for what?" Kiersti asked, peering over her shoulder at the bar.

"Bad weather when you're out on the water," I lied.

"I'd freak out if we got caught in a storm," Diane said.

"Don't you have a rule about always being able to see land? How bad could it be if you did get caught in a squall?"

"That's true, but John wants to go up to the San Juans. It's like eight hours in the boat."

"Friday Harbor?" I asked John.

"Roche."

"So romantic." I fluttered my lashes at him. He was so whipped. Everyone knew Roche Harbor was romance central in the San Juans. I think they pumped subliminal romantic messages over speakers hidden all over the resort.

"We should all go together!" Kiersti suggested, clearly oblivious to my sarcasm.

Diane and John smiled at me from across the table and waited.

"Yeah, sure." I gave her a half-smile.

After I dropped her off at the ferry, I'd probably never see her again. I wouldn't leave her hanging. I'd text her and let her down easy. Tell her it was me, not her. Or something like that.

I wasn't an asshole.

As we walked out of the tavern, I caught Ashley's eye and gave her a wink.

Kiersti was pretty cold on the walk to the boat slip.

Okay, maybe I was a little bit of an asshole.

Oh well.

Cats don't change their stripes.

Or was that tigers?

TWO

Confession:
Doesn't matter the place or time, I will check out a beautiful woman.

Saturdays were for working in my wood shop. Or if it was fall, watching college football. WSU was playing this weekend and a bunch of guys planned to get together to watch the game, drink beers, eat burgers, the usual.

Sounded great.

Unless you were me.

My mother called me twice before noon to remind me of my youngest sister's baby shower and how devastated Lori would be if I didn't show up.

Yeah, right.

Why would she want her brother at her baby shower? My uncle duties didn't begin until the kid would be able to speak and ride in a boat. Same rule as applied to Cara's and Amy's kids. No diapers, no vomit, no babysitting, and limited interaction until they were human. From what I could tell, that started around five, maybe six.

Oh, and no dolls. I'd teach them how to gut a fish, kill a

crab, and carve a tree branch when they could hold a knife. Fun uncle, that was me.

I glanced at the clock. Three sisters meant three weddings, and now what felt like endless baby showers. Not to mention all of my cousins and their weddings and showers. Any recent population explosions on South Whidbey were the direct result of Donnelys marrying and breeding.

My ninja skills were well honed by this point—the curse of a big family. If I timed it right, I could show up at my parents' farmhouse at the end of the shower, be a good son and brother, then grab the leftover snacks to bring down to John's on the beach for the second half of the first Cougars' game of the season.

If I'd stalled long enough, the party should end twenty minutes after I turned up the long, fern-lined, dirt road. My grandfather, Clifford, grew up in the house and had passed it down to my dad when it got to be too much for him and Gramma Ellie. They had built a smaller house on the property where they could still be close to family. Lots of history here.

The woods opened up to reveal the wide meadow surrounding the house where it sat on a high bluff overlooking the shipping lanes. Over the years, the land had been divided amongst siblings into smaller lots invisible through the dense trees. Paths used by us kids to get to the cousins' houses were overgrown now, but still there if needed. The land was worth millions, but we lived like average folks. Donnelys didn't flaunt their wealth. In fact, we never talked about it. To get those millions meant selling land that had been in our family for generations, and that would never happen. Not even in the lean times, when loans and second mortgages were taken out, was losing or selling this land ever an option. Sure, some of the other property on the island had been sold and developed over the years, but mostly for family, or donated to the county as open space.

My place sat on three acres in the woods across the road and down a ways, the land a gift from my grandfather. I built the house myself from an old barn we converted. I preferred to live in the woods. No one walking by on the beach. Long ass driveway and only a moss-covered mailbox to mark the entrance suited me fine.

I parked by the weather-beaten barn near the edge of the clearing. Mini-vans and nicer sedans crowded the driveway near the house. Weird to think of little Lori as a married woman with friends who drove mini-vans.

Passing one of the ancient apple trees on the property, I remembered how Lori and Cara would climb up and pelt anyone who walked by with the tiny, bitter fruit. If her kids were anything like her, she was going to be in trouble.

I snuck in through the open kitchen door. Laughter and female voices carried from the living room. Needing fortitude, I grabbed a beer from the fridge and opened it on the wall-mounted bottle opener. The snacks and food in the dining room had been picked over, but I found enough to make a plate. There would be plenty to take for the game. My eye roamed over the offerings on the table and buffet. Tiny pink and blue cupcakes caught my attention, and I snorted.

They really were the puffy hearts of baked goods.

I popped one in my mouth in a single bite.

"Hey! Those are for dessert," a female voice scolded me.

I chewed and swallowed before turning around.

The voice belonged to a tall woman wearing shorts and a sleeveless shirt. A slim line of pink lace peeked out from the edge of her shirt. Nice. I let my eyes wander down past her shorts where her tan legs went on for miles. Her tits were small, but she made up for it with the legs.

"TC Donnely, stop checking out my legs." Her voice was throaty. Sexy and unexpected. Wavy brown hair ended above her shoulders and angry green eyes greeted me when I managed to tear my mind from the fantasies of those legs wrapped around me.

"Do I know you?" I licked frosting off the side of my thumb and then took a long pull from the bottle.

Her eyes focused on my mouth and throat as I swallowed.

I flashed a grin. "Cat got your tongue?"

"I see you haven't changed." She crossed her arms. Smoky, her voice was smoky like she'd smoked a pack a day, but not masculine, more like an old film star or singer. In one word: sexy. Illegally so. She could make big money doing phone sex. Hell, maybe she did.

"I'm at a disadvantage here. You know me, but I can't for the life of me remember you. And with legs like yours, I think I'd remember." I let my gaze travel south again.

"Tom, you made it!" Lori's voice cut through the tension.

"Hi, sis." I hugged her, but kept my eye on the angry amazon.

"I see you and Hailey remember each other."

"Hailey?" Impossible.

"I'm not sure Tom remembers me."

No way was the woman standing in front of me the same annoying as fuck friend of Lori's growing up, whom I called Idaho. Hailey King. You named your daughter after a town in Idaho, you were asking for the nickname. Growing up she'd been all gangly limbs and scowls.

"Of course he remembers you. Right?" Lori smiled and curled herself around my arm, her full belly bumping into my hip.

"Of course. Yeah. How's it going, Idaho?"

Green eyes narrowed at me. Guess she still didn't like the nickname.

"Idaho! No one's called you that for ages." Lori laughed and bounced. Pregnancy clearly made her crazy.

While Hailey scowled at me, I gave her a wink. Idaho sure grew up nice. As kids she was a true tomboy. She fought like a boy, never minding getting dirty, and didn't put up with any bullshit from boys, even being four years younger than the pack of us. Her dad worked for the ferries and swore like the former sailor he was, a trait Hailey had picked up and taught Lori. Until Mom found out, and Lori had to wash her own mouth out with soap.

"I see you haven't change, Thomas Clifford." With nonchalance, she picked up my bottle and took a swig.

I ignored the use of my middle name. No way would she provoke me so easily. "That's my drink, you know. Wouldn't want you catching cooties."

"I figure the alcohol will kill anything you might be carrying." She finished the bottle.

Lori's focus bounced between the two of us. "Right. You two need to go to your separate corners. Mom's been asking about you. We've been waiting for you to arrive to open the presents."

I glanced at the clock. "Mom said the party ended in fifteen minutes. You haven't opened presents yet?"

Lori laughed. "Oh, she totally lied to you. We know your tricks. The party doesn't end for another hour." Her dimples were identical to mine and I knew she used them the same way I did … charming her way out of situations where people wanted to throttle her.

I closed my eyes and exhaled.

"You've been outwitted, TC. Again." Hailey stood next to me; a warm, clean scent from her encompassed me. She smelled like fresh rain or summer.

"Nice to see you, Idaho. Now mind your own damn business."

Tom's ninja skills, zero. Mom, one. Outwitted by my mother at the age of thirty-three.

Added bonus: extra time with the snarky amazon.

Good thing? Bad thing? Hard to call yet.

———

"TC!" Mom greeted me with a big hug when we walked into the babypaloozed living room decorated with all sorts of cute animals. "When did you get here?"

"A few minutes ago. He's been hiding out in the dining room eating the desserts," Lori ratted me out.

I tossed a purple almond-shaped candy at her.

"Hey, no throwing things at the pregnant woman." She batted away the sugar missile.

I scanned the room for my dad or a brother-in-law and found both standing in the far corner near a bowl of dip. Smiling at the ladies on the way, I made a beeline for my kind.

"Hey."

"Hey."

"Hey."

Greetings out of the way, we ate dip and stood awkwardly in a little pocket of testosterone.

My oldest sister Amy clapped her hands and declared it time to open the gifts. Her dark hair contrasted to the rest of ours. She inherited her coloring from Mom while the rest of us favored our dad's light hair and blue eyes. Lori and I inherited the curls. Little Mom, as we all called Amy growing up, bossed us around more than our actual mother. Some things never changed.

"Dad, Tom, Nick, come sit."

We grumbled and made our way over to a row of dining chairs behind the sectional. I sat closest to the hall for an easy exit.

"Where are Doug and Greg?" I asked.

"Doug's out of town, and Greg had a charity golf tournament," Dad explained.

"Greg got excused from this circus to play golf?" I asked, miffed.

"Yeah, talk to your mother about that. Had I known it was an option, I would have joined him."

"You and me both," I said.

"We could have made it a foursome," Nick said.

I laughed. "Nah, you had zero chance of parole from this, man. Welcome to the rest of your life."

"Nick, come sit with me and open gifts," Lori called from the love seat.

I spread out and stretched my legs into the space Nick had occupied. Dad had his head turned away and leaned in his chair to peer into the family room on the other side of the door. I tipped my chair to see behind him and let out a chuckle. Sneaky bastard had the game on mute in the family room.

"What's the score?"

He faced me and smiled. "14-3 Cougars, beginning of the second quarter."

"Why is it grown men can't speak up for what they want? We're here in the house, we should be able to watch a game of football without getting in trouble."

"One of life's great mysteries, son."

I shook my head and thought about grabbing a beer. Idaho had finished my last one before I could drink half.

"Cougars winning?" her voice asked from behind our row of chairs.

"Hailey!" Dad greeted her warmly. Since when had she become everyone's favorite?

"Ken, I thought you might be thirsty." She held up two beers and a cider. "And I owe Tom a beer." Before sitting between us, she handed me a bottle and then passed one to my dad.

"Thanks." I gave her a side-long look. "Did you spit in it?" I closed an eye and stared into the bottle.

"I'm not twelve anymore."

"That's not a no. Dad, switch bottles with me." I reached for his bottle.

"No, I didn't spit in your drink. Honestly. Give a girl some credit."

"Girl? Idaho, you were never a girl."

She smiled to herself and leaned closer to whisper in my ear, "Thirty-six inches."

Thirty-six inches? What does that have to do with anything? "Um... what?"

"My inseam." She lifted her eyebrow knowingly before excusing herself.

I choked on the liquid in my mouth and started coughing, feeling like hacking up a lung was a viable option. My eyes watered and I felt my dad's hand slap my back. I caught Lori and Cara's disapproving stares. Mom appeared worried.

"He'll be fine," Dad explained. "Wrong pipe."

I gave the room a wave to carry on as I watched Hailey walk into the kitchen. Her legs were really long and her shorts weren't.

Not thinking about it, I followed her.

"You okay?" she asked, filling a glass of water for me.

"Why did you tell me that?" I drank the water, leaning against the sink. My eyes wandered over her lean body again. Her arms were long and sinewy like her legs.

"I'm saving you the effort of trying to find a tape measure. From the way you've been staring at my legs, I figured you were curious." Her eyes didn't glance away from mine. She was calling me out for checking her out earlier. "I feel bad you choked and almost died. I didn't think anything could shock you."

"Talking about your inseam in front of my father? You didn't think it would get a reaction out of me?"

"First, I said thirty-six inches. I could have been talking about a bookcase or changing table. Second, you were obviously checking me out in the dining room." She held up three fingers. "Third, your reputation precedes you."

"First, my reputation has nothing to do with you. Why would what I do and who I do it with matter to you? You're my sister's friend and none of my business." From her frown, I could tell my tone sounded more defensive than I'd intended. I exhaled and then finished the glass of water. "So how are you, Idaho? Long time no see."

She raised an eyebrow at me.

I held up my palms. "Let's start over? I shouldn't have been checking you out at my sister's shower."

Her eyes scanned over my chest and shoulders before making contact with me. "Okay. Fair enough. I shouldn't have said the inseam thing in front of your dad."

I snorted. "Ya think?"

She shook her head and rolled her eyes. "Sorry."

"No worries." I stuck out my hand. "Fresh start?"

"Okay." She met my grasp and shook hands. Her grip was strong and warm. "No more Idaho, right?"

I pulled my hand away. "Sorry. The name's too good not to stick."

"Great." She exhaled.

"We should probably get in there. Lori might string us both up for missing out on a few oohs and aahs over adorable shit."

"You're a sweet brother for showing up today."

"I didn't have a choice. Mom would cut me off from Thanksgiving if I didn't come to these things. Have you had her stuffing? No way am I missing out on her sausage stuffing."

"You're a simple man. I'm going to ignore any talk about your love of sausage stuffing."

It sounded like it could be a put down, but since we'd declared a truce not five minutes ago, I'd let it slide.

"Don't underestimate simple and straightforward, Ida— Hailey." I cocked my head in the direction of the living room. "Shall we? We're missing out on some good stuff from the sounds of it."

She gave me a small smile and gestured for me to lead the way.

She joined my dad and me in the back row, and laughed at our inane questions about diaper containers and ointments. I glanced down at her finger and saw an engagement ring, but no wedding band. Part of me wanted to ask Lori what her situation was, but I knew that would be opening a giant can of pain-in-the-ass. Not that I was interested. I also knew better than to touch any of my sisters' friends. Or cousins' friends. Island was too small and this family was too big.

———

An hour later and I could finally make my escape. The Cougars were down in the third quarter. My mom grabbed some containers and filled them full of leftovers for the guys. Dad and I discussed the WSU season and how the Huskies looked pretty good, too. I even carried a load or two of baby gifts out to Lori's car like a good brother.

Family duty finally over, I texted Ashley before pulling out of the driveway.

You free later?

A few seconds later a response chirped.

Hi to you too. What did you have in mind?

Hi. I hit send. ***Your place around 9?***

I tapped my fingers on the steering wheel while I waited.

9 is late for dinner.

I smirked. ***Who said anything about food?***

Her next response took longer. I hoped I hadn't pissed her off. She knew the deal. Hang out, sex, hang out. Easy.

Okay.

I smiled. Easy.

THREE

Confession:
I have a long list of rules when it comes to women.

R un by another branch of the family, Donnely Boats had occupied this location on Holmes Harbor since the fifties. Custom boats and bigger contracts typically kept the company busy, but the boat business had slowed with the recession. At least a recent tugboat contract meant we'd be hiring new staff, including the random assortment of welders and pipefitters.

I could have moved up to management years ago, but I like welding and saw no reason to sit in an office all day dealing with other people's bullshit and politics. As long as the new hires weren't dumb-asses or incompetent jerks, we'd be fine. They probably wouldn't be in my gang anyway. Being a Donnely had its perks. I got the pick of jobs and crew, but most of the time people left me alone to get my job done.

Monday morning, an assortment of trucks filled the spots closest to the office when I pulled into the lot at the boatyard. I squeezed my vintage Triumph Bonneville around them and parked on a sliver of weeds and gravel on the far side of the building.

A fresh pot of coffee sputtered and steamed in the break room. I filled a Styrofoam cup with black coffee, no sugar. Alone for a few minutes, I sat at one of the round tables in an orange plastic chair and put my feet up. The local paper sat open to the police report where the typical small town crimes were reported. Sure, more serious stuff, like domestic violence and drugs, happened on the island, but we still had people calling the sheriff over their missing goat or an eagle's nest on their property.

The sound of heavy boots and male voices carried down the hall. I glanced at the clock. Shift started in five minutes. I finished my coffee, smashed the cup in my hand, and folded the paper.

Time to play with fire and molten metal. Much better than sitting in front of a computer all day.

I worked for a few hours on the hull of the tug in dry-dock. With my helmet down and sparks flying, I got into the zone.

A few hours later, I took off my gloves, flipped up my visor, and hopped down to grab lunch. Ahead of me, a group of newbies walked on some sort of tour with Al, our HR manager.

"Hey, Al," I called out to him. "These the new hires?"

Al stopped and the group of six guys with him halted, too. "You guessed it. I'll introduce you."

He told me a bunch of names I probably wouldn't remember tomorrow. Most were journeyman, and had been around boatyards for years. They worked on a couple of projects and moved on to the next gig, always going after the better money. I honestly stopped paying attention after the second guy.

"And last, but not least, is King."

King.

I wondered if Idaho had a brother. I couldn't remember if

she did or not. Maybe a younger one? I focused on where King stood at the end of the cluster of guys.

Well, I'll be damned.

"What the hell?" I blurted. "Idaho?"

All eyes turned toward her. "Hey, Tom. Long time no see."

The other guys snickered and I could tell they were probably thinking I was a sexist pig about women working around boats. I might have been a pig about other things, but it didn't matter to me what you had in your pants if you worked hard and didn't act like an asshole.

Al glowered at me.

"Oh, no. I know her. She's friends with my kid sister," I explained, lamely. "Since when do you weld?"

"Hailey comes to us as a project manager. Lots of welding experience, but not on boats." Al continued talking, but I was too busy staring at Idaho. She wore a baseball cap like two of the other guys and given her height and long legs, she blended in with the rest of them in her canvas jacket, jeans, and boots. No sign of any lace. Pity.

She smiled at me, and my focus moved to her full lips. Definitely not a guy.

"Well, shit. You're full of surprises these days."

"Yeah, Lori told me you were still working here. I guess I should've mentioned it last week."

"Guess so." I shrugged. "No big deal. Not to me anyway. You're not the first woman to work here."

"And she won't be the last." The discomfort in Al's voice revealed the reality that most women who had worked here didn't stick around. Working in a shipyard was tough work, inside the office or out. Not to mention the majority of the guys around here were sexist pigs. Too many cocks turned any place into a locker room.

"Right. Welcome." I gave them all a wave and headed inside for lunch.

Most of the chairs were already filled by dirty welders who

had soot stains on their sleeves and packed lunches in front of them. I located my bag in the fridge and sat with the usual crowd.

"You couldn't see her tits at all. Maybe she doesn't even have them."

"Yeah, but that mouth could make up for the lack of boobs. I can think of a few things I'd have her mouth do."

"Fuck the mouth," pausing for laughter, the speaker continued, "I'd like to see what those legs look like around me."

Typical assholes. A hen in with a group of roosters meant a lot of feathers got fluffed up. Most of it was just talk, but some of these guys had lower morals than I did. Married? Didn't matter, they still stared and talked like they stood a chance.

Took me a few minutes to realize they were talking about Idaho. I cleared my throat to get their attention. "Not to spoil the fun, but I've known King most of my life. She's one of my kid sister's best friends growing up. Can we lay off the talk about her?"

Four faces stared at me in stunned disbelief. I didn't engaged in that kind of talk on a daily basis, so I didn't understand what was so shocking. The women in my family both set the bar for respect and instilled fear in me, so unless a woman did something to make me lose it, I respected women in general.

"You pulling the off limits card on King?" Stu, a real old timer, who didn't like women except in his bed or kitchen, asked.

I thought about it for a minute. "Yeah, I guess I am. Sorry to be a drag, but it's weird hearing that shit about her."

"Donnely, your balls shrinking into a vag?" Jay joked.

"No, they're doing just fine. Your sister couldn't keep her hands off of them all weekend."

For the record, Ashley wasn't related to Jay, and Jay only had brothers.

The table broke up in laughter that only followed men being inappropriate. Issue over. Talk moved on to a new waitress at the

Chinese restaurant in Freeland and whether or not she wore underwear. Three votes to one she didn't.

Break over, back to work.

Repeated five days a week.

Idaho being here could make things a little more interesting. Curious to what she was doing working here, I'd have to figure out a way to get more information about her from Lori. Wait, I didn't research women. I didn't care about their story when I knew there wouldn't be more than one chapter. No, Idaho wouldn't have her own chapter. I didn't sleep with other guys' women. Not intentionally at least. Once I saw a ring, I bailed. Plenty of single girls out there looking for fun.

Speaking of, I texted Ashley.

Thanks for this weekend.

I always remembered my manners. Please and thank you went a long way.

———

At the end of the day I stood next to my bike in the parking lot. Movement down the row of cars caught my eye. Idaho was walking with Daryl from my crew. From the looks of things, he didn't know his boundaries. Or didn't care. I paused with my helmet in my hands.

"Hey, Ida— Hailey," I shouted.

They both stopped and stared at me.

"Hey, Daryl. Mind if I steal Ms. King for a minute?"

Daryl frowned. He probably thought I was ruining his shot. His problem was he didn't have a shot to be ruined.

"Ms. King?" she asked, leaning against a truck next to my bike.

"You like that?" I grinned at her. Daryl still stood near the bumper of a silver SUV I assumed to be hers at the far end of the row. I nodded in his direction. "He giving you a problem?"

"Daryl?" She laughed and the sound of it made me smile. "What is he? Eighteen? Twenty? He's harmless."

"Having been an eighteen-year-old guy, I can assure you he isn't harmless. Or innocent. You've got to watch yourself around here. Be too nice and he'll follow you home. Be too mean and he'll hide in the bushes outside your window."

"What's with the protective bullshit?" She curled her hands around her biceps.

I pouted my lips. "You're Lori's friend, so that puts you under the sister umbrella. I don't put up with morons disrespecting my sisters, and the same applies to you since you work here."

"Great," she mumbled.

"You don't sound too thankful." Her sarcasm confused me.

She plastered on a smile. "No, by all means. Thanks for the warning."

"You're new. It's the least I can do." I furrowed my brow at her weird smile and the disappointment in her voice. "Let me know if any of the guys get out of hand and I'll take care of it."

"I can hold my own, Donnely. All grown up now."

I fought the urge to scan down her body, and lost. Damn work clothes and this angle meant I saw nothing of interest. When I met her eyes, she raised an eyebrow, and I gave her a lopsided smile.

"Right. We're done here?" she asked.

I glanced over her shoulder at Daryl kicking rocks with his boots. "Sure."

"Have a great weekend."

Of course I tried checking out her ass as she walked away. She glanced over her shoulder, and I smiled to myself. Her stupid jacket blocked my view. I strapped on my helmet and started the bike. I rocked it off its kickstand and let the engine rumble, stalling for a minute to make sure Daryl walked away. Idaho shot me a dirty look and waved with her middle finger.

Nice. Still one of the guys.

I revved the engine and let the gravel fly behind me as I pulled out of the lot, accelerating when I hit the smooth pavement. Instead of turning south on 525 toward home, I made a right and headed up island. I leaned into the curve, letting the wind coil its cold fingers around my neck.

FOUR

Confession:
I hate set-ups.

Sawdust circled in the air as my chainsaw cut through the soft pine log, bouncing off the plastic of my face guard and covering my jacket and jeans in a fine layer. Earmuffs muted the screeching of the saw to some degree, but it was still loud. Loud enough I didn't know John had showed up until he crossed my line of sight.

I quieted the saw, but left it running. It purred like a cat while I pulled the hard hat and protective gear from my face. After killing the motor, I set it down on a nearby stump.

"Nice eagle."

In front of me stood a six-foot eagle I'd been carving for a client. Its wings spanned almost seven feet from tip to tip. A classic Donnely spread eagle—my signature piece.

"Thanks. I need to add more to the feathers and details on the face, but I'm pretty proud of this one."

"Who's it for?"

"A couple building a place up in Greenbank. High bluff. Nice property."

He nodded in appreciation and walked around the sculpture.

"Want to grab a beer?" I gestured past the wood shop to the house. The constant mist had stopped long enough this morning to get some carving done outside. My shop opened on two sides and had a large overhang where I could carve in the rain, but I preferred to be outside. Stumps of various sizes and woods sat stacked under the wide eave along with half-started projects of typical island designs: salmon, bears, and of course, eagles. I'd carve anything for the right amount of money. I'd even done a mermaid for a house near the ferry on Columbia Beach. Her tits were glorious.

We sat on the porch of my house in a pair of custom Adirondack chairs I built last summer. I sipped my beer and waited for John to talk. I didn't need the conversation. He was the one who stopped by.

"You have plans tonight?" he asked after we were about half done with our beers.

"You have something in mind?"

He scratched his neck and smoothed down his beard on either side of his mouth. "Yeah. Not really. Diane was thinking about going to the Dog House to play pool tonight."

"Sounds like a fun night. What's that got to do with me? It's not Thursday." Our standing pool night had been Thursday for years.

"Well …"

"No."

"You don't even know what I'm going to say."

"Does it involve a set-up?"

"Not a set-up per se. More like she's tired of always hanging out with the guys."

"So let her go shopping or drink martinis at Primo with the girls."

"She does all those things. It's just, she has this friend …"
He cringed.

"Is she hot?"

"Not really your type. At all. But she's nice. And can play a decent game of pool."

"You didn't answer if she was hot."

"Yeah, I guess so?" It sounded like a question. "She's blonde. Talks a lot."

"How much is a lot?"

"You wouldn't have to talk all evening if you didn't forcibly interject."

"Nice tits?"

"I honestly haven't noticed. The talking overwhelms everything else."

"Man, you're whipped."

"Not going to deny it." He drained his bottle and set it on the stump next to his chair that served as a table. "So you'll meet us there?"

I thought about it for a minute. I didn't have any better offers in the works. Other than probably calling Ashley later. I saw her last weekend. Two weekends in a row would be weird for us. Too regular. Regularity led to a slippery slope of dating.

"Yeah. I'll show up."

———

Blonde. Check.

Nice boobs. Check check.

Talker. Check.

John had been right. Diane's friend talked a lot. Like non-stop chatterbox.

I learned she had a dog named Sprinkles and a cat named Precious.

In the first five minutes.

Mostly I nodded and tried to get a glimpse down her shirt.

31

Diane kept giving me an apologetic look, but she didn't need to feel bad. I'd probably still sleep with her friend.

Confession time: It takes a lot for me not to want to sleep with a woman.

Size didn't matter if she had confidence.

Age didn't matter if she didn't act old.

Language barriers? Not a problem and sometimes a bonus.

As long as there was chemistry, I could make it work.

The only real deal breakers for me were married and lack of self-respect. I had learned early and painfully not to fuck another man's woman. Split lip and a few cracked ribs proved the point.

And self-respect?

I didn't do desperate, needy, addicted, or tragic.

Sex was sex. Purely physical. A clear understanding between adults meant mutual pleasure. If we could have a conversation, laugh together, and enjoy each other's company when our mouths weren't occupied, even better.

Sub-category under self-respect: hygiene.

A trim, some attention to the important areas went a long way.

Where was I? Right.

Diane's friend.

The talker.

I knew a way to get her to shut up.

"Hey, babe, it's your shot." I leaned closer and put my hand on her shoulder.

She turned and gave me a small smile. "I'm not sure which ball to go for. Can you help me?"

Four solids sat on the table, one lined up perfectly with a side pocket. I raised an eyebrow at her and she shrugged.

"Side pocket from across the table. You've got this," I whispered close to her head. She shivered and chirped like a little bird. I think it was her laughter.

Her body language told me I had her if I wanted.

She made the shot easily and bounced over to hug me, pressing her curves into my side.

Easy as giving catnip to a kitten.

To prove my point, she rubbed her chest across my bicep and purred. "You're my good luck charm."

I slung an arm around her. "Nah, you did fine on your own."

Her lips rose in a smile and I was pretty sure she batted her lashes at me.

"You have another shot, you know."

She scratched, and we lost the game when Diane cleared the table on her turn. The woman was a pool shark.

"Sorry to kick your asses." Diane high-fived John, who picked her up and kissed her. Show off.

"I'll buy the next round of drinks," I offered.

Diane followed me. "So do you like Jessica?"

I glanced over my shoulder and took in Jessica's ass in her tight jeans. "Yeah, sure."

"That didn't sound all that convincing."

"What's her deal?" Normally I didn't care, but Jessica lived on the island, and nothing was smaller than this island in the winter months. The last thing I needed was a level ten clinger.

"She's cool. Moved here to teach at the middle school. Originally from Minnesota."

"Let me guess? She teaches English?"

"No, social studies and world history. Or something like that."

In my experience, teachers were the marrying kind. But they could also be freaks in bed.

"Divorced?" Divorced would be better. More freaky and less likely to be looking for a long term relationship.

"How'd you guess?"

"The talking and the touching."

"You really are something."

I cocked my head, waiting for her to continue.

"This wasn't a set-up, but I figured some flirting from you would be better than binge watching another season of some random TV show. The island isn't exactly bursting with eligible bachelors."

"You sure she only has the one cat?"

"Positive." She patted my arm. "Tom?"

"Yeah?"

"If you do sleep with her, be nice, and don't lead her on."

"I never do. Scout's honor."

"Were you ever a Scout?"

"Eagle Scout." I gave her the salute. "I've taken a vow to help others and be trustworthy."

"What about loyal?"

"Only to a select few." I winked.

She studied me with her warm brown eyes. John lucked out with this one. "Okay. But you mess with her head, I'll ask John to punch you someplace it'll hurt."

I rubbed my side in memory of the one and only physical fight we'd had years ago. John had tackled me in school and shoved me into a locker. We'd both weighed less than a hundred pounds soaking wet. I couldn't remember what the fight was about. I'd always been a lover and not a fighter. Basically, I was a fast runner as a kid and good at deflecting the trouble my mouth got me into even back then.

"John's lucky he met you first. You're the real deal."

She gazed over her shoulder at the man she clearly loved. "Maybe things would have turned out differently if you'd used a different line."

I couldn't stop my laugh. "The line works more than you'd believe!"

"It never works," Olaf, the bartender, commented. "You want to close up your tab or keep it open?"

Olaf had seen and heard more than he should have over the years tending bar here. The tavern was over a hundred years old, and Olaf had been here for at least a third of that time, if not more. If anyone ever needed to blackmail someone, they should head directly to Olaf for dirt. He'd caught me having sex in the women's room and under the stairs, and once under the deck on the beach below. He'd seen my naked ass more than any other man I knew about.

"We'll keep it open." Facing Jessica, I said to Diane, "Watch in wonder."

"Oh no, what are you doing?"

I returned to the stools near the pool table, carrying our drinks.

"Babe, I know you're new to the island and all, but have you ever been geoduck hunting?"

John muffled a snort and Diane groaned, but Jessica ignored them. "I've never heard of such a thing. What is it?"

I pulled out the dimples. "Well, it's really something which needs to be experienced more than explained. And it's best done at night."

"Sounds interesting. I'm up for anything," she replied, playing with her hair.

"Young lady," Olaf called from his position at the bar, "Tom Donnely is making an illicit offer to you. Don't you fall for his nonsense. No one in their right mind would go digging for clams at night."

Both John and Diane cracked up, but Jessica continued to stare and slowly blink at me. Geoduck hunting or not, she said she was up for anything and I intended to find out what exactly she meant.

Ignoring Olaf, I said, "Well, in that case, what are you doing now?"

"Let me get my purse."

I smirked at Diane on our way out the door. She gave me the two finger eye to eye gesture. I waved at her.

And that was how I picked up women with the geoduck line.

FIVE

Confession:
I have a sixth sense about relationships. That's why I avoid them.

Halloween meant a visit to the farmhouse to see all of the kids' costumes, say hi to Pops, steal some candy, and get a few gold stars in the family column.

It also meant lots of sexy costumes at the Rod & Gun Club party, and later at the Dog House tavern in Langley. Something about the holiday turned women into minxes. Guys had it easy. A scary mask and maybe some fake blood, and we were good to go. The R&G party had been a tradition since my parents dated, probably even my grandparents. Every year spiderwebs transformed the clubhouse and they played the same soundtrack of monster songs since the seventies.

This year my costume consisted of a Crystal Lake Camp Counselor T-shirt, jeans, boots, and a hockey mask. I left the hockey mask in the car when I stopped by my parents' house. My mother accused me of being a Halloween bah humbug—whatever that was—but my dad and Amy laughed when they saw me.

"You were so the one who got killed having sex," Amy said between snorts.

"Probably. I'd like to think I'd have outsmarted the killer and lived." Standing taller, I rolled my shoulders.

"TC, not likely. One hot female counselor in those short shorts and you'd be a goner. Remember, we've known you since puberty."

I think my older sister called me a slut. "Nice, Sis. Remember, I know stuff too. Like the time you were on the band trip to Olympia."

Amy's eyes widened. "Don't you dare mention that in front of my kids. That was a long time ago, a lifetime ago."

Apparently the slut genes ran in our family. "No worries. I'll wait until they're out of high school."

She scowled at me.

"Cool uncle, remember?"

"Thomas Clifford!"

What was with these women and using my middle name?

"Why is your sister using your middle name?" Dad asked. He was dressed as the Grim Reaper with a smiley face mask. He said it made it less scary for the little kids, but in my opinion, it was creepier.

"Nothing. We were reminiscing about Halloweens past."

"Ah, good stuff. Like the time you and John got caught TP-ing the Methodist church in Langley?"

Vandalizing a church with toilet paper hadn't been the smartest decision. Worse was doing it on a busy intersection. Teen boys were not the smartest creatures in the kingdom.

"Well, on that note, I'm going to the Rod & Gun."

"Have fun," Mom said, patting my shoulder. "Lori said she and Nick were going, too. She doesn't have many weeks left before the baby and wanted a night out."

I wondered if they'd be dragging Idaho with them. I hadn't seen her much around at work other than passing in the lunch-room and parking lot.

When I got to the club, a few cars were already parked on the gravel drive leading to the main road. Pulling around to the kitchen entrance, I found a spot next to the dumpster. The tune of *Monster Mash* carried out from the open kitchen door and I smiled. Some things never changed. I lowered my hockey mask and prepared for some fun. A couple of tipsy women tumbled out of the door and screamed when they saw me standing by the dumpster. I lifted my mask to apologize.

"Donnely!" the blonde dressed as a German beer garden girl hugged me with so much force we nearly fell over.

I knew her. I'd slept with her. I ran through a list of names.

"Debra, how you doing? I didn't mean to scare you."

She giggled and her friend held her hands to her chest like she was trying to control her heart rate. "Funny, Tom. Standing out here in the dark, waiting to scare innocent women."

"Innocent?" I grinned at her.

Both drunk girls laughed. "Oh, you know us so well." Hands curled around my biceps.

"Maybe we should ditch this party and go somewhere more private," tipsy girl number two suggested.

"Sounds like a lot of fun, but I promised my friends I'd meet up with them inside."

Pouting lips and exaggerated sighs responded.

"Boo," Debra said.

"You know where to find us," drunk friend chimed in.

I had no idea where to find them, but their offer flattered me. I lowered my mask and lurched at them, sending them into another wave of screeches and giggles. Sometimes falling into bed with a woman, or in this case, women, was too easy. And a little boring.

Inside, a stuffed walrus head hanging above the popcorn machine leered down at partiers with an expression of surprised contempt. If I were a walrus and ended up guarding a popcorn machine for eternity, I'd be pissed off, too.

I scanned the room while waiting in line for the bar. People in various costumes stood around or danced on the small dance floor under a single, sad disco ball. Upon first glance, I couldn't tell if I knew any of them until my eyes rested on John's bearded face above the crowd. Bastard wore a red and black plaid shirt and a knit cap. Was there an axe over his shoulder?

"Hey, lumberjack!" I shouted over the music. He turned his head and flipped me the bird before excusing himself from the conversation.

"Hey, Donnely."

"How'd you know it was me?"

"I recognized the mask. You've had that stupid thing since middle school when you wore it to the Clyde and scared the shit out of Mrs. Erickson. Didn't she punch you in the face?"

I lifted the mask. "Yeah. I still have the scar on my eyebrow." I pointed to a narrow line of clear-cut at the end of my left brow.

John laughed and shook his head.

"Where's Diane?"

He craned his neck and studied the room. "Over there, by the elk that Pops shot."

A lot of taxidermy decorated the Rod & Gun. A polar bear of questionable lineage stood in the corner behind John, glaring at a spot up and to the left. Salmon and other fish swam frozen on various walls. This was where dead animals came to live on forever.

I followed his finger. Diane, dressed as a sexy girl lumberjack, or a lumber-jill, stood next to a tall, all-black ninja.

I laughed. "I'm not going to be able to resist all the wood euphemisms tonight. I'm warning you now."

John frowned at me and grumbled.

"Dude, you wear matching costumes, you're going to get shit."

"I know, you don't have to say it."

I held my tongue. He and I both knew Diane owned him.

"Who's the ninja?"

"One of Lori's friends. Your sister and Nick are the baker and bun in the oven."

I groaned. "That's got to be the most ridiculous costume ever."

"Yeah. Poor Nick. I'm pretty cool in comparison."

"You're mocking your own profession. Not sure how cool that is. Are you wearing ladies' underwear to at least make it funny?"

John punched my arm. "No."

I ordered a pitcher of IPA and we wove our way through the crowd to Diane and the gang. With a sympathetic smile, I handed Nick a glass.

"Don't start, Tom."

"Nah, it's too pitiful, dude. Drink up." I clinked my glass against his.

Lori and the ninja stood off to the side. I couldn't see her face, but ninja girl looked familiar. By the way she waved her arms around, their conversation was heated.

"Hey, Tom Cat. No cat costume?" Diane teased.

"Har har. I'm a scary serial killer. Watch out." I lowered my mask again and snuck behind ninja girl to scare Lori.

They continued their conversation and I caught pieces over the music about "don't let him get away with that" and "you deserve better". Girl stuff. No way did I want to get caught in girl and relationship drama.

I was halfway in a turn to sneak away when Lori squealed in surprise and ninja girl spun around. Her fist made contact with the side of my face. I didn't see it coming because of the shitty vision in the mask.

"Oh, fuck." I whipped the mask off my face and rubbed my cheekbone.

"Ouch!" Ninja shook out her hand and wiggled her fingers while Lori shot a dirty look at me.

"Tom?" they both asked at the same time.

"Who punches someone in a mask at a Halloween party?

41

That hurt!" I held my glass to my cheek. At least the skin wasn't broken, but there was going to be a mark.

"I'm so sorry." Ninja pulled off her hood.

"Fucking Idaho? I should have known. You always hit like a boy. Your talents were wasted on volleyball. You should've been a boxer."

Laughter from the rest of the group pissed me off. "What are you laughing at?" I attempted to cross my arms, but with the beer I ended up dropping the mask. When I went to pick it up, I slammed my head into something hard. "Fuck."

"Shit," Idaho cursed when she stood up and rubbed her head. Something about her soft, raspy voice and the cursing combined to be extremely sexy, and aggravating.

Lori held the sides of her oven costume and laughed. "You two really need to avoid each other before someone breaks a tooth or loses an eye."

"Shut it, Lori." I didn't know whether to rub my head or my cheekbone.

"Oh come on, I'm teasing." She pouted and I swear her eyes teared up.

"Don't cry, crazy, pregnant woman. No crying on Halloween." I hugged her with one arm and spun us so she stood between me and the death ninja. "Idaho, try not to hit the pregnant woman."

She stuck her tongue out at me and pulled her hood down again. "I apologized. You have a hard head, by the way."

"You don't even know," Lori said.

Conversation resumed and I nursed my injuries with another beer. A guy dressed as a football player sidled up to Idaho and put his arm around her shoulders. She shrugged him off, but let him hold her hand. The fiancé?

He faced me and I realized he was dressed as a zombie football player from *Beetlejuice*. Then it hit me. Growing up with three sisters and one TV between the four of us, I had been forced to watch a lot of chick movies and TV shows.

"I love my dead gay son," I quoted *Heathers.* I mean, come on. Dead football player? That had to be his costume.

"What?" he asked.

"I love my dead gay son," I repeated.

"What the hell is that supposed to mean?" He stepped closer and tried to appear taller than me, but I had at least a couple of inches on him.

"Hey, man, just quoting the movie *Heathers.* You know. From the '90s? It's a famous line." I didn't back down, but my tone told him he was an asshole for making this a thing.

"Oh, right. Okay, I get it." He slapped my shoulder like we were buds. Who was this guy?

"Everything okay over here?" Idaho asked, a worried expression on her face as she glanced between the two of us. She didn't know me well enough to be worried about me starting shit. Okay, maybe that wasn't true given she had been friends with my sister forever, but whatever she heard had been greatly exaggerated. Lover, not a fighter. Runner, not a confronter.

"Nothing." I pressed my lips together and shook my head. "Simple misunderstanding about costumes."

"Don't worry, baby. We're cool."

Baby? Babe was one thing, but baby? For a grown woman? Who was taller than he was barefoot? Again, who was this guy? I mean, the baby answered the question, but my brain had a hard time wrapping my head around them as a thing.

Huge bank account or huge dick.

I guess my poker face had left the building because Lori poked me in the side. "Kurt, this is my brother, Tom."

I choked on my beer. "Kurt?" He had to be fucking pulling my leg he didn't know *Heathers.* He had dressed as the very character at the center of the line I quoted. That was hysterical. I laughed, or started to, but when he didn't say anything or break his blank, boring expression, I realized he had no idea. None.

Oh, irony, thy name is Kurt. I stuck out my hand. "Nice to meet you."

After an overly firm handshake from him, I wiped the sweat from his palm on my jeans.

"Always nice to meet another Donnely."

What was I missing? Before I busted a few brain cells over Kurt dressed as dead Kurt, a pair of freckled arms encircled my waist and squeezed. Red hair bounced around the side of my arm.

Ashley.

I didn't know she'd be here, but things were looking up.

She had dressed herself as a cat and wore a smug smirk on her pretty face. "You like?" She twirled around and showed me her tail.

Ashley came dressed as a ginger cat. Or a piece of tail. Either had my cheeks hurting from grinning. Unlike No Clue Kurt, Ashley owned who she was. I poked the painted nose on her face and pretended to scratch her stomach. She in turn purred and nuzzled against me. I was half a second away from licking her face when I realized we had an audience.

"Wow, Tom, who knew you were into the furry scene," Diane commented, attempting to hold in her laughter.

"Furry? What the hell is a furry?"

"You know, people who get off on pretending they're animals and dressing up in giant fuzzy costumes."

John snorted next to her.

I reflexively stepped away from Ashley. "No way, man."

"Weirdos," Kurt muttered under his breath.

Now he was pissing me off. Who was he to judge me or Ashley for having some fun? *Fuck him.*

I rubbed my nose against hers and kissed her, long and deep; deep enough I bent her back to go deeper. The kissing lasted long enough to prove my point. Her eyes were wide as saucers and her expression was not unlike the deer head mounted by the dance floor: surprised and delighted.

I ignored Kurt, but instead faced Diane and John.

Idaho whispered, "Don't forget to spay and neuter your animals, folks."

Oh, for fuck's sake. Those two needed to let go and loosen up, or get laid.

Ignoring her snark, I declared, "It's Halloween, people! Let's do shots!"

Normally, I believed shots were for girls to get drunk enough to do the things they really wanted to do sober but were too "good" to do. Sometimes an occasional shot of whiskey and a beer were exactly what the night called for.

Tonight needed a round for everyone.

Lori spoke up, "Well, none for me, obviously, but I'll help you carry them." Her expression told me she wanted to do more than carry a tray of shots.

"What's up with no sense of humor guy? Is he Idaho's man? And if so, are you kidding me?" I asked when we were out of ear shot of the group.

"Nice PDA, brother. I thought you might start humping like the Tom Cat you are."

"Nah, PDA isn't my thing. But no limp-handed man is going to call me or my friend a weirdo."

"I think you proved your point."

"Good."

"To answer your question, Kurt is *Hailey's*," she emphasized the name, "fiancé."

"I don't like him."

"I'm sure she'll be very concerned about your opinion."

"He's bad news."

"He's fine. Big real estate developer, self-made, super smart, and has lots of money. In fact, he's building a beach house here on Whidbey for her."

"Maybe he can use some of his money to buy a sense of humor. Or a Netflix subscription. If he has money, what's she doing working down at the yard?"

"It's the 21st century, women work." We moved up a few steps as the line for drinks shifted. "Seriously, why do you care?"

"She's your best friend. And he's a douche-nozzle."

"You don't know him. He's ambitious and driven. Unlike some guys."

I ignored her barb. "I can tell when a guy's an asshole."

"Takes one to know one?"

"Exactly." We reached the bar and I ordered shots. "Have they set the date?"

"No." She stared down at her round belly.

I lifted my eyebrow in question.

"Hailey's been stalling."

No woman ever stalled to have a wedding. Once a ring was on her finger, it was a speedy downhill on the matrimonial roller-coaster.

"It's all moved really quickly and I think she's adjusting." Lori glanced away again.

"You don't like him either."

She met my eyes and shrugged. "He's okay."

We returned with the shots and passed them out. Raising mine, I made a toast. "To bad choices."

Lori gave me a side-long glance, but lifted her glass of soda.

"To bad choices," everyone said and downed their shots. Everyone except Clueless Kurt.

"I don't like whiskey. Only Scotch." He set his glass on the table.

"Scotch is whiskey," I muttered under my breath.

Idaho shook her head and picked up his shot. "More for me." She swallowed and a shiver ran through her. "Let's dance."

Kurt sat down.

I knew then she'd never marry that loser, even if he was Mr. Successful.

SIX

Confession:
A confident woman is a turn on.

A couple of weeks later, John and I were three-quarters of the way through our pitcher and a few games of pool into the evening. Once again the Dog House was packed: the two of us, three random guys at the bar, and Olaf. Another wild Thursday night during the dark months on the island.

"Last call. You don't have to go to your own house, but you can't stay here," Olaf announced. The clock said we still had a half-hour until eleven, his typical weeknight closing time.

"What's up with closing early?" I asked as the three guys put on their jackets.

"My back's bugging me and y'all are boring. Go home or call one of your booties," he grumbled and turned off the old neon sign outside.

"I'm heading out," John said. "Gotta drive up to Anacortes tomorrow morning."

"We're not finished with our game."

He studied the table. "You'll win."

The double doors hadn't stopped swinging when the front door opened again and a cold wind blew into the bar.

"What'd you forget?" I asked, expecting him to be standing there. Instead of John, a windswept Idaho greeted me with a stare. She swept her hair away from her face and growled.

When she walked toward me, I was ninety-percent certain she wanted to slap me. I spread my stance and tensed for the impact. Sadly, she wouldn't be the first woman to smack me or attempt to. Good thing I was pretty fast at dodging and weaving.

I held her gaze as she got closer. Part of me wanted to close my eyes and turn the other cheek ... literally. Or back down the hall and hide in the men's room. Ah, the men's bathroom. A place no woman dared to go unless absolutely necessary. Urinals freaked them out.

I took a big step and then another until the darkness of the hall to the back room enveloped me. I wasn't running. Far from it. I moved slowly and kept my eyes on my assailant stalking toward me.

I probably should have asked myself why she wanted to slap me. Had I stopped to think, I might have realized unlike most women with the same expression on their face, I hadn't actually given her a reason to be mad at me. At least none I knew about.

Her eyes narrowed and she cut the distance between us in half with two long strides. To my left was the door to the bathroom and potential salvation. Further behind me stood the backdoor and freedom. While I debated hiding or fleeing, she made the decision for me by grabbing the front of my shirt.

"Hey, Idaho. What's up?" Always act innocent. In this case, I didn't have to act.

"I've been looking all over for you tonight."

I raised an eyebrow. "You have?"

She stared at my mouth and pressed her lips together. "I have. Why is a good man hard to find when you need him?"

Her words rearranged themselves in my head after she'd

spoken them. "Don't you mean a hard man is good to find when you need him?"

She snorted out a laugh. "Exactly. You read my mind." Her hand not clutching my shirt touched the bared skin above my belt.

"Hey, whoa, Idaho. Where you going with that hand?" I jerked my hips back to escape her wandering fingers.

"I need a good man. And since I don't know any good men, I decided I needed a hard man tonight."

"Okay." I grabbed her hands in mine to protect myself from her assault. "Can I ask you one thing?"

"Sssure."

The subtle slur answered my question, but I asked it anyway. "Have you been drinking?"

"Tommm, don't be mean. You sleep with everyone on the island. I need you to sleep with me. Now." The slight rasp to her voice had strengthened into a sultry purr.

Definitely not sober. "What happened to your own man? Have sex with him."

She wiggled her left hand out of my grasp. "No more boyfriend. No more ring."

"What happened?"

She pressed a finger to my lips. "No talking, more sex."

"More implies there's some sex to begin with." I couldn't figure out why I bothered to argue. Sex without strings was my thing.

But could I have stringless sex with Hailey? I had rules. She was my kid sister's best friend, and engaged.

While I was lost in some sort of moral debate, she kissed me. *Shit.*

Worse, my body responded, and I liked it. A lot.

She was an amazing kisser—even buzzed and with grabby hands, her lips and tongue teased mine with a balance of aggression and skill.

When she bit my bottom lip, I did the smart thing. I kissed her back.

Our bodies met and I forced hers against the far side of the hallway. We bumped into the wall and I pinned her with my hips. With her height, I didn't have to lean down. One of her long legs wrapped around my thigh like I'd imagined when I first saw them at Lori's shower.

Shit.

Lori would kill me. I'd always respected the code of not fucking my sisters' friends.

Idaho reached between us and stroked my hardening erection through my jeans.

To hell with my rules.

I waved the white flag. Smart idea or not, I surrendered. If she wanted a one-night stand, who was I to let her have it with someone else? That would be like catching a King and throwing it in another man's boat.

I chuckled at the unintentional pun of her name and the king of salmons.

She shifted and kissed my neck. "What's so funny?"

Like an idiot, I told her.

"You're making out with me, grinding your erection into my hip while thinking of me as a fish?" She pinched my nipple. Hard. She had perfect aim.

"Ouch." I jerked away, giving her enough room to escape down the hall toward the bar. "Hey, where are you going?" I grabbed her hand and halted her. How did this go from her attacking me to me chasing her?

"For years I've heard how amazing you are in bed, all about your great moves and talents. I figured you were a sure thing. Instead I get fish talk. If I wanted a limp fish, there's plenty of men on this island to choose from who don't know what they're doing." Fire lit her green eyes. Her cheeks were flushed with emotion and perhaps a little beard burn. Her bottom lip appeared stung and swollen from our kiss.

A noise to my left reminded me we had an audience. Olaf tipped his head and met my gaze.

"Nothing to see here." I answered his silent question. "I think Hailey needs a ride home."

"I don't need anything from you." Her tone edged belligerence.

"Yes, you do. You need me to take you home." I stared at her. "And you need to remember I haven't said no."

Her mouth opened to speak, shut and opened again, and then clamped closed.

"We good? I'll drive you home and we'll go from there?"

Her eyes narrowed and her nostrils flared. She was either mulling over my offer or about to charge me with her horns. I hadn't seen them yet, but I was certain she had them.

I bet she would be amazing in bed.

If I had any say in it, that's where we were heading now.

"I have a confession," I said when we reached my truck.

She buckled herself in and faced me. "Yes?"

"I have no idea where you live."

Her laughter filled the small space. "I thought you were going to confess something serious. I'm renting a place on Goss Lake."

I joined her in laughing. "Maybe we should keep the questions and conversation to yes/no for now so you don't end up wanting to punch me like you did back there."

She nodded. "Yes."

"Great."

SEVEN

Confession:
Size matters, but paying attention matters more.

M y high beams lit a narrow path through the cedar filled woods around Goss Lake. Tucked between Holmes Harbor and Langley, Goss and Lone Lakes were further off the tourist path. Idaho gave me directions, our only conversation during the drive. She didn't fidget or bounce with nerves. If anything, a steely resolve settled around her and she stared straight ahead. The headlights passed over a hulking mass between the cedar trees along her drive.

"Whoa, was that a deer?" I asked, trying to see it in the red glow from the taillights.

"It's nothing."

"Are you sure? Could be a bear," I joked.

"Trust me. Park behind my car."

I stopped behind a small Ford SUV. "How'd you get to the Dog if your car is here?" At least she hadn't been driving under the influence.

"A friend drove me. And for the record I had two shots over

an hour ago. I'm not drunk. Far from it." She sighed. "What happened to our yes/no pact? There's a lot more talking going on here than I anticipated."

I shrugged. "I'm a curious guy."

"Well, Mr. Curious, how about we go inside?"

"Alrighty." I reached over her lap and opened the glove compartment. Inside, I fished out a few condoms.

"Magnums?" She sounded more curious than doubtful.

"Yes."

"Oh." She quickly unbuckled her seatbelt and had the door open in a flash.

I smirked. My bravado and confidence were firmly based in reality. My reputation was well earned.

I followed her down the path to a cedar-shingled A-frame house. She'd left the porch light on, but still fumbled with her key in the lock. Hating to see her nervous, I leaned into her and rested my hand over hers. "Here. Let me." My breath tickled the small hairs by her ear and she shivered, but instead of moving away, she rested her head on my shoulder. I kissed her temple, lingering there for a moment despite the door swinging open in front of us.

She reached for the light switch on the wall next to the door.

"Leave it off," I commanded, gently guiding her forward into the dark space. Despite the clouds, enough light filtered in from the wall of windows facing the lake that I could see the outlines of furniture.

"Just one," she argued and walked over to a table lamp. "I have a thing about shadows in the corners turning into serial killers."

I scanned the room, Amy's words about being the first to be killed in a horror movie running through my mind. Seeing nothing but a few dust bunnies in a corner, I declared the room killer free.

"What if you're the bad guy?" she asked, moving to the coat rack near the door.

"Me? No, darlin', I'm the knight in shining armor."

"Prince Charming?"

"Sure."

"Ugh. I'm not some damsel in distress who needs rescuing." She hung up her jacket and gestured for me to take off mine. "Boots, too."

"You're too bossy to be a damsel."

"Damn straight." She stripped off her sweater and threw it over a chair. Boots followed and joined mine by the door. "Drink?"

"Sure. What do you have?"

"Whiskey and tequila."

Revenge sex, if that's where we were heading, and I'd bet on it, required tequila. "What were you drinking earlier?"

"Tequila." She grabbed the bottle and poured two shots, lined up two limes slices, and grabbed the salt shaker.

Yep. Revenge sex.

Fine by me.

"What should we toast?" I asked, watching her lick the side of her thumb and pour salt on the wet skin.

"Magnum condoms works for me." She licked, drank, grimaced, and shook her head.

I took her hand and licked the same spot, tasting salt and something essentially her. Meeting her eyes, I poured a thin line of salt and licked the skin again, pausing to suck and gently bite the fleshy part of her thumb. The shot followed and I maintained eye contact while I finished with the lime. Her breathing was shallow and her tongue peeked out from her slightly parted lips.

"Damn," she whispered before pressing me into the counter.

Our mouths crashed together in a tangle of tongues and teeth. She bit my bottom lip and then sucked away the sting. I ran my tongue along her front teeth before owning her mouth, dominating the kiss and switching our positions.

With my hands on her ass, I lifted her up on the counter.

She was the same height here and we aligned perfectly. I ground myself into her and trailed my hands under her thin, long sleeve T-shirt. I could see her black bra beneath the material, her nipples creating shadows where they peaked. My thumbs rolled over them and I pinched both between my fingers, causing her to suck in a breath. Small tits were often more sensitive than their bigger sisters. What was the saying? More than a mouthful was a waste? I couldn't wait to get my mouth on hers. I jerked the material up and over her head. A flash of black under her left breast caught my eye.

"You have a tattoo?" I leaned forward so I could see it more clearly.

"Um, yeah." She lifted her arm and tilted back. "*A chuisle mo chroí.*"

"A hush lemo cree?" My tongue twisted with the unfamiliar sounds of another language. Using my fingertip, I outlined the small black letters flowing over her rib. My eyes met hers and her cheeks flushed. "What does it mean?"

"Literal translation in Gaelic is 'pulse of my heart'."

I traced the letters with my tongue. "Seems a logical place for it."

I blew warm air over the words. Such a romantic quote for a tomboy like Hailey. She chose to hide her tattoo on her skin in a vulnerable place. Bold, yet protective.

"Were all your friends getting them?" I shifted to see her face again.

She straightened and barely met my eyes. "No, just me being a rebel. I wanted something to remind myself I'm alive. I'm here. I exist."

"You definitely exist." I kissed my way down her neck, lingering at the top of her shoulder, before continuing my journey south. My mouth found the swell of her tits and I licked a line down to the center between her bra. "You're a bad ass."

Her hands reached behind her and I stilled them. "Let me." Seeing a beautiful woman naked for the first time was better than Christmas, and no way was I going to let someone else unwrap my present. I flicked open the closure with one hand and pulled the delicate lace away from her skin. A toss over my shoulder made the offending garment disappear.

"Your turn," she whispered into my neck.

"Not yet. You're still wearing clothes."

"Hmmph. I can't remove my jeans if I'm sitting on my ass." She pouted, but made a good point.

I picked her up and held her thighs. Those long, gorgeous legs tightened around my hips. I could screw her standing here, but she still wore her jeans. "Bedroom?"

"Upstairs."

I carried her up to the loft bedroom, not listening to her protests of being too heavy or big. That was bullshit. I tossed her down on her bed, mainly to watch her perky breasts bounce when she landed.

My fingers found the button on her jeans and I yanked down the zipper before shimmying them over her hips. Enough light carried over the railing to create shadows and highlights around her curves. Before I could flip her over to see her ass, fingers grabbed at my flannel, tugging at buttons, and threatening to rip them off.

Chuckling, I slowed her hands. "Slow down." I finished what she started and my T-shirt joined the flannel on the floor. All that remained were my jeans and socks. Regardless of the chill, I had a no socks rule. No pants, no socks.

She rolled over and snuck beneath the covers, hiding her gorgeous body under a layer of quilts and blankets.

I dove under and found my way to her, centering my face over her middle. One hand skimmed over her stomach, while the other pulled her legs apart. Her body tensed and I kissed whatever skin I could find, stomach, hip, thigh, inner thigh to soothe her. She laced her hands through my hair and I accepted it as encouragement to continue.

Her hesitation—despite her hands guiding me lower—told

me she wasn't used to getting this. Any man who expected blow jobs but didn't love going down on women was a dickhead. We'd already determined Kurt fell into that category.

One-night-stand or not, I'd make her come hard enough to never accept anything less.

A nip to the skin at the top of her thigh told her I meant business. This wouldn't be two licks and done. I would stay down here until I finished what I started. With each lick, suck, and swirl I paid attention to her reactions. Every woman reacted differently. What worked for one, left another cold. The reason women loved me was simple: I paid attention.

And I was a very fast learner.

Idaho relaxed and her body told me exactly what she loved. Her hands tightened ever so slightly when she liked what I did and eased up when she didn't. Or pushed when she wanted my mouth to shift. Her hips began to grind off the bed, seeking more. I gave it to her with one, and then two fingers, curled and pressed inside of her. *Ah, that was it.*

I slowed my rhythm, but increased pressure. Muffled below layers of fabric, I could hear her soft moans and whispered swear words. I lost myself in pleasuring her until her hips rose off the bed and I felt her tense all over. I continued doing exactly the same thing until she shuddered and her thighs tightened around my head.

She called out "I'm coming."

I smirked. *Oh, darlin, I know. Trust me, I know.*

"Sweet damn. That's what all the fuss is about," she swore and shifted her legs.

I grinned and kissed her stomach, then shrugged off the covers. Sweat dampened my forehead. I wiped my beard on my arm.

"Satisfied?" I flopped on the pillow next to her.

Her eyes were closed and she smiled. "I'm not through with you yet."

"Oh, we haven't even begun." I rolled over and set the condoms on the table, then pulled off my jeans and socks.

"Three?" Excitement or disbelief echoed in the question. Maybe both.

"I like to plan for every possibility."

A few hours later, one condom remained unopened when I put on my jeans. I'd leave it there as a reminder.

Hell, I'd leave it there for someone else to find.

On her back, with one tit exposed above the quilt, Idaho softly snored.

I tucked her fully under the covers and kissed her forehead. "Thanks for the good time."

She stirred and opened one eye. Sitting up, the quilt dropped and exposed both breasts, which she quickly covered.

"No need to be shy, nothing I haven't seen already."

"Are you leaving?" Her voice croaked with sleep. "You can stay."

"Nah, but thanks. It's better I leave now. I'd hate to see regret in your eyes in the morning. You have some ibuprofen?"

Her brows furrowed. "I'm not drunk. I made this decision completely sober."

"I'm sure you did. You've been lusting after me since high school." Making up stuff, I teased her. Or so I thought. She ducked her head and gazed out the window.

Okay. That was news to me.

"Listen, you'll be happier to wake up alone tomorrow. Want me to give you the pep talk about it being the first day of the rest of your life?"

She threw a pillow at my head. "Get out."

I ducked and heard her laughter. "You know I'm right."

With a sigh, she nodded. "Thanks."

"For what?"

She gestured at the bed and me, and her body.

"No need to thank me." I rubbed my lips together and

dragged my teeth over the scruff of hair right below my bottom lip. "It was my pleasure."

I stood to leave.

"Tom?"

"Yeah?'

"Can we not tell Lori about this?"

"No problem. It'll be our little secret." I leaned over and kissed her forehead. "A one-night-stand between old friends."

Her frown returned for a split-second before she gave me a smile. Maybe I imagined the frown.

I let myself out and sat in the truck for a minute before putting it in reverse. In the red-lit darkness, I caught sight of the shadow in the woods again. I swung the truck around so I could use the headlights to illuminate whatever lurked there.

Beyond the first row of cedars lining the driveway stood a giant pinecone about as tall as me. I hopped out again and walked over to it, stepping between ferns to get to the open lawn. I knocked on one of the scales. It answered with the sound of flesh on steel.

The sculpture was welded metal.

I walked around in a wide circle, letting my hand trail along the surfaces.

Whoever made this had talent.

And shouldn't be working in a boatyard.

Idaho didn't make sense to me.

I glanced at the dark house, tempted to crawl into her warm bed and ask all kinds of questions, which would break the pact.

Instead, I returned to the running truck, and headed home.

EIGHT

Confession:
Turns out, I'm not all that wild when it comes to sex.

***L**et's go to a party.*

I got Ashley's text on Saturday afternoon.

What sort of party?

I felt like I was seeing too much of Ashley. Hanging out on weekends felt like dating.

I didn't date.

Dating led to relationships.

It's down on Scatchet Head. Come. You'll have fun. Promise.

I ran through a list of people I knew who lived down there and who also might know Ashley. Coming up empty, I agreed.

Give me the address and I'll meet you there.

———

"You never told me what kind of party this is," I said as Ashley wound her arms around my neck to kiss me.

"Does it matter? Me, you, booze, food, other people. What more do you need to know?"

I'd parked at Bailey's Corner to meet her per her instructions. Seemed a bit complicated to go to a party. She explained away the oddness by saying the house was at the end of a private road and there wasn't a lot of parking. Made sense, so I didn't question it further. Another car pulled into the parking lot. A couple I didn't recognize got out of their beige Camry and walked toward us. Ashley greeted them warmly and introduced me. Short and round Molly let her hand linger in mine after we shook hands. I flicked my gaze to her husband, Kyle, who looked like a bored accountant, to see if he noticed. I doubt he did because he was busy checking out Ashley's chest.

"Nice to meet you," I said, drawing his attention away from her cleavage.

"Hey. This your first party at the Wrigley's?"

I stuffed my hand in my back pocket to break the contact with Molly. "As far as I know. I don't think I've met them."

"Oh, you're in for a fun night!" Molly's hand stroked my forearm. Wow, she was a touchy one.

I stepped slightly behind Ashley. "Well, let's get this evening started then. Who's driving?"

Ashley drove us down the hill to the beach. Parked cars filled the narrow driveway.

"Big party," I said.

Molly chuckled from the backseat. "I love it when there's a big turnout. So much more fun than standing around eating guacamole and chips."

While Ashley parked, I made a note to avoid Molly for the rest of the night by standing near the chips and dip.

We followed a lit path to the door of a nondescript rancher. Kyle knocked three times on the door and paused, then slowly knocked twice more.

I studied Ashley from the corner of my eye. Her fingers gripped mine, but she didn't look at me.

A man a few years older than me, or maybe early forties if he was in really good shape, swung open the door. "Welcome, I'm Stephen. Leave your shoes by the door here. Coats on the rack."

Inside the lights were low and some random country music played. The paneled walls were typical island, but that's where any familiarity ended. The living room had four sofas and more beanbag chairs around a central rug. *Wait, was that a rug or a wrestling mat?* A shiny silver pole stood alone in what should have been the dining room if it had furniture. I'd never been in a total party house like this before.

Ashley tugged my hand and we moved further into the house, passing through a galley kitchen, its counters laden with trays of snacks, including chips and dip. I grabbed one and Ashley swatted my hand. "Those are for later."

I chomped on the chip, swallowed, and smiled at her. "I ate the evidence. No one will ever know."

We followed our host into a family room with more couches and wood paneling. A few other groups of people stood around with red plastic cups like the world's most low-key fraternity party. A woman with a swarm of blonde hair circling her head and a black jumpsuit barely containing her tits waved at us and rushed over.

"Oh, Ashley, I'm so happy you're here." Blondie leaned around me and kissed her full on the mouth.

Okay, that was weird.

Stephen smiled, watching them. "Brandi, you know everyone, I think, except Tom."

"Hi, I'm Brandi. With an 'i'." She had a little bit of lipstick smudged on both her cheeks and near her collarbone.

"Hi." I gave her a wave, and, having learned my lesson after Molly, stuffed my hands in my back pockets.

"Not much of a talker, is he?" Brandi asked Ashley. "Not that it matters in this crowd!" She laughed at her own personal inside joke. Kyle and Molly joined her. Ashley chuckled and color pinked her cheeks in embarrassment.

Still chuckling, Stephen put his hand on Brandi's ass. "It's still early. Grab some food inside; there are coolers on the deck with beverages. Remember, our two drink maximum, so pace yourselves." He winked at Molly. "If you drove, keys go in the fishbowl by the door."

"Is this a key party?" Molly asked with fake shock.

"This isn't the seventies, honey." Kyle draped his arm around her shoulders, letting his hand rest on her boob.

The whole crowd was very touchy-feely. "I'm going to grab a beer. Ashley, you want something?"

"Sure." She grabbed hold of my belt loop and trailed close behind me as we wove our way through the crowd of mostly couples toward the sliding glass doors.

Despite the cold breeze, I felt more relaxed being outside and away from our hosts and Ashley's "friends".

I popped the top off of an Alaskan Amber. "How do you know Brandi with an 'i' and Stephen?"

"She's a regular customer at the Clinton location."

"And Molly and Kyle?"

"Same thing. He commutes over to Shoreline and stops by every morning." She shrugged. "You get to know a person seeing them consistently."

Ashley owned two coffee huts with her brother Jonah on the island and one over in Mukilteo. They had built a mini-empire from scratch on the wallets of mocha loving housewives, tourists, and commuters. Her staff often featured perky girls in tight T-shirts. I guess she was the Hooters of coffee.

"This party is not at all what I expected," she said, sipping on her bottle.

"It's a little weird." We leaned against the deck railing and stood in silence, watching the other party-goers through the window.

Brandi and Molly were dancing with Kyle. Stephen sat on

one of the couches between two other women, his arms stretched behind them both.

"They seem friendly, if not a little handsy."

She spit out her beer and choked, coughing while I patted her back.

"Swallowed wrong," she sputtered.

A skinny, dark-haired young guy with tattoos on his neck slid the door open and poked his head out. "Mind if I join you?"

I shrugged. "Sure."

"I'm Casey." He introduced himself. He sat on the railing next to Ashley, really close to her.

In fact, his thigh bumped her arm. I scratched my neck and watched him. He caught my expression and shifted a few inches away, creating a sliver of space between them.

I listened while they chatted about the coffee business. A few more people joined us outside. Two women came over and started chatting to me. One of them was the beer garden girl from Halloween. The other one graduated high school a year behind me. Damn small island was small.

I finished off a second beer while we all talked. The girls said they were cold and invited me inside with them. I noticed Ashley and Casey were deep in conversation, and his hand rested on the railing behind her ass. Her hand sat on his forearm.

How cozy. I felt a cold trickle of possessiveness run through my body. He had some nerve. Clearly we were together when he got here. Of course, she wasn't my girlfriend, but unless this was a swin—

Holy shit.

I peered in the window where Kyle had his arm around the waist of another woman who was most definitely not Molly, because she was kissing Brandi in the middle of makeshift dance floor. Was there a ferret cage in the corner?

No way.

I coughed loudly, drawing Ashley's attention. When she met

my eyes, I jerked my head to the window behind me. Her eyes widened and she hopped away from Casey so fast he lost his balance, nearly falling over the deck on to the sand below.

"Can I have a word with you?"

"Um ... yeah ... of course ... sure." Her words tumbled out of her mouth in an awkward stream of nonsense.

I pulled her down the stairs to the wet sand in our socks. She had some explaining to do. With my arms crossed, I waited.

"Tom ..."

I waited.

"I really didn't know what to expect, but it wasn't this. I thought we'd come and it would be a bunch of hot young people, maybe lots of sexual tension, and it would be exciting."

I remained quiet, feeling a cross between fuming and duped. She'd brought me to the island version of *Eyes Wide Shut* without the masks, money, mansion, or hot naked women. Although I suspected if we hung around long enough, some nudity might be inevitable.

"And I didn't tell you it was a special kind of party, because I figured you'd say no out of some misplaced sense of propriety." Her voice became squeakier. "Which is ridiculous because you're all about sex. You don't do relationships, or hell, dating. What's wrong with coming to a party where that's everyone's focus? This should be cool with you. It's just sex."

My eyes widened and I lowered my hands. I swung my arms as I exhaled a cloud of warm breath. With each inhale and exhale, I stared out over the water. Lights from Everett and Seattle sparkled across the wide black expanse.

I rubbed both hands over my beard. "Yeah. I've got to go."

"That's it? Really? I'm giving you the kind of fun most guys dream about."

"What's that?"

"Freedom. Space to have fun, explore."

"By watching you have sex with some guy you just met?"

"Whoa, who said I'm having sex with anyone tonight besides you?"

"Isn't that the whole point? I get to watch you with another guy."

"Or woman," she offered.

I paused to think about it. Was that one of my fantasies? According to the porn industry, yes. What was I complaining about? I thought about Brandi and Molly. They weren't hideous, but neither turned my crank. Some fantasies might be better left in the imagination.

"A head's up would have been nice is all I'm saying."

She coiled around me like the snake in Eden. "So we can stay?"

I burst out laughing. "No way."

"What if I don't want to leave?" She pouted.

"Then stay. Get your rocks off, but I'm out of here."

She followed me up the stairs. Casey had disappeared. He'd probably found another offer.

I rubbed the sand from my socks on the mat and opened the door.

"Tom, I can't believe you turned out to be such a prude," she shouted after me, her feet stomping on the wood floor. Her voice and antics drew the attention of a couple making out in the hallway.

"Have fun, Ashley. Don't call me." Searching for my shoes, I made the mistake of glancing in the front room. A couple was going at it on the mat while another couple watched from the couches. The man, who had his hand down his pants, made eye contact with me. I recognized him as Stephen, but didn't know the woman.

"Thanks for the chips and dip!" I waved and shut the front door behind me. I didn't bother putting on my boots until I was on the main road.

It was at least three miles up hill to my truck. About halfway there, I burst out laughing and had to double-over to catch my breath. *What the actual hell just happened? Did I dodge a bullet back there? Or walk away from the opportunity of a lifetime?* The night promised sex and lots of it, and I was hoofing it to my truck alone. I'd seen orgies in porn, but never been to one in real life. Of course, I'd thought about it, but the reality tonight seemed a lot less sexy.

I'd heard of swingers before, but on the island? Geez. John would never believe me if I told him. Oh shit, no way was I telling him about tonight. He'd never let me live it down. That kind of material couldn't be passed up. Ever. I'd never stop busting his balls if it happened to him.

Maybe it had. Growing up here, we knew pretty much everyone. Now, I'd never be able to go to Red Apple or Payless Foods for groceries and not wonder who was and wasn't a swinger. I shook my head. What if you ran into someone you knew? What if you ran into a family member at one of those things? Did whoever got there first get to stay? Did you draw straws? Or both leave and never speak of it again?

What if I ran into Hailey at the party?

Would I have stayed? Made out with her in front of Ashley? After last weekend, I didn't think she was kinky, but maybe she was. Her nipple twist had been accurate and painful. Maybe she liked to boss around men and make them serve her. Hadn't that pretty much been what happened? *Shit.* My mind spun all sorts of crazy scenarios as I trudged up the hill.

Headlights brightened the road behind me and I stepped further toward the edge of the shoulder. I had another mile plus of walking and decided to stick out my thumb. Single guy walking along the road a night, it would be a long shot to get a ride, but I had nothing to lose. My dignity lay on the beach behind me.

A familiar fender came into view.

What were the odds?

A yellow dog head stuck out of the passenger window, looking happy to see me.

"Hey, Donnely, what are you doing in the woods?" John asked.

"Listen, you give me a ride to Bailey's Corner to get my truck, and don't ask any questions or I walk there. Deal?"

John laughed and told Babe to scoot over. I climbed into the cab and held up my hand. "Seriously, don't ask."

"Husband catch you and you had to climb out a window?" He continued laughing, clearly amusing himself. At my scowl, his face grew serious. "Oh, no, please tell me it wasn't some girl's father. That's all sorts of wrong."

"One time when we were in high school. Once. I've gone out a window once. I was seventeen."

"And landed ass naked in a bush of stinging nettles." He slapped my shoulder. "Best idea ever. I swear, if I have a daughter, I'm planting those all around her window."

I joined him laughing about stupid teenage me. Easier than the grown man me being a fool. At least it hadn't been Hailey picking me up. At least I had a small shred of my ego left.

When he dropped me off, I thanked him, and he said, "For what?" before driving away.

With friends like him, who needed swingers?

NINE

Confession:
I have a photographic memory for sex.

irst thing Monday at work, I stopped in the break room for
a cup of coffee. Our dry spell ended overnight with sideways rain and high winds. Tree branches had been dropping all
over the island and power outages were likely if the storm ended
up being as bad as the doomsday weathermen forecasted. At
least this week my work was inside the hull of the tugboat, a
small blessing.

Pouring coffee into my mug, my ears perked at the sound of
soft cursing and the muffled thump of folders landing on the
carpet in the hall a few feet away.

Idaho stood there staring at me. I smiled and she dropped to
her knees to pick up the papers around her feet.

"Morning," I said with a smile, liking the vision of her on
her knees.

"Hi," she mumbled, not making eye contact. That I didn't
like.

We hadn't discussed how to deal with working at the yard

together. I hadn't given it much thought at the time, but we probably should've discussed not making it a big deal. She came to me and I gave her what she wanted. In my eyes, that made us even-steven.

"Hey." I squatted down to help her.

"It's fine. Don't help." She snatched the papers from my hand.

"Hey." I tried again.

This time she allowed her gaze to land on my face. I waited while she slowly made her way up from my mouth to my eyes. "We're okay, right?"

If she was having regrets, I needed to know, so I could make it right.

Her slow exhale brushed across my face. She blinked a few times and then straightened her spine in resolve. "We're fine."

"Good." Standing, I reached my hand down to help her up.

"I got it." She rose and stepped away. A minute passed before she spoke again. "Thank you."

"For what?"

"You know."

"My pleasure." And it had been. Frozen images of her above and beneath me from the other night flashed through my mind. I smiled at the memory and skimmed my index finger over my lips. "Anytime."

Her mouth fell open before she clamped it shut. "It was a one-time thing."

"Never say never." I handed her the pen she'd dropped. "You know where to find me."

She shook her head and walked down the hall. I let my eyes land on her ass. No jacket today. Not one to deny myself, I dropped my gaze to her long legs and thanked whoever invented the idea of tight jeans.

Someone cleared his throat beside me. Al from the main office stood there. Clearly, I'd been busted.

"Tom, do we need to go over the fraternization policy?" he asked.

"No, not an issue."

"Good to hear. The last thing this company needs is another sexual harassment accusation."

I nodded. I had a couple cousins who thought the last name Donnely meant they were above the law around here. Sadly, to save the family name and pride, Pops had bailed them out more than once. He had a three strikes rule: first time, you were probably a dumb-ass; second time, you were stupid; third time, better learn from your mistakes. There were probably twenty first and countless second cousins, and only two had ever made it to the third strike: Bob had served time; and Clark served as a state representative down in Olympia.

"How's she working out?" I gestured down the hall to where Idaho had disappeared.

"She's one hell of a project manager. I think she'll get us there under budget and early."

Figured she was smart, too. "Good. I've been keeping an eye on her."

"So I observed." His voice was serious.

I faltered. "I meant around the rest of the guys."

"I know what you meant, but honestly, she doesn't need it. The woman can hold her own. Saw her put Stan in his place so fast he didn't realize what had happened until the end of lunch."

Go, Idaho.

TEN

Confession:
Most of everything I know, I learned from Pops.

Every November, Lori and Nick hosted a Leonid meteor shower party at their house down the road from mine. Hidden deep in the woods, the location was perfect for stargazing away from Seattle's light pollution. A large open field held a pyre of wood for a bonfire on one side, and blankets, pillows, and inflatable air mattresses for meteor watching on the other.

I had been instructed, under penalty of death by purple-nurple, there would be no hanky-panky on those air-beds. Of any kind. For that reason, I usually went by myself to these events.

Rather than drive, I grabbed a flashlight by the door and headed into the woods, following the familiar path to my sister's house. A few yards from the edge of the trees, the glow from the fire brightened the path, and I turned off the light. People walked toward the blaze or stood around its edge. Lori's round belly stood out against the warm glow, so I aimed for her profile.

When I reached her side, I kissed her head. "Hey, baby sister."

"My favorite brother!"

"Only brother." I grinned and her smile mirrored mine.

"Same thing."

I greeted other familiar faces, landing last on Idaho's.

"Hey." I gave her a slight head bob, not knowing if we were cool.

She rolled her eyes, but smiled, returning my gesture.

"Funny running into you here," I said.

"Why's that? Lori invited me. It's her house."

"Don't get me wrong, I'm glad you're here. It's just funny how we don't see each other for years and now here we are again."

"I'm living on the island, we work together, and I'm best friends with your sister. It's inevitable we'll be in the same place at the same time a lot. Like five days a week and some weekends."

"Sounds like a custody deal." I frowned.

"You have kids?" Her eyes widened.

I gave her a sly smile. "None I know about."

"Right. There could be hundreds of Tommy boys running around out there."

"Hundreds? You flatter me." I rubbed the knuckle of my index finger against my jaw. She might have been fishing for her number. To be honest, I didn't keep track. No notches in my bedpost or in the frame around my bedroom door. Actually, there wouldn't be. I rarely brought women to my house. John joked I needed a "he-man woman-haters" sign above the door like we had in our tree house on my grandparents property. It wasn't that bad. Women who were related to me visited all the time, much to my annoyance.

Idaho studied me.

"I swear, not hundreds." Not sure why I needed to emphasize my point, but it mattered.

With a shrug and a small smile, she walked away, and joined a group standing on the far side of the fire.

What did her shrug and smile mean? I furrowed my brows and stomped out a glowing ember on the grass. The party had shifted and I stood alone. Fine by me. I found a Deschuttes in one of the coolers. Plates of hot dogs and sausages filled a nearby table, along with metal skewers and old school sticks for toasting marshmallows. I speared a sausage and joined the crowd around the bonfire.

"You should see a doctor if you have a burning sensation in your wiener," Diane bumped my hip.

I gazed down at her and she pointed to where flames encompassed my sausage.

"Damn." Pulling the flaming meat toward me, I waved it around and blew on it to extinguish the fire. What remained looked like a charred, black dog turd. "You think it's still good?"

She waved the smoke away from her face. "No."

I shrugged and threw the carbonized chunk of meat into the fire. "Want one?"

"Nah, I'm all set with meat right now, thanks."

I smiled and glanced over her shoulder. "Where's the big lumberjack?" These days wherever Diane was, my best friend was sure to be lurking close by.

"He's over there somewhere talking about fishing with your grandfather. Those two could talk all night about lures and weights."

I stared through the flames and found them. Pops sat in a folding camp chair and gestured broadly with his hands. From here it appeared he was telling the famous Sitka halibut story from '84. There were the ones who got away, and then there was the big fish story. The biggest, baddest gilled monster that broke your heart and ruined you when it swam away. We all had one.

"I should go say hi."

Pops was hands-down one of my favorite people on the

planet. He didn't talk a lot and he didn't like most people, or things, but we had a bond. His eyes lit up when he saw me.

"Hey Pops." I squatted down in front of him so he'd be able to hear me better. We chatted about nothing for a few minutes.

"I met John's young lady. She's quite the catch, I think. Pretty thing. Reminds me of Ellie when she was younger. Although, when I was your age, I'd been married ten years and was raising a family."

John and I both glanced down and fumbled with our beers.

"Now, I know your generation does it differently, but for the life of me, I can't figure out what you boys are waiting for. Or running from." The lenses of his glasses reflected the fire, but I knew he was giving me his patented Clifford stare. "Women keep their looks longer. Men? We lose our hair, get a paunch," he patted his belly, "grow fur in our ears, and those pretty girls aren't going to look our way anymore, at least not for the right reasons." He paused to cough. "You wait too long, you miss the best titties."

I choked on my beer. John stared at me with amused disbelief.

Clifford Donnely called it like he saw it.

I said a prayer of thanks he didn't talk about trouble getting it up with my grandmother.

"At least now with those drugs, you don't have to worry so much about losing your ability to salute your woman."

Ah, there it was.

"I enjoy your company, but go talk to those young ladies of yours." He pointed with his thick, gnarled fingers across the fire to where Diane stood talking with Idaho.

"Oh, that's not my girl, Pops. She's Lori's friend, Hailey King. You know the Kings, over in Freeland?"

"She the one marrying the no good land-grabbing city boy with his big ideas about progress?" He glowered.

"I think she called off the wedding," John said.

"Good. Came to her senses. The last thing we need is his

kind destroying what took generations for this family to build. Now, one of you give me a hand out of this goddamn-cheapass-rickety-prick-chair. It's past my bedtime."

We each took an arm and gently tugged him out of the folding chair. He hacked again and patted the pocket on his chest for his smokes.

"You quit smoking. Five years ago," I said.

"Damnit. One of the worst mistakes I've ever made. I miss the days when smoking was accepted and appreciated. Like a stiff drink at lunch. Nowadays nothing I do isn't regulated by doctors or the government. Too many bureaucrats messing in my business."

I had to laugh at his grumblings. He was a man of strong opinions and stubborn as all get out. Open-heart surgery with a quadruple by-pass had been the final push for him to quit smoking. Nearly scared us all to death, but he took it in stride like he did with most things.

"Nice to see Pops. The man never changes. He's exactly as scary and funny as he was when we were growing up," John said as we walked over to Diane.

"Man used to scare the living crap out of me as a kid, but he was a pussycat compared to Gramma Ellie. She had a spatula she kept aside special for us kids. 'Go see your Gramma' were the scariest words a Donnely kid could hear." I rubbed my ass in memory.

"No date tonight to rub your ass for you?" Diane teased, wrapping her arms around John.

"Har har. You're beginning to remind me of one of my sisters." I narrowed my eyes at her. "And I don't need another sister."

"I tease with love. Speaking of dates, where's your firecracker Ashley tonight? She was all over you on Halloween and I didn't see you complaining. Or acting like you were being attacked by bees. What's going on there?" She showed her teeth in what someone might mistake for a smile. The Cheshire Cat had nothing on her.

"No idea, haven't talked to her. You know me, I don't date."

"Look!" Lori shouted and pointed to the sky.

A silver streak and then another flashed across the darkness. The crowd strolled over to the viewing area and claimed blankets and mattresses. Couples coupled together like they were animals on the arc. I found a spot on a blanket on the ground and lay down, propping my head on my arms. Another bright flare blazed and burned out above the tree line. On the mattress next to me, a body shifted under a blanket. Ugh. If people were making out two feet away from me, I needed to move. Lori would not approve of this becoming an orgy. Chuckling to myself, I sat up and folded my arms around my knees, trying not to glance to my left.

"Tom?"

Idaho.

I turned my head to see her. "Whatcha doing there, Idaho?" I whispered as I lay down.

"Watching the stars. You?" She rolled to her side to face me, and the airbed dipped.

Our faces leaned close together and her eyes sparkled in the dim light. I stared for a moment, maybe two. She didn't break eye-contact, and she didn't make a face to deflect.

"No, you're not." It was the first thing to come to my mind. "Stars are up there." I pointed above her head, and smirked. "You should make a wish."

"Maybe I already have." She flipped on her back.

I couldn't help it. Teasing her felt like breathing. I didn't think about it, the words flowed out of me. "Scoot over a little."

"I'm not spooning with you," she whispered, crossing her arms.

"No spooning. I want a pillow." I shifted my legs so my head could rest perpendicular to her hip. I kept my eyes on the sky and the stars streaked above me while I listened to her breathing.

Unlike fireworks, meteor showers didn't have crescendos and encores. The frequency increased and the bright paths of meteors incinerating lit the sky, but there was no reason to ooh or ahh. Meteor watching was a quiet, mostly solitary activity. A few "look!" and "over there" pierced the quiet, but otherwise the fire crackling, murmured, intimate words and the soft rustle of branches in the wind were the only sounds.

Something about observing the stars blinking their limited light and lying on the ground combined into a creeping loneliness. I arrived alone and I'd be leaving alone to return to my house, alone. Would anyone mark my disappearance? Would anyone notice if I faded away?

Then again, I'd rather be alone than one of those couples that walked and ate in silence, and appeared more sad and lonely together than if they were solo.

The cold earth and wind snuck under my clothing. I shivered.

"Want to share my blanket?" her soft voice asked.

"Nah, I'm good."

"I can see you shiver, and you're jostling me. Come on, I won't bite."

"You can't make that promise. I have a distinct memory, which would contradict your statement."

"Shh. Someone might hear you." She half sat up and peered around at the couples near us. No one was paying attention. I could have told her so.

I rotated so my body lined up parallel with hers, but remained on the ground. I plotted my quick escape in case I needed it.

She sighed and the blanket landed over my torso. "That didn't come out right. I'm not ashamed of what happened. I'm a grown woman."

I waited. Typically what followed "I'm not ashamed" proved otherwise.

"It's complicated. Kurt, Lori … it would be a mess if they found out."

"Don't worry about it. No one will hear it from me, if you're concerned. I'm not one to kiss and tell. Trust me, the last thing I want is to be the center of the gossip circle."

"I … I wasn't worried."

"No problem. Honestly, I'm pretty clear about how things work. Don't beat yourself up. From what I remember, we had fun, a lot of fun. Don't taint it with some girlish guilt about getting off with someone you don't love. That's bullshit."

"Will you hang on a minute?" Her voice rose above a whisper. "You're putting words in my mouth, and you have no idea what I'm trying to say here. If you did, maybe you'd shut up for five seconds and let me get the words out." Her voice trailed off in a frustrated huff. "Never mind."

"Now you've piqued my curiosity."

"Curiosity killed the cat, Tom."

"I'll take my chances." I reached over and searched for her hand under the blanket. I found it resting on her stomach, tightly clasped with the other one. She didn't unwind her fingers, so I lay mine on top. "Tell me."

"I never said I didn't like it. You know you're good in bed. You shout it with the way you flash your dimples at every woman you meet, in your swagger, in the 'I don't give a fuck' attitude you have about relationships. And for the record, I did have fun."

I didn't contain my grin. "You mean these dimples?" I gave her both barrels.

"Stop. You already charmed me out of my underwear once."

"And? You want another go?" I pried her fingers apart and wove them with mine.

She whispered something so quietly it got lost in the night.

"I'm sorry, you're going to have to repeat that."

"Yes."

"Again, didn't catch that," I teased.

"Yes, I wouldn't mind another go."

I squeezed her hand. "They always do."

She pulled her hand away from me and threw off the blanket, kicking at it with her feet. "Don't be an asshole."

Shit.

"Okay, I shouldn't have said that." And more quietly, under my breath, "Even if it's true."

"I'm going home."

"Fuck." I've messed this up. "Don't. I'm sorry. Let's hang out again."

She didn't respond.

"I'd like it, too," I said.

"I don't want to be a pity fuck. That's the last thing I want. Don't ever make me feel like I'm some sort of charity project for you. Just. Don't." She struggled to keep her voice low, the history of past hurts staining her words.

"Never. No way." I held up my fingers in a salute. "Promise."

Her eyes narrowed, but she relaxed again. I pulled the blanket up to cover us and leaned closer to her ear. "Come over after this. Better to drive over and park behind the shop than leave your car here, and have people ask questions. I'll walk home on my own. Nod your head if you agree."

In the darkness, with the sky burning up above us, I waited for her signal.

She was right. This could be a shit storm if people found out. On the other hand, we were adults. We had chemistry. They could mind their own business. She moved her head in a subtle nod with eyes fixed toward the sky.

After a few moments, I bounced up and stretched, yawning loudly. "Okay, kids, Tom Cat's heading home. You behave yourselves. Or don't. You know I wouldn't."

A few groans and good-byes responded. The spell of the night broken, others stretched and stood too, Idaho amongst them.

Lori shouted at everyone to leave the stuff on the lawn for the morning, but I folded our blanket and put it on one of the chairs near the fire. With a wave and a sweep of my flashlight, I headed off into the woods. Leaving alone like always. Better alone than lonely, as Pops would say.

ELEVEN

Confession:
I make a mean breakfast.

I sat on my porch in the dark and waited for car lights to slip through the woods surrounding my driveway. She should have been here by now. My leg bounced as I counted to sixty again and again. The light over the shop highlighted one of my works in progress: a six-foot otter rested across two sawhorses. I liked this project and lost myself in plotting the cuts I still needed to make.

Lights blinded me as her car bounced over the ruts of the unpaved drive. I stood and pointed to the side of the shop where she could park. "What took you so long?"

"I ended up folding all of the blankets to annoy Lori. Or that's what she accused me of doing. Woman is almost nine months pregnant, I couldn't leave her with a mess." She strolled toward me on the porch.

"You're good people, King."

She took the steps two at a time until she stood in front of me. "Maybe I don't want to be good." Her mouth met mine, warm and wet.

I let her take control as she slammed our bodies into the door-frame. I reached behind myself to open the door, and pulled her inside with me. Still kissing, we stumbled into the living room and landed against the side of the couch. I lifted her by the hips and she spread her legs to wrap them around me. Her tongue stroked mine, and I let my hands wander everywhere, shoving fabric out of the way as I went. Her coat, sweater, and shirt flew across the couch, landing on the floor and coffee table. She reached around to unclasp her pink lace bra. My hands cupped her warm flesh while hers undid my belt and lowered my zipper. Cool fingers reached inside to grasp me. I jumped at the shock of the contrast between warm and cold. She leaned too far and tumbled over the couch, landing in a soft heap on the cushions. I jumped over to follow her, my laughter joining hers as we made out like horny teenagers, half-dressed and rounding second base for third.

Her phone vibrated and rang from the floor. We paused in our kissing, and I waited for her to say something.

"Ignore it. Nothing good comes from late night phone calls."

I shifted to release some pressure where the zipper of my open fly ground into my skin.

"Take your pants off," she commanded.

I paused. "Bossy much?"

"We're going to end up naked eventually. Why wait and prolong the inevitable?"

"The inevitable sounds like the ice shelf melting or polar bears going extinct. Doomsday and disaster. Not hot sex."

"Who said the sex was hot?" She smirked at me.

I nipped her shoulder. "I believe you did less than an hour ago. Isn't that why you're here?"

With a gentle shove, she encouraged me to roll to my side. She shifted to the edge of the couch and said, "Actually, I only needed to use your bathroom."

Laughing, she moved out of range before I could pull her to me. With a few quick movements, she dropped her jeans and stepped out of her underwear. I sat up fully to watch her, attempting to figure out her next move. She both confused and intrigued me.

Before I could stand, she dashed over to the stairs and up the first few steps. I nearly tripped over my own jeans trying to catch up to her, and then face planted on the first stair, barely bracing myself with my hands in a semi-pantsless push-up. After an awkward struggle, I kicked off my jeans and boots, following her upstairs in only my boxers and socks.

Both the bedroom and bathroom doors were closed. I peeked into the bedroom and found it empty. Waiting for her, I propped myself up on the pillows and stripped off my remaining clothing. The house was cold, but my skin felt flushed when I took myself in hand and stroked. Running water and the faint squeak of the door opening announced her return. She strode into the room and studied me for a few seconds before flopping on the bed next to me.

"Here, let me." She moved my hand out of the way, and again, her cool skin contrasted against mine.

"Shit, why are your hands always so cold?"

She paused and loosened her grip. "Want me to stop?"

"No, but you should get them checked out. Maybe you have a heart condition." I pulled her toward me and kissed her. Her hand set the rhythm and our mouths echoed it. I slowed down the pace and touched the tops of her thighs, dragging my hand slowly up and over her hip before settling in the space between her legs. My fingers met with smooth skin below a small patch of hair. I paused. Hailey had waxed since our last meet-up. She was definitely a single girl now. I briefly wondered if she had other men besides me.

I stretched my arm to reach the top drawer in the night-stand, but she leaned over me to grab the condom. She pulled out a long row of them and gave me a sidelong look. "Jeez, do you buy them in bulk?"

"Of course. Those things add up."

Her eyes flashed to mine and I shrugged. We'd already been over this. Without breaking eye contact, she tore the edge of the wrapper with her teeth.

That was hot. I loved when a woman took charge. Sometimes. Better than lying there like a log and making me do all the work. Where was the fun in that? Sex, after all, was about fun, not work.

She straddled my hips, beaming down on me. I matched her grin and gripped her thighs, urging her up, wanting to be inside of her.

Her hands covered mine and she whispered, "Patience."

"Patience is a virtue and I'm not feeling particularly virtuous right now. Don't tease." I flicked her nipple.

With a smooth movement, she impaled herself on me until there was nothing left of me outside of her. She paused and I felt her open further to accommodate me. I fought the urge to thrust and grind myself into her, seeking a way to feel more of this amazing sensation. I wanted to feel her without the condom. Would she feel like silk or velvet?

I stopped. I never had sex without a condom. Ever.

Well, not since high school and the pregnancy scare. After, I ruled I'd never trust a woman when she said she was on the pill.

"Tom?"

I still hadn't moved. I opened my eyes to meet green ones.

"Did I do something wrong?" She shifted her position as if to climb off me.

I held her in place and thrusted. "No, nothing wrong. Everything right."

Holding her lower back and hip with one hand and the other on her boob, I moved her above me. She arched her back and tossed her head, tweaking her nipple.

"You're beautiful." The truth slipped out without thought.

Her eyes flashed open and she leaned forward to kiss me, bracing her arms near my head. It changed the angle and I went deeper. I wanted more.

I rolled us over and lifted her legs to my shoulders. Ah, there it was—the sensation where I couldn't tell I ended and she began. So deep I wished my dick was bigger, longer, thicker to feel more of her. Not that I had a small dick.

She closed her eyes, and I studied her face, prolonging this feeling. She had a small dark freckle on her cheekbone near her left eye. Her lips parted and I noticed the bottom one was much fuller than the top. Her front teeth bit into the plump flesh and I envied them. I leaned forward to claim it for my own, causing her to moan and tighten her arms around me. My hand snaked between us and I stroked her clit. Her palm lay on top of mine and she showed me how much and where, releasing me when I figured it out.

This was different than the first night. Last time, I didn't feel I had to prove anything. I knew I would show her the time she wanted, even if she believed she was using me for sex. Tonight, she took charge, but I won.

Her teeth found her lip again when I pinched her nipple and pressed against her with my thumb. She tensed and tightened around me before she came. I stared at her face, gorgeous in ecstasy, and felt myself near the edge. I paused and pulled out for a second. Her eyes fluttered open.

"Did you come?" she asked.

I shook my head. "I need a break before you go for seconds."

A slow, blissed-out grin spread across her face. "Pretty cocky, aren't you?"

I raised a shoulder and stroked myself. "Roll over and we'll see if it's cockiness or confidence. Or both."

She lifted on all fours like a good girl with her face peering over her shoulder as I stroked her ass. "What are you waiting for?"

"Simply admiring the view." I gave her cheek a slap and she replied with a soft moan. When I slapped the other one she moaned louder.

"I like that."

"Which part?" I spanked her at the bottom of the curve of her ass.

"That. And when you take charge."

"I know. Ready?" I plunged into her again, quickly finding our rhythm. As much as I loved this position, I wasn't sure if I could keep my promise of another orgasm. Bracing on one arm, she reached up to stroke herself, arching against my thrusts.

Good old-fashioned teamwork brought her another orgasm before I felt myself tip over into my own. I lost myself, pulled under by pleasure, as I grunted and moaned. Exhausted, I fell on top of her and she collapsed beneath me. Our chests heaved and a fine layer of sweat sealed our skin together. I moved her hair from her neck and lightly bit her shoulder.

"Hi," she whispered. "You're crushing me."

———

I stretched, my arms and legs taking up the middle of my king bed. A slight ache reminded me of the sex last night. Blinking open my eyes in the bright morning light, I listened for sounds of water in the bathroom. Normal stillness in the house answered me. I lifted my head and studied the space for signs Hailey was still here.

"Idaho?" I called out.

Nothing.

I located my boxers on the floor and stepped into them. The floor was cold and I hopped around to avoid making prolonged contact on my way to the bathroom. I didn't smell coffee or breakfast cooking on my way down the stairs. Her clothes were gone from the coffee table and floor. The couch cushions had been fluffed into their normal positions. I threw on my shirt from last night that smelled of smoke from the bonfire, and padded over to the kitchen to make coffee. No note on the counter either.

Huh.

I spun around and studied the rooms. No sign she'd ever been here at all.

Little did she know, I'd planned to make her breakfast.

Oh well.

Her loss.

I found my phone and scrolled through to see if she'd texted.

Nothing.

I realized I didn't have her phone number. Why would I? I had no need to call her before. I guess I could get it from work on Monday. Not that I needed it. I wasn't going to chase her.

I smirked, confident there would be a next time. Sex with Hailey was different, better.

TWELVE

Confession:
I'm a sucker for my family.

Holidays could be torture for the single man, or they could be prime time to fill the needs of lonely women. Thanksgiving meant a day of football and eating at the farmhouse. A day when men could be men and sit around watching other men play sports, with a never-ending supply of snacks, beer, and sanctioned post-meal naps. Dad and Pops claimed the two recliners in the family room while I stretched out in the corner of the couch and rested my feet on the coffee table next to the bowl of chips.

My phone chirped with a message. A local number flashed on the screen, but I didn't recognize it. I punched in my code to unlock the phone—couldn't be too careful—and opened the message.

Happy T Day. ~H.

Ducking my head, I smiled to myself. Nick sat next to me, but he leaned forward, intent on the game, shouting at the coaches and arguing with the announcer's take on the last play. I quickly typed a message.

Hank, is this you?

I smirked and waited.

Who's Hank?

Sorry, Howard.

I drummed my fingers on my leg.

You know a lot of men with names beginning with H. Guess again.

I tapped the phone against my cheek, trying to think of another guy's name with an H.

Hector, sorry man. Or is this Horatio?

Hector's going to be pissed you don't have his number saved. Js

Damn. I'm out of guys. Heidi?

A full play went down on TV and a commercial break aired before my phone lit up with another text.

Har, har.

I'd gone too far. Time to confess.

Hailey, I knew it was you. You at your folks?

She replied right away. ***Yep. You?***

Not at your parents. Sitting on the couch with the men while women make us a feast. I knew it would rile her up, but I couldn't stop the teasing if I tried. I was having too much fun. Around me, cheers and high fives erupted for a touchdown. Or a field goal. I'd completely missed it.

"Woot," I shouted, lamely after the fact.

Pops shot me a dirty look. "You going to watch the game with the rest of us or play on your gadget?"

"Ooh, busted," Nick said next to me. "You making plans for a hook-up later?" He leaned over, trying to see my screen.

I turned my phone against my chest in case he recognized Hailey's number. "No, just a friend."

Another text arrived.

Sounds like a classic sexist set up you've got going there. Dinner's ready. Thanks for the chat.

I frowned. I didn't want our conversation to end even if I got teased.

Maybe if you're bored, we can hang out this week-end. Happy Thanksgiving. I hit send before I talked myself out of it.

No immediate response, so I tucked my phone under my thigh and got into the game, shoveling chips and crab dip into my mouth.

"Slow down, Tom, your mother's going to be mad if you can't have seconds and thirds at dinner," Dad chided.

Something about being in this room with Dad and Pops brought me right back to being a kid. Feeling chastised and annoyed, I got up and walked down the hall to take a piss. Female voices carried from the kitchen and I paused. Normally, I couldn't care less what they gossiped about, but I thought I heard a familiar name.

"Hailey said it was completely over. Kurt became more and more controlling after he proposed. She returned the ring right after Halloween." Lori continued their conversation.

Like a creeper, I crept down the hall to hear more.

"Oh, that's a shame," Gramma said. "And at her age, it's not as easy to find a nice man. The good ones are all taken."

I frowned and crossed my arms.

"Tom's still single," Mom said, defending me.

I could always count on Mom to take my side. A burst of laughter followed her words.

"Right. And for good reason, Mom." Amy's voice joined the conversation.

Cara was still laughing.

"What's wrong with Tom?" Mom asked.

"Um, how to say this in front of Gramma." Lori's voice hesitated. "He's not a bad guy, he's just a—"

"He's one of those bachelors, honey. You know, the kind you

call for a good time and a little hanky-panky, but don't introduce to your parents."

My grandmother had called me out.

Amy, Cara, and Lori cackled in unison.

"Oh, that's not true." Mom chuckled. "He hasn't met the right woman yet."

"Yet? How many women does he have to try out? He's running out of females on the island. Plus, he's not twenty-two anymore," Amy said.

"You know, Pops was a real ladies' man when I met him. I think your mother is right. It takes a special kind of woman to tame a Donnely man."

"I have to agree with that," Mom said. "Your father—"

"Mom, do not say anything about Dad. Please!" Lori screeched. "La la la la."

I could picture her standing with her fingers in her ears like she did as a kid.

Cara's voice spoke over Lori's singing. "I guess time will tell with Tom. I'd never set him up with any of my friends. That's for sure."

Gee, thanks, Cara.

I'd had enough and went into the bathroom. Staring in the mirror, I cocked my head and rubbed my beard. Who were they to label and judge me? Their words stung. Screw them. I never told them how to live their lives.

Getting married, having kids, and settling down wasn't for everyone.

And definitely not for me.

I thought about texting Ashley to meet up later, but after her "special" party, I wasn't sure it would be a good idea. We hadn't spoken or been in contact since.

"Dinner's ready," Mom called from the dining room. I popped my head through the doorway from the hall and she gave me a guilty smile. "Tom, mind calling the kids in from outside?

The family poured into the room and as people took their seats, it became apparent we were a chair short at the grown-up table.

"Mom? We're missing a chair for Tom," Cara pointed out as I entered the room, kids shoving past me to their table in the kitchen.

Mom's face dropped. "No, that can't be right. We're always ten. Oh! I forgot to adjust for Nick."

"It's fine. I can sit at the kids' table." With a hollow laugh, I walked toward the breakfast nook. Sitting around the kitchen table were my five nieces and nephews, each with a pre-made plate of food and a glass of milk. One chair sat empty at the head.

Squeals of "Uncle Tom" greeted me when I sat down among the Lilliputian Donnelys, the future of the family.

"Did you know the turkey's name was Tom, too?" Sam the smartass asked me.

"I'm pretty sure this one was named Butterball." I stole Sam's roll and he kicked me.

"Mom!" the little bugger yelled. "Uncle stole my roll!"

"Don't be a tattle-tale," Amy shouted. "Tom, give back the roll."

I took a bite and put the roll on his plate with a smile. A small shoe made contact with my shin again. "Ouch," I mumbled through gritted teeth.

Pops' deep baritone rang out with the words of prayer and a blessing for the food while I rubbed my leg, and gave my nephew the stink-eye.

After grace, I took a plate and filled it in the dining room. Lori and Cara gave me looks of sympathy, going so far as to offer their chairs at the table.

"Nah, you two need the break. I can handle the kids."

———

It would never be clear how or who started the great mashed potato fight at the kids' table. My money and version would always be that it began with little Lily with her blonde curls and cherub cheeks. Yes, she was under two, but had a mean arm and a spoon she knew how to use. In the aftermath, it became clear I'd borne the worst of the attack. My hair and beard were covered in gravy laden spuds and melted butter.

Perhaps there was a small part of my brain which felt smug over the potato incident. The disapproval and tsking from the sister/mom brigade made me chuckle, earning me dirty looks and threats of having to bathe all five kids. Dad laughed and threw me a kitchen towel while Pops reminisced about a food fight in the Navy, which earned him a short stay in the brig. While my sisters cleaned up their various children, I wiped down the table, chairs, ceiling light, wall, along with a framed watercolor of a pig, and a spot on the ceiling ten feet away that I blamed on Lily, aka future champion softball pitcher.

We adjourned to the family room to stretch out and rub our swollen bellies before dessert. My phone laid abandoned on the couch cushion where I'd left it. It flashed with a notification. Not wanting to get my hopes up, I stuck it in my shirt pocket and waited.

Uncertainty weighed heavy in my chest where my phone tugged at my pocket for the next five minutes. Unable to wait any longer, I pulled it out and saw two new text messages. One was from Ashley, which I ignored. The other was from Hailey.

Sure.

One word.

Four letters.

A whole world of possibilities.

THIRTEEN

Confession:
I don't always want to be in charge.

Friday dawned clear and blue. The brisk air snuck through leaky windows and gaps in the floor. Sunny days would be rare over the next few months. With a day off and no plans, I decided to take the Triumph for a ride up the island. Dry roads, clear skies, and the perfect day lay ahead of me. In preparation for winter's long, dark, damp days, islanders spent as much time outside on the non-wet days as possible, storing up Vitamin D and the feel of warmth on our skin to last us for months.

After breakfast, I tugged on my leather jacket over a thermal and flannel. The cold air required extra layers, and I sported long johns under my jeans. I tucked a thermos of coffee in the saddlebag. Gloves on, visor down, I revved the engine and plotted my route north.

I took the left after Freeland and drove up past the State Park. At Greenbank, I stopped at the store and grabbed a sandwich. I sped along Ebey's Spit before Fort Casey. Nowhere to be, I meandered to Route 20, and headed north. On the open road,

I let the bike go, leaning down and into the curves. Out of nowhere another motorcycle passed me on the left, leaving me in their exhaust as they took the curve around Penn Cove fast. The bike appeared to be an orange painted vintage BMW. I accelerated, hoping to catch up with them.

The driver turned his head and gave me a wave with a gloved hand as we passed the old drive-in. Wearing an insulated suit and black helmet with the visor down, they could be anyone, but seemed to know me. I lost them in Oak Harbor, but guessed they'd gone north.

Near Deception Pass, I finally caught up to the bike. Finding out who was riding had become more than curiosity. This game of cat and mouse both intrigued and annoyed me.

Right before the bridge, the BMW pulled off the road and stopped fast, creating a small spray of gravel on the shoulder. I slowed to a stop about five yards away and waited with my engine purring.

If the mystery rider were a woman, all sorts of dirty thoughts floated through my mind. I bet we could find a secluded spot in the park, maybe over a picnic table. If the mystery rider were a man, who the hell was he and why the random chase?

I didn't have to wait long. With a kick to the stand, she stood up. Right, she. Even with the nondescript, ill-fitting cold suit, I could tell she was a woman. Long legs and a nice ass.

We might need that picnic table after all.

Gloves off, she reached for her helmet as she walked toward me. I kept mine on, liking this game we were playing. She flicked the chin strap and tugged off the helmet, revealing familiar brown hair.

"Hey, Tom." She greeted me with a smile.

I removed my helmet. My own, slow, sly smile returned hers. "Hey, Idaho. Didn't know you rode."

"No? Funny the things you don't know." She continued her slow walk to my bike.

I cut the engine. "You drive a R90s?"

She grinned. "I do."

"You paint it that hideous orange color?"

Her smile faltered and her eyes narrowed. Her bottom lip pursed in a sexy pout. "You disappoint me, Tom. You should know Daytona Orange is factory."

"Where'd you get a vintage BMW bike?" I studied the swoop of the polished chrome twin exhaust pipes.

"It was a gift. Pretty sweet ride you have there, too."

Did the ex buy her a motorcycle? Kurt didn't seem the kind of guy to approve of them unless it was a new Harley to impress his friends. Maybe a previous ex?

"Thanks, it was my dad's," I answered.

"Mine too."

"Your dad gave you a motorcycle?" I imagined my sisters' faces if Dad gave them such a gift. Delight would not be top of their reactions.

"I asked for it when I went to college. Didn't want or need a car in Seattle, but a motorcycle? That—"

I cut her off. "Made you the coolest girl on campus."

She laughed and swung her helmet by its strap. "Something like that."

"Why the long chase to here?"

"I recognized your bike when you pulled on to 20, so I passed you to make sure it was you. I didn't think you'd follow me. Or is that something you do? Chase random women on motorcycles?"

"I couldn't tell if you were a girl or a guy," I said in defense.

She raised an eyebrow and licked the corner of her mouth.

"Wait, that didn't come out right. I meant, I was more curious about the passing and waving. You seemed to know me."

"You were curious."

"Always."

"What if I had been another woman?" She stalked closer.

I waited like a lion watching a gazelle cross my line of sight. I shrugged. "Hard to say, but I'm more than happy you're here."

"Why do you always expect me to make the first move?" she whispered a few inches away. Her warm breath brushed my cheek.

"I think you like it." I turned my head and trailed my nose against her jaw, but when I got to the tender flesh under her ear, her head jerked away.

"I think you're used to women throwing themselves at you and you've never had to work for it before."

She had a point.

I tipped my head and gave her my slow, easy grin, guaranteed to incinerate underwear. Steel ran through her veins. No smile, no frown, not even an eye-twitch. I released the second dimple and ducked my head.

The last thing I expected from her was laughter. With her head thrown back, she laughed so hard she snorted.

"What?" I asked.

She'd lost her mind.

"You're ridiculous." She swallowed the last of her laughter and attempted a serious face.

Not a word any man wanted to hear when he worked his tricks. "Ridiculous?"

"Does that look really work?"

I frowned.

"It does!"

"You're great on a man's ego." I scowled. "Didn't hear you complaining before."

"Your ego will be fine. I'll tell you a secret." She stepped close again and I could smell a warm, floral scent. "I did have a crush on you when we were younger. You were a junior and I was in middle school. You didn't know I existed."

Suspicion confirmed, I smirked.

"Cocky suits you," she said.

I reached up and grasped her neck. No escaping me now. Her helmet clattered on the ground at our feet. I had her attention. No more laughter. Her eyes focused on mine and then closed. My lips found hers, rough, determined and completely in control. She softened against my leg and I shifted to face her, wrapping my other arm around her waist.

I pulled away. My lips barely brushed against hers. "Speaking of cock, ever since you got off your bike, I've been thinking about your mouth on mine."

Her gasp sucked the air from my mouth.

"Let's find someplace more private." I dropped my arms and started the bike.

She stood there, arms at her sides, lips swollen from my mouth, windswept, beautiful, and stunned.

"If the dimples don't get them, the dirty talk always does."

———

I could hear her bike behind me as I slowly wove my way through the campground. A few RVs were parked in the larger sites, but most were empty and exposed. Deep in the woods, a lone picnic table sat in a small clearing. Perfect.

I flipped down the stand and swung my leg off the bike, but leaned up against it while Hailey parked hers. Muffled sounds of waves against the shore below and the scent of pine greeted me when I removed my helmet again. I inhaled deeply, filling my lungs with the clean, fresh air.

This time I stalked over to her. If she wanted me to take control, I would. The expression on her face when I told her what had been on my mind confirmed she may have liked taking the initiative, but like many women, she wanted to give up control, stop thinking, and be told what to do once in a while. I had no problem with that.

She glanced around and cocked her head to listen to an eagle in the distance. "You sure this is private?"

I shrugged. "It's private enough." After setting her helmet on her bike, I tugged her forward to the picnic table.

"What did you have in mind?" Her voice hesitated and paused.

"I think I made myself pretty clear up on the road." I leaned against the table and waited to see what she'd do.

"Give me your jacket," she demanded.

I unzipped and shrugged off the leather, arching my eyebrow when she wadded it up and dropped it on the cement platform at my feet. I loved that jacket.

She smiled and knelt.

Oh.

She looked amazing from this angle. Any man who said he didn't love this view lied.

I braced my arms behind me on the table as she unbuckled my belt and slowly unzipped my jeans. Closing my eyes, I waited for the warmth of her mouth to engulf me.

Her laughter greeted me instead.

I opened one eye and then the other. No man ever wanted to hear giggling near his stuff.

Her hands rested on my hips and her eyes focused on my red long johns. Right. Forgot about those.

"Yes?" I asked.

"I thought men only wore these in the movies."

"Apparently not. It's cold on the bike." I shrugged. "Things need to be kept warm."

Her hand reached into the fabric and brushed against my skin. I jumped from the contact of the cool air and her fingers gripping me. Her other hand shoved the fabric down and out of the way.

She teased and poked out her tongue to touch the tip, then licked down to the base. The warmth from her tongue faded as the air chilled my skin. I rested one of my hands on her shoulder. Understanding my silent plea, she stopped her teasing and encircled the head with her mouth, her hand moving to cover what she couldn't accommodate.

My fingers wove through the strands of her hair. I needed the extra contact to ground myself from the incredible sensations she was creating with her mouth and tongue. Being outside with the possibility of being caught amplified everything. Each lick from her tongue, drag of her teeth, and squeeze of her hand brought me closer to coming. Her moans vibrated around me and her eyes met mine.

Game over.

Like the gentleman I was, I gave her a warning. "I'm close."

She responded by sucking in her cheeks and pulling me further into her mouth by my hips.

Answer received.

I let my hips gently thrust forward, needing more. Finding it, I closed my eyes and moaned, deep in my throat, completely lost in the sensation coursing through my body.

When I slowly blinked them open, she released me with a soft kiss and leaned on her heels, a satisfied grin on her face. With a light touch, she tucked me inside of my long johns and patted the cotton covering my waning erection.

"Did you pat me?" I asked, zipping up and adjusting myself.

"Maybe. I'm sure he's very cozy in there."

"It's my dick, not a person, you know." I offered her my hand to stand and watched her stretch.

"You didn't name it?" She handed me my jacket, then brushed her mouth against my shoulder.

"If I did, I'm not telling." I grabbed her face and kissed her … hard. My tongue met hers and I silently said my thank you. "That was amazing. We should definitely do that more often."

Excitement lit up her eyes. "What are you doing later?"

FOURTEEN

Confession:
Most of the time I'm not interested in the whole back story.

We rode together down the island. Clouds had rolled in and the temperature dropped on the ride. I let her lead the way around Holmes Harbor to her house. I wanted to get another chance to inspect the sculpture in her yard before it got dark. Hailey pushed her bike into the garage and I stepped through the ferns toward the giant pinecone.

"Tom?" her voice called out through the trees.

"Over here.."

Her footsteps stomped over pine needles and leaves. "What are you doing over here? You better not be peeing in my woods."

"I wasn't, but that's a great idea. I really need to take a piss." I turned and faced a tall cedar.

"Donnely!"

I hadn't unzipped my jeans, so I turned around to show her. "Trust me, I don't announce it when I piss in the woods."

"But you do?"

"What man doesn't pee outdoors? Why wouldn't you?"

"It's different for women."

"Sucks to be you. Peeing outdoors is one of life's great pleasures."

She grimaced. "I'd like to think there are much better things to do outdoors than relieve your bladder."

I stepped closer and gave her a peck on her check. "I can think of at least three things, and one we did earlier today."

Her eyes softened and she gave me a shy smile. "So what are you doing wandering around my yard?"

"This." I gestured behind myself at the giant pine cone. "Where'd it come from?'

"A really big tree." She joked.

"It's amazing." I touched one of the spiked scales.

"I made it."

"What's it doing hidden here in the woods?" I smiled, feeling pride and awe at her talent.

She stood on the other side and ran her hand along the cupped surface of another scale. With a shrug, she met my eyes. "It was a college project. Senior year."

"Wow. Seriously?" I paced around the metal until I reached her side. "Why is someone with your talent working at the boat-yard as a project manager?"

"I applied to be a trainee welder and didn't get the job."

"You wanted to weld boats all day?"

Another shrug. "Sure."

"That's a waste."

"You don't sculpt for a living either." She tried to stuff her hands in her pockets. Talking about her art seemed to make her insecure and this was a new side to the woman who'd always hit like a boy, didn't take my shit, and had enough nerve to walk into the Dog House to proposition me.

"I fool around with a chainsaw. My signature piece is the spread eagle, for Pete's sake!"

"Who's Pete?" Her eyes crinkled up in amusement.

Holding her hands in mine, I stretched her arms above her head, and leaned into her so she bowed over the sculpture's curve.

"I'm trying to be serious here."

"And I'm deflecting. Obviously."

"Stop doing that."

"Can we talk about it another time? I'm cold and hungry."

I stared into her eyes, trying to figure out the whys and hows she wasn't sharing with me. A pale brown rimmed her irises and tiny flecks of gold floated above the green.

"Give me the short version and I'll get you tell me the rest another time."

She eyed me warily. "Okay. Short version is an art major pretty much equals poverty, so I took what I learned managing a sculptor's studio, and translated it to project management. Turned out, I'm really good at organization and bossing people around. I know, shocking. Work and making money took precedence over playing with metal. But I still have studio space over in Seattle."

I smirked at her bossy comment. "One more thing."

Her long lashes blocked the clear green when she narrowed her eyes. "One."

"If you had the rich boyfriend and then fiancé, why was money an issue?"

She scoffed. "Right." Her exhaled breath lifted a strand of her hair. "I never wanted his money. After we got married, it would have been ours, but it felt weird to have him support me. Not that he would. He didn't really get my sculptures. Sure, he thought it was cool to be with a woman who was air-quotes *artistic*. I guess it gave him some sort of rich guy cred to be with a wild metal sculptor he could show off at parties" She rolled her eyes.

"What a fuckwad. Oops, I said that out loud."

"You're not sorry."

"No, I'm not." I moved closer. "One more question?"

"Is that your question?"

"No." I let my lips skim her forehead. "Why did you move back? Other than wanting to live out your lifelong dream of being a welder at Donnely Boats."

She tried to kiss me, but I dodged out of the way. "Fine. I'd always wanted to move back here. Start a family. Have a pretty house. Be close to the water. All the super sentimental girly stuff. That's why he bought the land for the house. For me."

"At least he did that."

"Why?"

"We wouldn't be here now, would we?"

I leaned in to tug her bottom lip with my teeth. She answered by looping one of her legs around my thigh and tilting her hips into mine. We kissed against the unforgiving metal, losing ourselves in the moment. I forgot what we were talking about. Breathing heavily, I pulled away and shook my head, trying to clear my thoughts.

"Let's eat," I said.

"You do owe me from the park earlier." A wicked grin crossed her face.

I pecked her cheek. "Later. I was thinking more about ordering pizza."

———

We flipped a coin for who would go out in the cold to pick up the pizza in Freeland. She won and offered me her car, but knowing my luck I'd run into someone who knew one, or both of us, at Sal's. Too complicated. Speaking of complicated, we'd ordered a half pineapple and jalapeño, and half meat lovers. Pineapple on a pizza was weird.

Dan behind the counter cocked an eyebrow at my order and gave me a knowing smile. "Sounds like you've got a date with sweet and spicy tonight."

I chuckled at his bad joke. "Nah, hanging out with a friend."

"The only other person I know who eats pineapples and jalapeños on a pizza is your buddy John."

On the island, the pizza guys knew how everyone took their pie. If they teamed up with Sally, Connie, and Sandy—aka the gossips—they'd have a flow chart of who was dating and hooking up with whom all over the south island. They could probably rattle off who was off gluten or vegetarian along with impending separations and possible affairs.

Speaking of the devil, a bluster of cold from the opened door blew in ahead of Connie.

"Well, if it isn't Tom Donnely!" She greeted me with an air kiss from about two feet away. "Hi, Dan. Hope Tom isn't giving you too much trouble here."

Dan and I had a silent conversation men tended to have around women like Connie. We both shook our heads and looked up at the ceiling.

"Hi, Connie," I said to be polite.

"How's your sister? Sandy says she's the size of a trailer and about to pop."

"Lori's good. The whole family's good."

"That's wonderful. After all of the scandal with your cousin last year, I'm glad you had a quiet Thanksgiving."

Last year's cousin drama would be material for years in the gossip circles. Much like the time a new ferry captain missed the dock and grounded near Columbia Beach. Or the time Sibley's bull got out and blocked traffic for an hour, charging cars and anyone who dared to try to get him off the road. I think he rammed the famous red door sculpture, which was exactly what it sounded like: a random red door near the edge of a field.

At this rate, our pizza would be cold before I left Sal's.

"I hope you had a nice day, too, Connie. Any word on Angus getting parole early? Be nice for you to have him home for Christmas." I smiled as her jaw dropped and then clamped shut.

Gossip went both ways around here.

Dan softly chuckled from behind the counter.

"Thanks for the pizza." I picked up the box.

"Tell John I said hello and thanks for the cord of wood." Dan gave me a wave.

Typical John. He was always dropping off cords of wood for friends and those in need. In this case, the wood went into the wood-burning oven of his favorite pizza joint. I was pretty sure he never had to pay for his pizza again. Smart guy.

I strapped the box behind me and blew on my hands while the bike warmed up. I'd left my gloves at Hailey's. I pulled on the road and checked my mirrors. Damn it. Connie's car trailed a few cars behind me. No way I could drive up East Harbor without raising her suspicions. I turned and back-tracked to the main road, knowing I'd have to take the long way to Goss Lake. Pizza would be frozen by the time I returned.

———

An unfamiliar ringtone and buzzing woke me up to an unfamiliar room and a body next to mine on a couch. I stirred and the body moved, rolling into the crevice between me and the back cushions.

"I can't breathe," a familiar voice mumbled.

I sat up and realized I was still at Hailey's. It hadn't been my first time to wake up in a strange place. Typically remembering my companions name took much longer.

"I think your phone was ringing." I yawned and stretched.

She struggled into a seated position, getting tangled in the throw blanket. "What time is it?"

The room was dark except for the faint glow from the TV. Right, after realizing we were both fans of Bill Murray, we'd been watching *What About Bob?* and fell asleep.

I found my phone on the table and glanced at the screen. "It's 11:30."

"Geez, we totally sacked out. Who'd be calling me now?" Standing, she stretched her arms over her head.

I ran my hand over the exposed skin on her stomach. She smiled down at me and leaned into my touch. I kissed her on the hip. "Maybe you should find your phone and find out."

My own phone began ringing and vibrating in my hand.

"Booty call?" she asked as she walked around the couch to her phone.

"Nah, they usually text." I muted the ringer. "It's Nick."

"He called me, too."

"That's weird."

We stared at each other in confusion for a few beats, and then she screamed, "Baby!"

"What?" I stood up and dropped my phone under the couch. Leaning over to retrieve it, I felt the floor bounce.

Hailey jumped up and down. "He texted me. Baby! The baby is coming!"

My phone beeped. ***Baby. Island Hospital.***

"Looks like she's having it here on the island."

She was already rummaging around for her keys and jacket. "Let's go!"

A gust of rainy, wet wind hit the windows. "Great. I'm not riding all the way to the hospital in this weather. I'll head home and get my truck."

"There's no time!" Her voice held a panicked excitement that scared me. Women had a weird desire to see babies as soon as they were born. I preferred to wait until they were fully cooked and could focus their eyes. Otherwise they reminded me of the time our dog had puppies and I watched her chew off the sacs covering each pup. I shuddered.

"I'll have plenty of time to see the kid. There's no rush."

"She's your baby sister. Nick wouldn't have texted if they didn't want you there tonight." She bounced over to me and hugged me. I didn't raise my arms, so she ended up wrapping hers around mine like a boa constrictor. Giving up the hug, she said, "If you insist, I'll drive you to pick up your truck. You can get your bike tomorrow."

"Deal."

We put my bike in the garage next to hers and hopped in her SUV. Once I got in my truck, she waited at the end of my driveway until I pulled out behind her. Halfway up the island, still staring at her taillights, it dawned on me it might appear suspicious if we arrived at the same time.

I parked a few rows away from her in the hospital lot and shut off my engine. I'd give it five minutes, maybe ten, and then go inside.

Ten became fifteen before my phone buzzed with a new text from Hector.

Okay, scaredy cat, you can come inside and meet your nephew. He's all cleaned up. Mother and baby are fine.

Smiling despite my dislike of babies, I exhaled and got out of the cab. If I was honest with myself, it wasn't only the yuck factor that kept me away. Babies and births were scary—so much blood and screaming.

Okay, so it was mostly the yuck factor. Stupid health class movie had scarred me for life.

Inside, my shoes squeaked along the empty hall toward maternity. I rounded the corner and a pack of Donnelys greeted me.

"It's a boy!" Dad handed me a cigar.

"It's a boy!" Mom hugged me as if it was my baby.

"Yay! It's a boy!" Cara and Amy screamed and bounced like Hailey had earlier.

Yep, some sort of weird woman gene existed. I guess if you were going to have to push a bowling bowl out of yourself you needed it.

"Lori doing okay?" I asked the room in general while glancing around for Hailey.

"She was a trooper. Short labor. Only ten hours." Mom

beamed and tears filled her eyes. I hugged her to my side and she cried into my shoulder.

I stepped out of the hug and brushed my hands over my jaw. "Good."

Hailey appeared at the entrance to the room. She covertly wiped tears from her eyes and gave me a weird smile before walking over to sit next to my dad.

He handed her a cigar, too. She took it, laughing and crying at the same time.

"He's perfect," she said to Dad, leaning her head on his shoulder. "Looks like Ellie."

People were weird when they said babies took after family members, especially ones of the opposite sex. They all resembled grumpy, bald old men.

"So, Hailey, what did you do today?" Cara asked.

My eyes flashed to the other side of the aisle where Hailey sat.

"Not much. Took the bike out for a short ride."

Cara studied her for a minute. "Tom, weren't you going out for a ride today, too? Good weather for it."

I leaned forward and clasped my hands between my knees. "Yeah. You know people with motorcycles around here, gotta go out when you get a nice day."

I couldn't be sure, but something in Cara's line of questioning told me she suspected something. I wracked my brain trying to think of a slip or where she could have seen us out. I'd ditched Connie and gave away nothing at Sal's. There was no way she could know we'd be hanging out.

My gaze flicked up to meet Hailey's. She mouthed "relax," and then turned to my mom to ask her about Thanksgiving.

Cara paid no more attention to me. Maybe her question was innocent, and I'd imagined the implied connection between Hailey and me.

A scrub-wearing Nick walked into the room with an exhausted smile. The family jumped up to greet him with hugs and back-pats. Mom burst into tears again. Dad and she went to see Lori first. The rest of us took our seats and the waiting resumed. I had no idea why I had to be here. Needing to feel useful, I offered to get snacks from the machines down the hall.

When I returned, arms laden with chips and candy, only Hailey sat in the chairs.

"Did everyone else go see Lori?" I asked, dumping my treasure of junk food on a magazine-covered table before sitting across from her. Better to keep my distance after Cara's comments.

"They did. I thought I'd wait for you. They're bringing Noah to the room, too."

"Great. As long as no one asks me to hold him."

"You really don't like babies, do you?"

I shook my head.

She laughed and kicked my boot.

"Tom? Hailey? Mom says you two should come and say hi before Lori falls asleep," Amy said from behind me.

I quickly shifted my foot away from Hailey's and stood.

"Right, let's go," I replied a little too enthusiastically.

"And Tom? No jokes about her vagina like you made when I gave birth to Sam."

Hailey burst out laughing.

"No, he really did. I thought Doug was going to punch him until I explained how Tom speaks before thinking when he's nervous." Amy gave me a sweet smile and then slapped my shoulder.

Inside the crowded room, the family stood around Lori's bed, collectively cooing over the sea monkey in her arms. I gave her a wave from the corner and a thumbs-up. She smiled and returned the gesture.

"I still don't see the resemblance to Ellie," I whispered to Dad standing next to me.

"You have to see the hair."

Overhearing us, Lori gently pulled away the baby's cap to reveal a swatch of bright red hair.

Noah Donnely Crawford was a ginger. Poor guy. I immediately planned to teach him mixed-martial arts in order to kick some elementary school ass if anyone teased him about being soulless. No way would one of my nephews get bullied. Not on my watch. My chest filled with a combination of protection and love for the little guy. The ginger sea monkey had won me over in record time.

FIFTEEN

Confession:
I don't repeat because I don't want to get attached.

The first week of the last month of the year loped along, uneventful and quiet. It rained and got dark at three-thirty in the afternoon. During winter on the island, people drank a lot of coffee and beer. Strange things happened when people stayed indoors for long periods of time. Plotting and mapping out trips to visit the sun took over conversations. Mexico, Arizona, California became one word questions. Pops and Gramma announced they'd head south to their condo on a golf course outside of Phoenix the day after Christmas, wanting to celebrate this year with their newest great-grandchild.

Hailey and I managed to avoid each other at work, or if we ran into the other, said a polite hello and that was it. The guys had stopped focusing on her after the first month. They'd finally resolved the great debate over the underwear status of their favorite new waitress. To their dismay, the answer was yes.

I finished the otter and installed the eagle at the property in Greenbank. Commissioned pieces slowed down in the winter, so

I carved a bunch of small eagles I'd stockpile for next summer's tourists.

A storm blew in on the second Sunday of December. Strong winds downed power lines and branches created obstacle courses on some of the smaller side roads. The farmhouse had a generator, but I had only a wood stove at my place. I could heat up food on the top and make a pot of coffee, which were the extent of my cooking skills under most circumstances. On Monday, we got hit with a layer of ice overnight, which turned parking lots into skating rinks. I watched the Seattle news and the annual shots of cars sliding in the wrong direction on bridges. Work shut down, along with schools and anyone not working for the first responders, highways, or hospitals.

I checked my cupboard and found the required loaf of bread to go with the gallon of milk in my fridge. Not sure why I needed either, but if it snowed or iced on the island, everyone fought to get both until the shelves of the stores were empty. I found a clean bowl and poured in some cereal. Taking my breakfast and mug for coffee, I walked into the living room and checked the pot percolating on the stove.

Nothing to do but hang around and wait out the storm.

You okay? I texted Hailey. She had a fireplace, so she should be okay.

Warm, but bored. What are you doing?*

We texted back and forth for a while, sharing nothing important.

If you're still bored, you should come over. I texted.

Roads are bad.*

I could come to you.*

I waited for her reply while outside a branch on one of my trees sagged and snapped with the weight of the ice. Part of me hoped she'd turn me down. The roads were probably a shit show.

Bring milk if you do.*

No wonder people were told to stay home. I had to backtrack twice before I got to the main road because of trees and branches. In spite of the truck's all-season tires, I slipped and slid a few times on straightaways. I took the curves around Bayview like an old man. Pump, brake, pump, pump, brake. Ice mixed with rain plunked on the roof and windshield like gravel. I was possibly the stupidest man I knew. If I crashed on my way to have sex, I'd never live it down. The power of pussy—no other reason could get me to leave my house on a day like today. Although, Hailey was more than sex.

Instead of twenty minutes, I arrived at Hailey's long driveway an hour later, and said a little prayer of thanks. Ice encased her sculpture and it appeared to be some sort of prehistoric skeleton trapped in a glacier. No doubt about it—the woman was talented.

Smoke curled from her chimney and puffed white against the gray sky. I knocked and held out the gallon of milk.

She swung open the door and grinned.

"Milk delivery." I kept my face serious.

She leaned against the door, blocking my entry. "I don't think I ordered any milk. You're not my regular milkman. Where's Dick?"

"Dick? The milk man?" I grinned at her.

Not breaking character, she said, "Dick always delivers on Mondays and Thursdays. His cream is the tastiest—so sweet and smooth."

I snorted and choked. "Yeah? Well, you've never tried mine. I can give you double-cream or triple-cream, it's up to you, and what you can handle. If that's too much, you let me know. I've never heard any of my regular customers complain." Her eyes panned over my body while my breath created clouds with each exhale. It was cold out here. "There's only one way to know if you like what I've got to offer."

"What's that?"

"You'll have to trust me and try it. Then if you prefer Dick's cream—" I couldn't hold in my smile or laughter any longer. "Let me in. It's freezing out here." I hopped from foot to foot to try to stave off the frostbite.

"If you wanted to come inside, all you had to do was ask." She smiled and scampered through the house, dashing to stand in front of the fireplace. "Close the door, you're letting out the heat!"

After taking off my wet boots, I set the milk down on the island and ran my hand over its cool surface, remembering the first time I'd been in her house. "Want me to put this in the fridge?"

"In there." She pointed to a cooler by the sliding door to the deck. Inside she had ice and a block of cheese. I couldn't help myself and lifted it up to show her. With a straight face, I asked, "Is this Dick's cheese?"

"Gross." She grimaced but laughed.

"Too far?" I joined her in front of the fire.

"Way too far. I regret ever having a milkman named Dick."

"Poor Dick."

"Dick jokes? This is where this has brought us?" She bumped her hip against mine. We hadn't kissed yet and I stared at her lips, wondering if this was a friend visit or more.

"You started it. Our milk man used to be named Charlie." I returned her hip bump, and took up more of the space directly in front of the fire, which needed to be stoked. I spied her poker and rearranged the logs before adding another. The new log popped and hissed as the flames engulfed it.

"My mom used Charlie, too," she said.

"I think every mom on the island did at some point."

"From what I remember, he wasn't a handsome man."

"Not like Dick?" I wiggled my eyebrows.

She exhaled an exaggerated sigh. "Can we drop it?"

"What?" I kept my face neutral.

"You know."

"I'm sure I don't."

"Do I have to say it again?"

"Please." My arm encircled her hip and pulled her closer.

"Dick. No more Dick."

"Are you sure?"

She spun in my arms and circled hers around my neck. "There's only one dick here I'm interested in."

I gave her my slow, one-sided smile. "So this wasn't about needing milk?"

"There's a half gallon in the fridge," she whispered against my mouth.

I could think of other ways to spend an ice storm, but none of them seemed nearly as much fun as whatever Hailey had planned for us.

My lips brushed hers and she pressed back, opening her mouth to escalate the kiss. Her hands moved to my belt buckle, my ass, and my thighs before cupping me through my jeans and giving a squeeze.

I shifted us as the fire began to burn my ass. Connected by our lips and arms, we waddled over to the couch where she fell and I landed on top of her.

"It's colder over here." She shivered as I pulled up her sweater and discovered three layers beneath before I got to bare skin.

"Are you planning to challenge me to a game of strip poker?" I nuzzled her exposed skin with my nose.

"That's cold." She jumped and snuggled into the couch.

"I'll heat you up. Promise." I pulled my green fleece over my head, leaving me in a single gray thermal. Under my jeans I wore the red long johns that amused her before.

"That's an excellent idea, but I think I only have Uno cards around here. Strip Uno?"

"Maybe later." I pulled her sweater up further with my teeth. "At least take off the outer two layers."

"Grab a blanket first." She pointed to a nest of them down by my feet.

I draped the blanket around my shoulders like a cape and stared down at her while she tugged all three layers over her head, leaving her in only a pale purple bra.

Leaning down, I cocooned us in darkness. I could hear the pops and wheezes from the crackling fire, but the rest of the world disappeared and ceased to exist outside our bubble. My finger traced the outline of the unexpected delicate lace. Her chest trembled under my touch.

"Still cold?" I exhaled warm breath over the swell of her breast and she shivered again.

She replied by pulling me up to her lips. I smiled and kissed the corner of her mouth, moving slowly centimeter by centimeter to her ear, leaving a trail of tiny points of contact. I licked the spot behind her ear and exhaled over the damp skin before pressing my lips to the same spot again. Her legs shifted, opening wider to contain my hips. I echoed her movement and tilted my pelvis to greet hers.

Finally having enough of my slow progress, she held my face in her hands and bit my lower lip. Not hard enough to draw blood, but it got my attention. Eyes open, I focused on her face in the shadows of the blanket. Her expression held something I couldn't pinpoint, but I felt the change in energy between us. Today was different than our previous encounters.

Her fingers danced over my stomach, rising and falling as she went over the muscles of my abs. With a flick, she opened my jeans and I held my breath while she explored. I raised my hips and her fingers slipped further into my pants, reaching down my thigh. She paused and I waited.

Her laugh began softly and built into more of snicker.

"Haven't we been over this? No laughing when your face or hands are near a man's dick area." I met her eyes.

Her hands threw the blanket off of us and we blinked at each other in the gray light. I held my serious expression for a few beats before her infectious laughter caught me. She shoved down my jeans and stared at the red cotton revealed beneath.

"I remembered how much you liked them before," I explained.

"I did. I loved them. They're seared on my brain." She slipped a finger beneath the waistband and tugged me closer. "But I really want the full view."

"Seriously?" I kissed her cheek, and she nodded.

"Whatever the lady wants, the lady gets." I hopped off the couch and dropped my jeans to the floor. Thick gray wool socks covered my feet and my gray thermal shirt ended at my hips.

She gestured for me to spin around and I complied. I faced her again and posed, flexing my bicep and bending my leg for the full body builder effect. A body-builder sporting wood, in long johns. Ridiculous or not, I tilted my head and laughed.

Curling up into a ball in the corner of the couch, Hailey rested her head on the arm and laughed until she wheezed. "You're ridiculous."

I nodded and leaned over her, bracing my arms on the back of the couch. "Don't tell anyone. I don't want to ruin my spotless reputation as a master seducer."

"I hereby promise to never reveal you're a goofball. No one would believe me anyhow."

"That's the beauty in playing into my reputation. I can do whatever I want as long as it doesn't challenge the preconceived notions about my whoring ways."

"I thought men were bachelors."

"Same thing if said with the same disdain, trust me."

She ran her fingers through my mop of curls. I flopped down next to her and pulled her legs across my red-cotton covered thighs. "I like secret Tom."

"I do, too. And he likes you."

She scrambled into my lap, dragging the blanket behind her, once again wrapping us in a warm cocoon.

"You're wearing too many clothes." I unhooked her bra.

"So are you." She lifted up on her knees and shimmied her leggings as far as she could without standing. Her legs got tangled and she face planted into my chest.

"You okay?" I asked, rubbing the warm skin of her back.

I felt her muffled laughter against my skin followed by an unladylike snort. Hands braced against my shoulders, she lifted herself away to stand. Keeping eye contact, she peeled off the final two layers covering us.

"Condom in my pocket," I instructed.

"Prepared much?" She rooted around and pulled out the condoms I'd grabbed before leaving the house this morning.

"Always."

She stroked me and then flung one leg over my hips, her thighs flanking mine as she lowered herself on me in one smooth motion. Moaning, I squeezed her boobs. She pulled the blanket over our shoulders before kissing me, sucking on my bottom lip, then swiping her tongue along the edge.

I loved kissing her. Each time felt exciting and new, but also like coming home. Familiar, unknown, and utterly captivating, I devoured her mouth until we were both panting and sticky from body heat. Her forehead tasted of salt and something sweet, essentially Hailey. I tightened my arms around her, my fingertips resting on her shoulder blades. I lost myself in her floral scent, the way her body moved effortlessly with mine, and her breath on my neck. My fingers stroked her, adding to her pleasure as she softly moaned and arched her back. Our rhythm faltered and stuttered as we both reached for our orgasms. I let my head fall forward and grasped her hips, controlling the pace and angle as every muscle in my body began to pulse with pleasure. She tightened around me and sent me tipping over into animal instincts. I bit her shoulder, moaned, and maybe growled as I came.

Her rocking slowed and ceased as she collapsed and snuggled into me. I cocooned her in my arms and kissed the top of her head.

The fire sputtered. I knew I'd have to get up to add more wood or it would die out soon. I couldn't imagine moving. Instead, I tapped her shoulder.

"Mmmm," she mumbled into my skin.

"Sweetheart, you need to move so I can take care of business and stoke the fire."

"No." She snuggled closer and stretched her arms for the throw.

I pushed it further away, and she snarled at me. "I'll be back in two minutes."

Finally, she rolled off me and became lost in the pile of blankets. Grinning, I ruffled her hair.

I hopped across the cold floor to the trash can, then tended to the fireplace. Fire reestablished and blazing, I crawled under the blankets.

"Shouldn't we put our clothes on?" She curled into my side.

"Nah, body heat is better for keeping warm. Trust me."

"I do. I trust you, Tom." Her voice trailed off with sleep.

I spooned behind her, wrapping my arm around her and resting my hand on her breast. Her hair barely hit her shoulders, its soft curls tickled my cheek. "Why the short hair?"

"That's a strange question. Why the beard?" She rubbed her cheek against my whiskers.

"I asked you first."

"Kurt loved long hair, was almost obsessed with it," she mumbled.

I chuckled. "So you cut it off to spite him?"

"I got tired of resembling a cartoon princess. It'll grow back."

I twisted a short strand around my finger. "It suits you. You're not the princess type."

"And the beard?"

"For the ladies." I dragged the rough scruff along the ridge of her shoulder, making her shiver.

She snorted and curled deeper into my chest. "Of course."

———

The hum of the heater kicking on woke me up. Outside it was dark and still. I blinked open my eyes and the light over her stove was on.

Thank God. The power had been restored. Hailey rolled into my chest and curled tighter against me. No reason to get up. I stroked down her side and over her hip and thigh before skimming around to gently squeeze her ass. She sighed and her hand trailed up my spine. I didn't want to get up and break whatever spell the ice storm had created. Feelings of contentment and peace spun a sticky web inside of me, pushing away the dark thoughts and loneliness.

With each pass of her hand down my back, the web grew larger, wrapping itself around my heart, then my lungs and ribs. My breathing paused and deepened as the sense of calm strengthened its hold on my brain. Normally, I'd be searching for my pants and saying my good-byes, but not today. This afternoon I had nowhere I wanted to be and nothing I wanted to do more than this. Lying on the couch in front of the fire, I settled into the moment.

Eventually, Hailey stretched and elbowed my rib so hard my eyes watered. In her attempts to adjust, her knee made contact with my balls.

"Ouch! Fuck!" I felt like I was under a ninja attack.

She struggled to free herself from the tangle of limbs and blankets, ending up falling to the floor in a heap of naked boobs and wool.

If I wasn't holding my breath from the pain, I would have laughed at her.

"Are you okay?" Her head popped above the side of the couch and she rested her chin on the cushion.

"I think I'll live, but I'm starving."

"Hey, the power's on." She stood, naked and glorious in the middle of the room, pointing at the light above the stove.

"Yeah, it came on a while ago, but you were sleeping. Good thing too, because the fire's about dead and you're out of wood."

"There's more on the side of the house. Do you think you can walk?"

I tossed a pillow at her, which she deflected with her mad ninja skills. "If I provide you with more wood, what's in it for me?"

"Hmmm…" She pulled her thermal and sweater over her head. When her mess of brown waves reappeared, she suggested grilled cheese and tomato soup.

"With Dick's cheese?"

"And we're back where we began." She tossed my long johns at me.

"Sounds like a deal. Can I wear my socks and boots, or only these?"

She scrunched up her mouth in exaggerate thought. "Fine. No shirt, though."

After shoving my feet in my boots, I ran outside to the neatly stacked row of split wood next to the house and filled the log carrier. In record time, I stood in front of the fire, brushing icy raindrops from my hair, chest, and shoulder. I rubbed my arms to get warm again.

She made grilled cheese and I opened the can of condensed soup, voluntarily stirring the pot to get rid of the lumps. I teased her about the songs playing on her docked phone on the counter.

"Allman Brothers? Really? Were you born when they were considered cool?"

"Let's say I've always had a thing for men with facial hair."

I stroked my scruffy beard. I'd let it get longer recently and discovered Hailey liked to tug on it when we kissed. She also squirmed and squealed when I ran it against her skin.

After dinner, neither one of us discussed my leaving. So I stayed.

As we fell asleep in her bed, I wondered what kind of cereal she had in her cupboards.

———

The next morning when I pulled into my driveway, Cara's car sat in front of the barn. From inside the vehicle I could see her face and glower.

Uh oh.

"Hey sis," I called as I got out of the truck at the same time she rolled down her window.

"Where have you been? Your phone's dead. No one could get a hold of you at all yesterday or last night."

Her tear-stained face and pink-rimmed eyes caused my heart to freeze.

"Shit. What is it? Is Greg okay? Mom? Dad?"

She shook her head as a fresh wave of tears spilled down her cheeks. "They're fine. It's Pops."

A cold chill crashed through the tenuous weavings around my heart, shattering the tender sense of happiness I'd had when I awoke this morning.

SIXTEEN

Confession:
I'm a sentimental idiot.

There are moments in life which remain crystal clear no matter how much time passes. Catching my first fish at ten. Driving a truck when I was eight. Cutting my leg with a chainsaw at fifteen. Pops had been there for most of them.

I remembered nothing of the drive to Coupeville with Cara. I sat in the passenger seat of her car, numbly listening to her say things. She could have been speaking Chinese for all I understood. Blood rushed through my ears, muffling my thoughts and drowning all sounds beyond the thrum of my heart beating.

Cancel that. I remembered the drive taking forever, and at one point yelled at Cara to quit driving like an old man. Wrong choice of words. She burst into tears and I had to hold the wheel while she searched for a tissue in her purse.

She parked in the lot, taking up two spaces, but I didn't comment. I fought the urgency to run into the hospital, but there was no point in running.

Cara led me down a different hall in the other wing, away from the new life in the maternity ward. Silence greeted us when we turned the corner into a quiet waiting room. It smelled of disinfectant and the sterile sickness of hospitals. Family occupied two rows of seats, but no one spoke. Some napped, twisted and contorted into the uncomfortable chairs. Others stared at the muted TV, sipping weak coffee from tiny paper cups.

My eyes settled on Gramma in the corner. Mom sat next to her and held her hand. Ellie was the strongest woman I knew, the matriarch and real head of the family. She was the heart and hope for us all. Today she appeared old and withered. Her hair, always perfectly done, was mussed as if she hadn't brushed it, and her clothes were mismatched as if she dressed with the first things she could find.

I walked toward them and crouched down to hug my grandmother. Her arms swept around my neck and she held on tight while my mother patted my back.

"Oh, Tom, thank God you're here. We've been so worried about you," Gramma said, giving me a tiny smile. In her hand she clenched a handkerchief she'd twisted with worry. "We thought you might have been hurt in the storm, too."

Mom stood and said she needed a coffee. "We'll find you some tea," she told my grandmother, who absentmindedly nodded. Amy came over and took Mom's seat. I scanned the room for Dad.

"Where's Dad?" I asked when we were away from the family.

"He's talking with the doctor." Her face crumpled and she sagged into my side. "Tom, it's bad. Really bad."

Words from Cara's ramblings in the car echoed in my head: head injury, stroke, coma, non-responsive in the ambulance.

"Mom, he's stronger than any of us. Pops isn't going to let a slip on some ice take him down." I ducked my head and gave her a confident smile despite my heart racing with fear.

She returned my smile, but her eyes filled with tears. "The doctors don't think he's going to make it. We haven't told Ellie yet. He hasn't been responsive at all, and he was out on the ice for over an hour before we found him."

I couldn't wrap my head around her words. "What was he doing outside in the storm?"

"They refused to come over and stayed in their little house. He went out to get more firewood for the stove and fell. Ellie was napping and didn't know. She called the house asking for him."

The image of my strong, larger than life grandfather lying cold and alone nearly broke me. My knees weakened and I faltered in my step. Clifford Donnely could not die. Not now. Not like this.

I punched the wall with my fist and then rubbed the sting with my other hand.

Mom stopped. I followed her gaze and saw Dad walking toward us with hunched shoulders and bloodshot eyes. When he saw Mom standing there, he shook his head and she jogged over to him, enveloping his six-foot frame in her petite five-foot-three one.

Dad's shaking body and Mom's sobs knocked me in the gut, and I staggered.

No, no, no.

This wasn't happening.

Tears skidded down my cheeks and ran into my beard. I bent over and put my hands on my thighs.

"No," I whispered like a small, scared child. Once again I was the little boy who got picked on in elementary school until the bullies found out Clifford Donnely was my grandfather, and left me alone. Pops had always been my rock and my biggest champion. Didn't matter if I didn't make State or messed up another car, Pops would take me out on his boat or for some chowder and give me the talk. Sometimes it was a pep talk, more often than not it was a straight talk about not making a mess of things. He was both good and bad cop.

Shoes squeaked on the floor behind me, and my sisters crowded around our sad little group.

"Dad?" Lori asked.

Cara rested her hand on my shoulder. I covered it with my own and then stood upright. She hugged me and I hugged her, pulling Amy into the fold with my other arm.

"He's gone, sweetheart." Dad's lip trembled and fresh tears spilled out. I'd only ever seen my father cry at happy times like the girls' weddings or the birth of a grandchild, or when the Seahawks won the Super Bowl. I couldn't stand to see him blubbering. I shrugged off my sisters and strode up to the man I'd idolized and knew I could never imitate. He pulled me into a hug, crushing my ribs. This wasn't one of those man hugs with the arm pats. This was parent and child, sharing sorrow, loss, and heartbreak. Tears flowed freely down both our faces, mixing and dampening our shirts before we pulled apart.

"I'm glad you made it, son."

I tried to speak, but my voice had disappeared and I coughed to clear my throat. "I didn't get to say good-bye." I snorted and tried to keep the snot from running down my face. Giving up, I wiped my nose and eyes on my sleeve. "I didn't tell him how much I loved him."

"He knew, Tom. He knew, trust me. None of us got to say good-bye, including Gramma."

At the mention of my grandmother's name, our collective eyes met. Mom's face went blank. "We have to tell her."

"I'll do it," Dad said, straightening his shoulders in resolve.

"We'll come with you." My sisters fell in step behind him. Mom and I stood for a minute in the hall. She and I were most alike. We buried our emotions down deep where they could be protected and not damaged. She patted my arm and handed me a tissue from her pocket.

As we gathered in the hospital room where Pops' body lay,

the collective space filled with sniffles and nose blowing. Cousins, aunts, and uncles who had been waiting or recently arrived crowded out into the hall. I was certain we broke some sort of hospital code, but Pops was a pillar of this community. Gramma stood near his head and said the Lord's Prayer over his still body. I fought my own tears by squeezing Cara and Mom's hands. At the end of the prayer, there was nothing more to say or do. We shuffled our feet; some touched Pops hands or rested a hand on his blanket-covered legs, saying a private, silent goodbye.

I had to get out of the stifling room before the walls closed in on me. I wove my way through family members until I reached the fresher air of the hall. Cara drove and I couldn't leave until someone gave me a ride. Exhausted, I flopped into an empty chair in the waiting room, and put my head in my hands.

I lifted my head to find a frazzled Hailey standing a few feet away at the end of the row, her eyes already watering and her nose pink from earlier tears. She covered her mouth with her hand and stepped closer. Without thinking, I stood and awaited the comfort of her arms around me.

"Hailey!" Lori sobbed behind me.

Hailey's fingertips brushed my hand as she passed me to hug Lori, who burst into tears, muffling her sobs in Hailey's shoulder. I stood awkwardly in place for a minute, then swept my hand over the back of my head. I rubbed both hands over my beard, exhaling before collapsing in the same chair. The two friends cooed and soothed each other as women do in these situations. My knee bounced and I fidgeted, listening to the sounds of comfort.

"I need to get out of here," I said out of the blue. "Lori, can I borrow your car?"

"It has Noah's car seat."

"He's not even here."

"I guess we could switch it into Mom's car." She frowned and I knew she really didn't want to bother.

"You can borrow my car," Hailey offered, digging her keys out of her pocket. "I'll catch a ride with Lori and I can pick up my car at your house." She held my stare for a few beats longer than normal, letting me know she'd stay if I needed her.

I caught the keys when she tossed them to me. "Thanks. I just … I need to be alone. I hate hospitals," I muttered, backing away from them until I ran into a row of chairs. Grief saturated their faces. I couldn't handle it. I stumbled and spun toward the exit. "Sorry. I'm sorry."

Standing in the middle of the parking lot, I had no idea where to find the car. I closed my eyes, inhaled and slowly exhaled, staving off a growing sense of panic swirling around me. The need to get out, to go, to run and never stop built into a riptide, pulling me under. I inhaled an unsteady breath and opened my eyes as I exhaled. Clicking the key fob, I studied the rows for the flash of lights. I spied my salvation in the shape of a silver SUV a few cars down from Cara's minivan.

At home I grabbed a bottle of whiskey and walked through the rain to my shop. I flicked on the overhead light and opened the doors to the cold, damp air. Sawdust clung to my wet boots as I paced the familiar space, touching old tools inherited from Pops, some he'd gotten from his father. Decades of use darkened the wood handle of a chisel. Knicks marred the top of a ball hammer. I spun the handle of the bench vice and chugged from the bottle. Every object held a story and wore its history proudly. I rubbed the scar on my left wrist, where I'd jabbed the blade into my skin while whittling with Pops on his porch. I'd needed ten stitches.

Bracing my hands on the bench, I hopped up and knocked over several newer tools that pinged and clunked on the cement floor. My boots beat against the uprights and rattled the bigger saws and tools underneath.

I was a coward. I didn't say good-bye to my parents at the hospital. I ran away like a kid. The whiskey burned my throat and the warmth reminded me of the coming numbness.

Tires crunched on the driveway. With the doors wide open, I had a clear view of Lori's car bumping through the ruts and puddles. I hopped off the bench and walked to the other side of the space, flopping into an old, beat-up recliner. I sipped from the bottle and then tucked it in the chair beside me. I didn't feel like talking to my sister or seeing the sympathy in Hailey's eyes.

Lori's car whined as she reversed down the drive instead of turning around. I waited for the sound of Hailey's engine starting.

"Tom?" Her fists pounded on the front door to the house. "You in there?"

I thumped my head against the worn upholstery of the chair. My head swam with the effects of too much whiskey, drank too fast.

"Tom?" she whispered from the opening to the shop. "You don't have to talk. I wanted to make sure you're okay." Her boots paused before clumping closer until she stood next to the chair.

"Hi," I said, glancing up, but not quite making eye contact with her. Instead I focused on her plump bottom lip.

"You want company?" She gestured to the bottle tucked next to me. "Or do you want to be alone with Jack?"

I shrugged and held up the bottle. "You want some?"

She took a small sip and squinted her eyes, coughing.

"Whiskey not your thing?" I swallowed more.

"No, I prefer tequila." She met my eyes, her meaning hanging between us.

Tequila and Hailey were happier memories.

"Just so you know, I plan to wallow thoroughly. You can stay if you want, but if you're disgusted by the sight of a grown man crying or put off by flying objects smashing pointlessly into walls and floors, you might want to leave now. I don't want the judgment and I can't stand the pity face."

Without another word, she crawled into my lap on the disgusting sawdust-covered chair. "What should we break first?"

Despite myself, I laughed and pulled her closer. I didn't know if it was from the booze or crying, but it didn't matter, I felt relieved she was here. Her eyes were bloodshot, her cheeks flushed, and the tip of her nose was pink. I leaned down and kissed it. She tilted her head and caught my lips with her own. My fingers found their way into her hair and tugged it, exposing more of her mouth to mine. The kiss fell into a desperate place, where we scrambled to find a hold to keep ourselves from sliding into the dark. I breathed like a drowning man, not sure if it was oxygen or her I needed more. My face dampened with tears, but I didn't know if they were mine. She straddled me and I grabbed her breasts, needing to lose myself in her, to crawl outside of my sadness.

We didn't speak, we only existed as bodies. My broken heart cried out, only to be muffled by her tongue in my mouth and her hand reaching inside my jeans.

With her hand enclosing me, she whispered against my ear, "Use me."

I clamped my eyes shut against the world, narrowing my existence to my hand in her pants and hers in mine. Nothing existed outside us. I focused on her touch, the warmth of her breath when she kissed my neck, the softness of her skin, and her dark hair cocooning us. I wanted to tell her I loved the way she felt and say thank you for no reason. Instead I kissed her harder, my tongue slipping deeper into her mouth as my hands gripped her tightly.

We didn't seek pleasure. We confirmed we lived.

When the shadow of death once again crept between us, a sob wracked through me. I tried to swallow it, and she stopped. I gave into my grief. Never had I felt so raw and vulnerable. Her fingers wove into my beard as she cupped my face in her hands. With a kiss to my forehead, her breath skimmed my skin, reminding me, showing me, we were still here.

She held me while I cried, and didn't judge. After I calmed down, I felt sheepish and tried to apologize, but she kissed away my embarrassment. With a soft good-bye, she carefully stepped around the broken glass of the bottle on the cement floor when she left.

SEVENTEEN

Confession:
Dating in a small town can be complicated.

S tanding at the pulpit felt wrong and weird. Any minute a
bolt of lightning would strike me down, incinerating me
into a messy pile of ash on the red carpet of the quaint
Methodist church where my family had been baptized, married,
and eulogized for generations. I took a deep breath, trailed my
hands through my hair, and stroked my beard. The words on
the page blurred together in fuzzy, blank ink caterpillars. A few
coughs and the rustling of clothing against the pews were the
only sounds as I stood still and tried to not lose my shit.

When I lifted my head and blinked at the crowd, familiar
faces stood out. My mother and grandmother smiled encourag-
ingly. I returned their smiles. John, wearing a suit, sat with
Diane behind the rows of family. He nodded and Diane gave
me a thumbs-up. I scanned the crowd for familiar green eyes
rimmed in brown.

Ashley sat a few rows from the back and gave me a little

wave. Across the aisle from her was Caroline, my high school girlfriend, and her parents. Two rows ahead sat Debra and her friend. Both made exaggerated sad expressions and tears ran down their faces. A few other women I'd slept with over the years sat with their families or husbands. The reception after this thing was going to be awkward.

Quickly focusing elsewhere, I found Hailey sitting near the Kelso brothers. A familiar older couple flanked her. Must be her parents. She nodded and tilted her head, waiting for me to begin. My gaze flicked to the standing people at the rear of the filled to capacity church. Kurt stood with a group of other men in suits. I would have missed him completely had he not been short enough to stand in front of his taller companions. My brow furrowed. What was he doing here? Did he know my grandfather?

I stared down at the eulogy my mother had asked me to read. It highlighted Pops' time in the service, his work with the Lions, Eagles, VFW, Rotary and every other community organization he'd participated in over his long life. Was it really a long life? Not long enough for me.

I met my dad's eyes and he gave me his patented 'let's get on with it' look: chin tucked, arms crossed, and an eyebrow arched. He hated funerals and wearing a suit as much as I did.

I tugged my tie near the knot and cleared my throat. I found Hailey's eyes again in the crowd and formed a small, closed smile only for her.

"Clifford Joseph Donnely, my grandfather, was a great man. One of a long line of Donnely men who settled, farmed, and worked hard to make this island what it is today. He did right by the land and people of Whidbey.

"Clifford was also a ladies' man, according to my grandmother, the beautiful Ellie Donnely. The ladies lined up at the dances, waiting their turn with Handsome Cliff. But he only ever had eyes for her, the woman who still made him smile and the rest of us blush over his inability to keep their PDA respectable in front of the children."

A few people chuckled and Gramma hushed me from her aisle seat a few feet away before giggling and fluttering her hands around her face. Mission accomplished.

After my ad-libbed lines, I followed Mom's notes, adding how much he'd be missed by his grandchildren and great-grand-children, who would only know him through the stories we told. Mom patted my leg when I took Dad's spot next to her as he said a few words, then invited everyone to the farmhouse for a reception and a chance to share more stories about Clifford after the burial.

———

Too many people were congregating under the heat lamps as mourners spilled out of the house on the wraparound porch and deck. All these people were here because of one man. At least fifty of them were related to him by blood or marriage. The Donnelys had been a prolific bunch of breeders in my grandparents' genera-tion. Some remote cousins introduced themselves for the first time. A whole flock of third cousins—or were they second cousins once removed—stood around telling stories about the family tree, and who was related to whom. I lurked in the shadows on the side porch overlooking the shipping lanes and watched a cargo ship head out to sea as I drank a bottle of beer. I hadn't bothered to read the label when I pulled it from the icy water of the drinks' bucket.

On the other side of the window, my sisters and mother moved through the crowd in their black dresses, picking up plates, handing out napkins, and patting arms, frowning and nodding their heads in sympathy.

I still wore my suit jacket, but the tie sat on the seat of my truck, rolled up and soon to be tucked away until the next funeral. Hopefully it would be a long time coming.

I sipped and swallowed the cold liquid, not thinking or focusing on more than getting through this circus long enough until I could hide away in the woods again.

Ashley's laughter cackled over the more somber conversation on the far side of the porch. I slunk further against the house, happy this corner was out of the sight-line from the main section. I cringed as footsteps from the opposite direction came closer. I braced myself with my "sad, but thank you for your kind words" face and hoped it wasn't one of the women from the crowd at the church. I'd managed to avoid Ashley other than a quick hug after the service.

"I brought you a beer." John's deep voice announced his arrival a few steps before he rounded the corner.

"How'd you find me?" I took the beer, setting my empty bottle on the floor.

"We used to hide in this spot as kids when your grandparents lived here. Best hiding corner because you can see inside the living room through the window and hear people coming from either direction with enough time to jump the railing into those rhododendron bushes."

"I forgot about hiding in those bushes. Or jumping the railing. We're lucky we didn't break more bones."

"You doing okay?" he asked.

I exhaled and nodded.

He took a long draught of beer. "It's okay if you're not. Clifford was everyone's favorite real adult. Damn, I'm going to miss that man."

Fighting the creeping tears, I raised my bottle. "To Clifford."

Our bottles clinked together and we fell into silence. Two grown men hiding in our childhood spot with no need to say anything more.

Laughter echoed from the big group under the heaters and he raised an eyebrow. "Is that Ashley?"

I scratched my jaw and nodded. "Damn island feels pretty fucking tiny today. Seems everyone knew Pops."

He chuckled. "Yeah, you must have felt like a mouse in a room full of cats at church. Saw Caroline and Ashley there along with a few other flames of yours. I was happy they didn't break out into a cat-fight over who got to console poor Tom."

He'd left out Hailey and the others he didn't know about.

I rested my bottle on the window ledge and rubbed my hands up and over my face, running them through my hair before reversing the gesture a couple of times. "You ever feel like your life hit a brick wall?"

"Yeah. I could say I have."

Oh shit. "Sorry. Of course you'd know the feeling."

"No problem. What's your point?"

"I'm not really sure. Remember at the bonfire how Pops talked about his life? He had a wife and a bunch of kids at our age, responsibilities, the farm, a business. I feel like a stupid punk compared to him. What do I have to show for thirty-three years walking around on this rock?"

"A bunch of kids you don't know about?"

I bumped his shoulder with my fist hard enough to knock him off balance a little. "Asshole. Seriously."

"You gave me that speech last year about relationships being work and not for you. Now you're going to settle down? Find yourself a nice girl who doesn't know about your catting around? Maybe a nice Mennonite or a pretty Canadian?"

"Like a mail-order bride?"

His low laughter made me smile. "Do those exist anymore?"

"How would I know?" I smiled smugly. "Right. No, not about women. I'm observing my life and not coming up with much I can claim as mine. Feel like I need a change."

"Change of scenery?"

"Yeah. Maybe? I don't know. Something." I didn't tell him how unmoored and adrift I felt over the past week. "Maybe I need to take off in the boat and go to the San Juans. Get away."

"Your mom would be pissed if you disappeared at Christmas."

"Damn, I forgot about Christmas. Shit. That's going to be depressing."

"I don't envy you. The first holidays and birthdays are the roughest. You can come to my Aunt and Uncle's. She'll feed you until you explode or pass out on the couch, unable to move for days."

Footsteps sounded on the wood boards of the porch and we both reflexively leaned further into the shadows.

Diane appeared around the corner. "Are you two hiding?" She stepped next to John and he rested his arm over her shoulders so she could tuck herself against his side. More footsteps followed her, and Hailey stopped a few feet away.

"Hi, Idaho," John greeted her.

She gave me a small, knowing smile. "You need a beer?" She handed me a fresh bottle.

John's eyes flicked to my face when she joined our group, but he didn't say anything. The three of them talked about holiday plans while I stood in silence, half listening and half staring at my family through the window. Mom met my eyes from across the living room and waved. She mouthed "need anything" and I held up my beer. She pantomimed eating. I shook my head and gave her my patented sad smile.

"We should have a party on New Year's," Diane said.

"I hate New Year's." John frowned.

"Me too," Hailey said.

"Tom's always up for a party." Diane teased, attempting to lighten the mood.

I shrugged, not sure if I'd be in the party or leave me alone mood in a few weeks.

"Party?" a new voice joined our conversation.

Ashley. Of course.

"Is there an after party? I'm always up for a party," she said. I nearly choked on my beer. John patted my back with his big bear paw until I stopped choking.

"It's a little wrong to be so excited about a party when

146

you've attended a funeral a few hours earlier, don't you think? And since when do funeral receptions have after parties? " Hailey asked.

"Who asked you?" Ashley snarked at Hailey. "No one said you had to go the party."

"There's no party. After this or otherwise," John clarified. He shot me a look over Ashley's shoulder I read loud and clear. I raised my shoulders and begged him with my eyes. "Hey, do you know where they put out the pigs in a blanket?"

I scrunched up my face. That was what he came up with?

"I think all the food's in the dining room," Diane said, oblivious to the faces John and I were making at each other. Unfortunately, Hailey and Ashley weren't.

"What's wrong with your face, Tom?" Hailey asked.

I sighed. "Nothing. I'm not feeling the fancy weenies right now."

"Oh, you must be starving," Ashley cooed while keeping her eyes on Hailey, who narrowed her eyes at Ashley's hand on my arm. "I should get you some food."

If I didn't create a distraction, Ashley's girl senses would start tingling and she'd ask questions I didn't want to answer. An awkward silence fell over the group.

"Sounds like a great idea. Why don't you go make Tom a plate?" Diane said, her eyes bouncing between Ashley and Hailey.

Ashley was stuck. She'd suggested getting me food. With a sigh and a sidelong glance at Hailey, she plastered on a smile and said, "I'll be right back. Don't go anywhere."

Inside, I observed her speaking with my mother, who then glanced at me and headed into the dining room. I probably had five minutes before she returned.

"I gotta take a piss. While I'm gone, anyone need a beer?" I took the long away around, avoiding the crowd, and went upstairs to the hall bathroom.

Someone knocked three times.

"Occupied," I yelled, turning on the faucet to wash my hands.

They knocked again.

"Hold on a minute." Wiping my hands on one of the fancy guest towels, I checked out my appearance in the mirror. I had dark circles under my eyes and my beard had grown scruffy, but damn, I looked handsome in a suit.

Another knock, and I scowled. "Give a person a minute to …" I swung open the door, "piss."

Ashley stood there, smiling. "Water sports have never been my thing." She gently pushed me further into the bathroom.

"Hey, Ashley." I smiled and plotted how to extract myself from the bathroom and this situation. She'd always been cool, but this felt like an ambush.

Her hand rested on the lapels of my suit jacket. "You never wear a suit."

"I know."

"You look good, Tom. Really good."

I gently grabbed her arms in order to switch our positions, placing myself closer to the door and freedom.

"Where are you going? I wanted to make sure you're okay. Everyone loved Pops. I'm here if you need a shoulder to cry on. That's all I'm saying."

My hand found the knob behind me and turned it. "Hey, let's not do this now." Thoughts and words spun through my mind as I attempted to escape with both our dignities intact. "I like you, Ashley, but my head's in a weird space now. And I think I realized last month as much fun as we've had in the past, maybe we're better off as more casual friends."

Her eyes widened and her nostrils flared. Combined with her long, red curls, her expression personified the term "seeing red." "Are you seeing that Hailey chick?"

My foot caught in the door as I attempted to swing it open. "Why would you ask about her?"

"She's always hanging around you. Halloween and now showing up for your grandfather's funeral."

"Right. And she's Lori's best friend. Maybe that explains it? Stop with the jealousy and suspicion. It doesn't suit you."

Leaving her standing there, I bounded down the stairs and smack into Hailey and Diane. Both their eyes were fixed to a spot above me on the landing. Reluctantly, I turned to see Ashley fixing her hair and wiping her mouth. The implications of her actions were evident on both Hailey and Diane's faces.

I closed my eyes and inhaled, my hands balling into fists by my sides. "It's not what it seems," I ground out through clenched teeth.

Diane rolled her eyes while Hailey shook her head.

Not now, I wasn't doing this drama now. I brushed past them and out into the cold air of the dark winter afternoon. Striding across the lawn, I found myself on the porch of my grandparents' little house. The old wooden swing called to me and I sat, pushing myself with my legs. From here I could see cars pull down the long driveway as guests left. When the number of cars on the lawn and circle drive petered down to less than a handful, I slowly strolled back to the main house.

Inside, my mother hovered over a team of women helping to clean the kitchen. I picked a sandwich off a tray and shoved half of it in my mouth. I found my father, sisters, and Gramma in the family room.

I stole a handful of chips from a bowl on the side table and settled on the floor next to the fireplace. An easy conversation continued around me while I ate. No one asked me questions or commented on my absence.

A short while later, Gramma yawned and everyone fussed over her. I offered to walk her home. We set off across the wide lawn, her arm tucked in mine. Her head reached only as high as my bicep but her grip belied her strength.

"Pops would have enjoyed today. It's always a shame we

can't attend our own funerals to hear all of the nice things people have to say about us. When we're alive we might get told how pretty our hair is or how nice our children are, but we typically only hear the bad things, the gossip and the criticism."

I nodded and patted her arm. "He would have been annoyed with everyone eating all his food and stomping around his house, snooping."

"I swear some of those people I met for the first time today." Her laughter brightened the darkness. "A couple of men even gave me their business cards. Can you imagine? At a funeral? My gosh, I've never heard of such a thing."

I didn't like the sound of that at all. "Did you know any of them? Recognize them?"

"No, I don't think so. Although one of the men seemed familiar. Very nice fellow. I think he grew up here."

I let the subject drop. Maybe someone else saw the exchange and could put names to the suits.

We arrived at her porch, and once she had the door open and the lights on, I stepped inside to kiss her cheek goodnight.

A little framed sampler needlepoint-stitch-thing hung next to the door. I peered at the familiar frame, reading the words for the first time: "*A chuisle mo chroí.*"

"The pulse of my heart," I translated the familiar words of Hailey's tattoo.

"I'd always thought it meant 'my love'. I made it for your grandfather when we were newlyweds."

My love. Such sentimental words for a tomboy like Hailey. Hidden near her heart, over her lungs, I'd missed the deeper meaning.

"It's a bit of sentimental stitching, but Clifford insisted it was the best present he'd ever received."

I kissed her cheek goodnight. "He loved you more than words."

She held my hand to her skin for a moment. "Don't feel too

sorry for your old Gramma. Clifford and I had a long life together, and all this is the outcome of our love." She patted my cheek. "I'll be okay."

I knew she would be. The question was, would I?

EIGHTEEN

Confession:
Sometimes I'm oblivious to the obvious.

The day after the funeral, I cornered Hailey in the break room. She stood at the coffee pot, pouring sugar into her mug.

"That's a lot of sugar for someone so sweet." Tom Cat's signature smile followed my over the top cheesy words. I needed to clarify something with her and wanted her on my side before I started talking.

"That's a lot of cheese you're spreading." She poured coffee into her cup of sugar and stirred before adding cream and stirring some more. "Can I help you?" Her words hung between us like icicles.

I scratched my scruffy cheek. "Yeah. I mean, no. You can't help me, but I wanted to clear something up from yesterday."

She leaned a hip against the counter and rolled her hand for me to continue. Today's outfit included a button down top and I could see the outline of her small breasts. Her nipples pushed against the fabric and I wondered if she was wearing a bra. Her throat clearing drew my eyes up to her face.

"Right, sorry." I gave her a sheepish grin. "I think you might have interpreted something wrong yesterday, and it's important you don't think what you think you saw is what you saw. Because it's not."

The skin between her brows creased in confusion.

"I mean, you weren't imagining things, but sometimes things look different than the thing they really are."

"Spit it out." Her arms crossed over her chest.

"Nothing happened with Ashley in the bathroom."

"So you weren't in the upstairs bathroom together?"

"No. I mean, yes, we were, but only because I was exiting when she was arriving, and we chatted for a minute."

"With her shirt open?"

"I swear everything remained buttoned and no clothes came off during our very, very brief talk."

She nodded. "It seemed like a lot more than a chat."

"I think that's exactly what Ashley wanted."

"What is she to you?" She sipped her sugar-coffee.

"Nothing. I mean, she's a friend, but she's not like a girl-friend. You know me, I don't really do the dating and girlfriend thing."

She paused with her mug near her mouth, then set it on the counter. "Right. Thanks for the reminder." Her lips lifted in an effort to smile, but her eyes remained blank.

"Nothing happened yesterday."

"Yes, you said so already." She exhaled long and slow. "Honestly, it's none of my business what you do or who you see. This," she gestured between us, "has been fun."

I nodded in agreement. "More than fun. You've been a great friend this past week."

"Friend. Right." She nodded and did her weird smile thing again.

"So we're good?"

"Great. We're great." She picked up her mug along with her files. "Merry Christmas, Tom. I know it'll be tough for your family, but you have them, and your *friends* to get you through it."

Feeling much better about things between us now that I'd cleared up yesterday, I bumped her shoulder with my fist. "Thanks. You too. Enjoy the time off from this place."

I walked out of the break room smiling. It had been a really shitty week, but at least Hailey was cool.

———

Christmas sucked.

Dad played Santa, filling Pops' suit with couch cushions and a layer of bubble wrap. When the kids sat on his lap, he popped and crinkled. The littlest nieces and nephews tugged at his fake white beard. They knew something wasn't quite right about Santa this year.

Burnt dinner rolls, overcooked, leathery roast beef, and dried-out mashed potatoes rounded out a mostly silent Christmas dinner. Mostly silent because Noah spent the majority of it screaming his tiny head off. How did lungs so small hold enough air to create a noise that loud and piercing?

Worst of all, my presents included socks. Knit by my mother, they were green and blue striped. *What was she thinking?*

When everyone else ran to the window in awe over the Christmas snow, a rarity on the island, I snuck out and headed home.

I lit the wood stove and put my feet up on the coffee table. A couple of fingers of Jack and the silence of the falling snow were the perfect companions for my mood. A small pine cone made of spoon-heads sat on the table. There hadn't been a card when I found it on my doormat, but there didn't need to be. I knew it was from Hailey.

I texted her to say thanks and wish her a merry Christmas. I thought about asking her over. I tapped my fingers on the phone's screen, debating hooking up on Christmas. Something about Santa and baby Jesus made it feel wrong. There were probably a handful of other women who wouldn't think twice about ditching their families to come over for some fun, but none of them appealed to me. Three years ago, I picked up a woman in a Target parking lot on Christmas Eve. A couple of spiked egg-nogs and a blow job later, we went our own ways to finish our last minute shopping. She'd been wearing a Santa hat. Merry Christmas to me.

I tossed the phone on the table and swallowed the last of my drink. I had to be careful with Hailey. After the bathroom incident with Ashley, Hailey had been cold and distant with me, which told me one thing: she was getting attached. Jealousy was the first indication feelings were developing. And I'd learned long ago, feelings led to trouble, and must be avoided at whatever cost.

Satisfied I'd made the right decision, I flipped on the TV to watch yet another round of *Elf* and *Bad Santa*.

NINETEEN

Confession:
I hate lipstick.

W ho the fuck poured sand in my mouth? I struggled to form enough saliva to swallow, and when I did, the effort made my head throb above my left eye. A vice squeezed my temples, but that was nothing compared to the thirst. When was the last time I had any water? A week? A month?

Shit.

I opened one eye to see if maybe I'd been smart enough to get a glass of water last night before coming to bed.

Only I wasn't in my bed. Or any bed. It felt like I was on a couch.

My other eye refused to open, so I peered up at the ceiling, and tried to figure out where I was. The plain white plaster gave no clues. I rolled my one good eye to the right and saw the blurry outline of a fireplace. A familiar plaid caught my eye and I held up the blankets covering me.

Hailey's. I was at Hailey's.

How?

I forced open the other eye and blinked in the bright light flooding through the windows. I rubbed my hands over my eyes and down along my beard.

This could not be good.

Wait, was I wearing pants?

I assessed and concluded I was. Okay, so we probably didn't have sex. I'd be in her bed if we had, right?

Where was she?

I rolled to face the cushions, and used my arm to pull myself up to see the other side of the room.

Nothing out of the ordinary, except a large glass of water and a bottle of ibuprofen sat on the island.

No Hailey.

Unfocused memories of last night struggled to the surface of my hangover.

———

Last night, I'd sat on a stool in the corner of the Dog House with John and Diane. Third wheel? Try tricycle. Being with a couple sounded like torture for New Year's Eve, but it worked out great for my new plan. Diane knew a lot of women on the island through her work. Any time one of them would come over to say hi, I'd flashed my dimples and offered them a kiss for the new year. According to John, I resembled a clown or a drag queen with all the lipstick stains on my lips and cheeks. Didn't bother me. The more the merrier.

A brunette leaned against my hip while she chatted to Diane. Nice tits, nice ass, and a voice that could strip paint, or barnacles off a boat. Nothing soft or sultry about this voice.

I swatted her ass to get her to move. "I'll be right back."

Squeezing through the crowd, I pushed my way to the men's room. I caught my reflection in the ancient mirror over the sink.

John was right. I had lipstick marks all over my mouth, cheeks, and neck, including one on the tip of my nose, making me look like a red-nosed reindeer. I half-ass rubbed them off with paper towel, laughing at how ridiculous I appeared.

In the dark hall, bodies packed together in a congested mess. I went with the flow to the back because it was easier than trying to squeeze around a cluster of women in line for the ladies'. Hands tugged at my arms and familiar female voices called my name. The lights were too low to pick out faces, and I might have been past the point of sobriety to remember names. I let myself be led closer to the dance floor. Pulsing rhythms and a steady drum beat had women all around grinding and bumping hips with each other or whoever stood close enough. More hands trailed down my body and grabbed my ass. I spun around, but my admirer had disappeared.

Normally, I didn't dance, but tonight I made an exception. This wasn't dancing, this was foreplay standing up. Someone handed me a flask. When the cinnamon heat hit my throat, I sputtered and had to lean over to keep from losing it on the floor. I stood up and the room tilted, lights flashing and spinning. Or maybe I was spinning. I couldn't be sure.

If I closed my eyes I might feel better—no, that was a bad idea. Very bad idea. I needed fresh air. The room smelled of stale beer and warm bodies. I shoved and pushed my way through the crowd as the band stopped playing to start the countdown. A female voice near the door asked me where I was going and who was she going to kiss at the stroke of twelve. I gave her a weak smile and leaned against the door to open it, tumbling over the threshold, and nearly landing on my ass. The deck railing caught me and I held on while I tried to get my head on straight.

Inside, the crowd shouted "Seven, six, five, four ..."

Fireworks exploded over Camano Island across Saratoga Passage, illuminating the clear sky.

"… three, two, one!"

A roar of noisemakers and cheers reverberated the windows separating me from the party.

The noise grew louder when the brunette from earlier opened the door.

"There you are. I never got my kiss." She swayed on her heels in my direction.

"No? That's a shame, isn't it?" I smirked exactly how I knew she wanted it.

She tasted of cinnamon and desperation. Loneliness filled my mouth with a bitter flavor.

Wrong brown hair. Wrong lips.

Wrong woman.

I needed to get out of here. There was someplace else I should have been tonight and someone else I should have been kissing at midnight.

I placed my hands on her shoulders and gently pushed her away. She slowly opened her eyes and blinked at me.

"Can you give me a ride?" I asked.

"Sure. We could go to my place." She ducked her chin and attempted a coy expression. The lust in her eyes and her hand near my belt buckle ruined any chance she had at playing hard to get.

"Maybe another time? I'm not feeling well and I need to go home."

"Want me to take care of you? I did a year of nursing school." She tried to touch my forehead with the back of her hand, but I caught it and held her wrist.

"Not sick. Just too much to drink. Can't drive."

"Where are your friends? Want me to get them?" She dropped the drunk girl act. Her voice had switched from seductress to concerned, nice girl.

"I don't want to ruin their night. Do you mind? It's up the road at Goss Lake."

· · ·

In my drunken haze, I managed to give her directions to the cedar-lined driveway, but told her to drop me off at the road. Bad idea. I stumbled and tripped on a root, landing on my side. I lay there, staring up at the stars peeking through the tall trees. I might have fallen asleep for a minute or two, then jolted awake. Clambering to my feet, I stuck to the middle of the gravel path until I arrived at the house.

The house stood dark except the porch light.

I didn't see a car in front of the garage, but rang the doorbell anyway.

I rang it over and over again. I pressed it and didn't let go, listening to the off key dong echo around the living room. When nothing happened, I pounded my fist on the wood door, then alternated with my knuckles, creating a rhythm a lot like a long Allman Brothers riff. I rested my head on the door frame and whispered, "It's me. Please let me inside."

Hope lost, I slumped to the concrete landing and rested my body against the door. From here, the giant pine cone stood out in the moonlight. I never had asked her why a pine cone. Or what she wanted to be when she grew up.

Or what she wanted from me.

———

This time I knew I had fallen asleep because I awoke to a boot kicking my legs.

"Ow, stop." I rolled away from the rude boot and curled my coat around my shoulders. Boy, I was glad whatshername grabbed it for me before we left the bar. She was so nice. Such a nice woman. I should thank her. Unlike the mean person who was still kicking me.

I pried open one eye and was met with green eyes blazing with fury.

"Thank God, you aren't dead. Now get off my porch."

"Don't be mad, Idaho. I was with the wrong woman tonight," I mumbled, trying to sit up, but my legs were asleep and my arms were frozen. "I only wanted to kiss you."

"I can see that. Were you running a kissing booth?"

I absently rubbed my cheek. "I tried to remove it. It wouldn't come off with the paper towel." I smiled at her shyly.

"Where's your car?" she asked, stepping around my legs to unlock her door.

I furrowed my brow. "I don't know. Not You gave me a ride here."

She held out her hand and I pulled myself up by grasping it.

"That was a bad idea." She walked through the door.

I attempted to pull off my boots, forgetting they had laces, and toppled over her couch. "Oomph." I rolled and put my feet on the floor by the coffee table.

"You're drunk."

I nodded, struggling to get the laces of my boots undone.

Her hands swatted mine out of the way. "Let me."

"You're the best, Hailey. I don't deserve you."

Her eyes flashed to mine. "Definitely not."

I pouted and petted her hair. "Don't be mean. I knew she was the wrong girl. I came to find you."

"Let's get you warmed up." She threw a blanket around my shoulders. I recognized it from our blanket bubble. I sniffed it to see if it still smelled like us.

"Did you sniff the blanket?" In the kitchen, she turned on the stove and filled the kettle with water.

"I wanted to know if it still smelled like us."

"I washed it."

I pulled the wool tighter around my body and shivered.

"I'll start a fire."

My eyelids drooped as she lit the kindling. I fought to keep them open as the flame caught, and burned orange and bright. The weight of my breath grew heavier and I let myself tip to the side, curling up under the blanket with my head on the arm of her couch. Unable to keep my eyes open any longer, they closed as the kettle whistled.

"You're the right girl, the only right girl," I mumbled to myself as sleep swept over me.

TWENTY

Confession:
Blue balls are not a myth.

Could I be more of an asshole? I should probably figure out a way to get out of here before Hailey woke up or came home. When I swallowed a couple of pills with the water she'd left for me, my stomach rolled in protest. I needed grease to absorb whatever alcohol still filled my belly. But, first, I needed a ride home.

Who could I call to come get me?

John? No way.

Lori? Worse than John.

Cara? Worst choice of all.

Mom or Dad? They wouldn't know the house, but I might as well hand over my man card for having my parents pick me up from a failed drunken booty call.

I could walk the couple of miles into Langley or hitch a ride to pick up my truck. The clock on the microwave said it was 9:00 a.m. Nothing suspicious about a hungover man walking along the road on New Year's Day this early in the morning. Nothing at all.

Staring out over the lake from inside the living room, I thought about throwing myself into the icy water. It would probably sober me up and the resulting hypothermia might freeze away this headache if I was lucky.

In the corner of the deck sat a hot tub I hadn't noticed before. I wondered if she ever used it naked.

Or if she and Kurt had had sex in it. If I had a hot tub, I would have sex in it. Not one of those public ones. That would be gross, but in my own? Hell yeah. I wondered if after last night, I'd ever have sex with Hailey again. If it were ever on the table, I'd request hot tub sex. After she drained the water.

Probably a long shot at this point, but there was always hope.

"Look who's alive and awake." Her voice deadpanned behind me.

Feeling sheepish, I gave her a small wave. "Thanks for not leaving me outside to freeze."

"Now why would I let you die? We're friends, right?" I didn't see her expression because her head was hidden behind the cupboard door where she pulled out the coffee filters. "Coffee?" The cupboard swung closed to reveal her messy hair and sour expression.

"You hungover, too?" I shook the bottle of pills at her.

"Not at all. I came home completely sober last night after spending the evening at my parents'."

"Sober on New Year's?"

"Shocking concept I know. How's the head?"

"Bad enough I've been standing here thinking about throwing myself off the end of your dock to see if the freezing water helps."

Her laughter caught in her throat. "Long walk off a short pier?"

"Kind of my own version of a polar plunge. Want to join me?" I wiggled my eyebrows.

"No, but thanks for the offer. Coffee?"

"Not sure my stomach can handle it. Before you came downstairs I was contemplating hoofing it to Langley to get my truck."

"I can give you a ride after the coffee finishes brewing."

That was soon. "No rush. Thanks for letting me crash on your couch."

"How'd you get here anyway?"

Whatsherface had given me a ride. "Some friend of Diane's brought me."

"Why would she think you lived here?"

I shrugged and studied the pattern on the linoleum floor. "I think I mentioned something about Goss Lake last night."

"Tom …"

I held up my hands. "I know. Shitty move randomly showing up here."

"And nearly freezing to death on my porch. What if I didn't come home last night?"

Jealousy flooded my veins over the thought of her being out all night with another man. I had no right to stake a claim on her.

She studied me with a curious expression. "Simmer down, I was speaking hypothetically."

I glanced at my balled fists resting on the counter. "Oh. Right. Hypothetically." I relaxed my hands and stuffed them in my pockets. "Well, I really owe you one for letting me crash on your couch."

"No problem. That's what friends do. They watch each other's backs."

The scent of brewing coffee filled the kitchen as a steady stream of brown liquid filled the pot.

"You want some eggs?" She opened the refrigerator. "Toast?"

"I don't want to put you out."

"Too late." At my frown, she continued, "It's fine. But you should go wash your face. Or if you can handle it, take a shower. You still look like you've been mauled by a makeup artist and you smell like the Dog House."

I sniffed my T-shirt. "I'm disgusting."

———

Upstairs, I tucked a towel around my waist, my decision made.

She sat on the counter, eating peanut butter from the jar with a fork when I returned to the kitchen.

"Where are your clothes?" The fork paused in her hand like a sparkler on 4th of July.

I swept my tongue along the tines, licking off some peanut butter. "I'm throwing myself in the lake." With a smile and a wave, I opened the sliding glass door to the deck. Cold air prickled my skin into goose bumps. "Damn, damn. Damn. It's cold."

"It's January," she yelled from the counter. "Close the door."

I slid the door closed behind me, and then ran across the deck, down the steps, and over the mossy path to the wide dock protruding into the water. Without hesitation, I dropped the towel mid-run and leapt.

The thin, icy surface crackled before water swallowed me whole, sucking me down into the freezing darkness. I surfaced, sputtered and kicked my numb legs to reach the dock.

"Fuckshitdamnmotherfuckingfuckingfucksonofafuckingice-bergshitshitshitdamnit."

My teeth chattered as I pulled myself on to the dock, and flopped there, attempting to expand my lungs enough to catch a breath.

"I have neighbors," Hailey yelled from the deck.

Glancing around at the few houses on the other side of the lake, I cupped my dick and laughed. "Darlin', they'd better have a telescope if they plan to see anything. Everything's crawled inside my body. I've created a new definition for blue balls."

"Come inside before you die out there." Her words were stern, but laughter crept around the edge of her voice.

I hopped up, still cupping my junk, and picked up the towel, already cold with frost. With the towel around my shoulders, held in place with one hand, I ran up the path to the house, the other hand hiding my goods from the eyes of curious neighbors with telescopes and binoculars.

"You're insane." She held open the door for me as I bounded up the stairs.

"Probably." I jumped from foot to foot to avoid frostbite I was certain had begun to take over my lower extremities.

"Go take a shower." She kept her eyes on the top of the cupboards.

I chuckled and waited for her to glance at me, then dropped my hands and the towel. Not my finest glory, but it wasn't anything she hadn't seen, or touched, or kissed before.

The sting of a dishtowel hitting my naked ass made me jump, but before she could reload, I ran out of the kitchen. Her laughter followed me up the stairs.

In the shower, scalding hot water poured over my head. I leaned into the spray and let my skin absorb the heat. It was barely shy of being painful, but distracted me from my headache. Thoroughly thawed out, I sniffed a bottle of her soap, and deciding it didn't smell too girly, I used it to clean my face. Suds stung my eyes when I rinsed. Another bottle held Hailey's familiar floral scent. I skipped it for something smelling like oranges. She had at least five bottles lined up on a shelf in the shower. I found some shampoo and after rinsing, called it good.

My clothes still reeked of last night, but I had no other options. At least all of the lipstick stains were gone.

The scent of eggs and sausage cooking greeted me in the kitchen. Over the speakers, some woman sang about hating the rain and Hailey sang along—loudly, and off-key—shaking her ass a little as she flipped the sausage. Oblivious to my arrival, she belted out the lyrics while I enjoyed the show from where I leaned against the fridge.

"Shit!" she screamed and dropped the spatula.

"Sorry." Giving her a little wave now that she spied me, I handed the spatula to her. "I was having too much fun watching."

"Great." She tossed the dirty utensil in the sink and pulled out a wooden spoon.

"It was awesome."

"Don't kiss my ass. I know I sound like a cat in heat when I sing. That's why I only do it when I'm alone, or think I am. I didn't hear the shower turn off."

"You were really into the music." I turned down the volume. "Believe me at my word. I won't lie to you."

She stared at me for a few beats and shook her head. "For some reason, I do believe you."

"Good. You should." I ran my fingers through my hair and scratched my scalp.

"Your hair's really curly when it's wet."

"I know. It was worse when I was a kid. Got picked on and called a mop head in elementary school."

"Moppy fits you."

I narrowed my eyes and snarled at her.

"Okay, Moppy, breakfast is ready." Right on cue, toast popped up from the toaster.

We ate in silence for a few minutes. The frozen lake, the hot shower, and now grease from the sausage restored me.

"So how cold was the water?" she asked, chomping on the edge of her toast.

"Fucking cold." I gave her a smile.

"You're crazy, you know."

"I think we established that outside."

She arched her brow. "We established it a long time ago, trust me."

I picked up a link of sausage and bit it in half. "Some people like crazy. It's a helluva lot more fun than normal and boring."

"Trust me, I know normal and boring. I almost became Mrs. Boring."

The energy shifted between us. Without meaning to, I'd referenced her ex, something I'd managed to avoid since the first night together over a month ago.

I dropped the sausage on my plate. "None of my business, but I called that on Halloween."

"What?" Her eyes widened.

"I told Lori you'd never marry him."

"What? She never mentioned it to me."

"Why would she? I'm not psychic or anything, but I do have a sense about relationships."

"Says the man who never, ever has them? Do you give marriage counseling, too?"

I sat there and took her words like the small assaults they were intended to be. "I've spent a lot of time around couples, often as the third wheel. People forget to play nice in front of me." I raised a shoulder. "From high school on, I've had a good sense of impending break-ups. Sadly, my skills are much less profitable than picking winning horses at the track."

"What about us said 'doomed' to you?" She crossed her arms in defense.

"You want me to discuss your ex with you? Are you sure?"

"Go for it." Her words were clipped and she stared me down in challenge.

"*Okay*." I drew out the word. "First, your costumes didn't coordinate. Second, he didn't understand the irony of his. Third, he's shorter than you."

She opened her mouth to protest and I silenced her with my hand. "You're still kind of a tomboy, and sometimes you like taking control in the bedroom." I swore her cheeks pinked, and I smiled because I knew I spoke the truth. "But at the end of the day, you want to feel feminine and cherished, not like a towering giant next to Napoleon."

Her mouth closed and I knew I'd nailed it.

"Where was I? Right. Fourth, you shrugged off his attempt to claim you by putting his arm around you at the party."

"Okay, point proven," she mumbled.

"Come on, Hailey. How could you seriously think about marrying a guy who didn't get a *Heathers'* reference? You and Lori were obsessed with that movie in middle school."

She shrugged, but chuckled. "I know. It's the reason I called off the wedding."

It was my turn to let my jaw drop.

Her throaty laughter made her eyes crinkle. "No! But your analysis of us is eerily spot on."

"See?" I resisted full out saying I told you so. "My other theory is all your friends are getting married and having kids, so you panicked. The first nice guy with a stable job, money in the bank, and the whole line about 'two-point-five kids, a golden retriever, and you staying home with the kids' sounded like everything you didn't know you wanted until the thought of being an old maid was staring you in the face at the ancient age of twenty-nine."

She huffed. "We started dating when I was twenty-seven. He is super successful, has money in the bank, and a golden retriever. After a string of starving artists and poor musicians, a guy who could afford to take me out, spoil me and want to take care of me sounded like heaven."

"You haven't mentioned having the hubba-hubba hots for him."

She focused on the table. "There's a lot more to relationships than sex."

I nodded. "Right."

Her eyes flashed to mine. "There is!"

I wanted to comment, but didn't care to know more about their sex life. No way. "When did he propose?"

"Early summer."

"And you were how old?"

She glowered at her plate and used her crust to stab a few small pieces of eggs. "Twenty-nine," she whispered.

"I'm sorry. I didn't hear that."

"Twenty-nine," she shouted.

I leaned against my chair and crossed my arms in triumph.

"Shut up." She matched my pose and pouted her beautiful, full lips.

"Told you I have a knack." I smiled smugly.

"If you have such a knack for reading people and seeing relationships play out, why are you perpetually single? Scared?"

Scared? Me? I chuckled. "I know myself well enough to know I'd be a disaster at the boyfriend thing."

She studied me, running her index finger along her bottom lip. I squirmed as her examination continued.

"What?" I finally whispered.

"Maybe you don't see yourself as clearly as you think you see others."

"We never do." I swallowed the last of my water and brushed my hands on my jeans. "So, you want to have sex now?"

Coffee sputtered out of her mouth and hit the table. "What? No!"

I pressed my lips together. "Didn't think so, but it was worth the shot."

"Have you not paid attention at all? To anything?"

"I'm teasing. Remember? It's what you and I do. You've made it pretty clear sex isn't going to happen. While I can't say I'm not bummed, I understand and respect it. Doesn't mean I won't still flirt with you. It's my first language."

A small smile appeared on her lips. "Ready for a ride?"

Guess I'd stayed long enough. "Sure."

TWENTY-ONE

Confession:
My family always comes first.

A few weeks after the first of the year, I sat next to Gramma on the couch in my parents' living room, watching the Seahawks in the playoffs. She wore a blue and lime green sweatshirt and matching wristbands in support of the team.

"Pops and I used to have season tickets when they first opened the King Dome. But you weren't born then, so you wouldn't remember." She patted my arm.

"Wish we still had those season tickets," Dad complained from his recliner.

"You could afford a box now if you wanted," I said. It was true. He had the money, but came from a long line of cheapskates. It ran in our blood.

"Nah. You see the game better right here in the living room." He dunked a chip in Mom's crab dip. "And the food's better."

My sisters and mom were in the kitchen, probably drinking white wine or mojitos, and gossiping. After what I overheard on

Thanksgiving, I knew to avoid eavesdropping on their opinions on my social life. Or lack thereof.

I had to admit, right now I had zero life. Cold, rainy days followed one after the other and nothing seemed to dry out, or warm up. Work sucked. I spent a week exposed to the damp, welding the hull of some rich man's yacht. Work, complaining about the cold, carving in the shop, eating over here … was the extent of it. I still played pool with John on Thursdays, but otherwise avoided the bar scene.

New Year's Eve and my polar plunge marked the turning point. I hadn't gone out and picked up a woman in weeks. It didn't appeal to me. Spending time with Gramma, listening to her tell stories about her life with Pops before I was born kept me more entertained than inane conversation to get laid.

"Someone wants to buy the old place overlooking Mutiny Bay," Gramma said out of the blue.

"What?" my Dad and I asked at the same time.

"Where the old barn still stands," she clarified.

"I know the property, Mom, but since when have you wanted to sell any land?" Dad sat up and flipped down the footrest, planting his feet on the carpet and leaning forward to focus on her.

"Oh, I hadn't given it any thought. It's always had a lovely marsh near the beach, and for years there was an eagle's nest in the cedar grove near where the house stood."

Sometimes I forgot how much land my family owned around here. The Mutiny Bay farm came down through Ellie's family and sat apart from the main holdings closer to Double Bluff. A crooked barn leaned precariously in an overgrown field, but the fifty acres of land around it were a jewel. We rented out the fields to a local family who kept up the tradition of farming on the island.

"Who's interested in the place?" I asked. Her comment after the funeral flashed through my mind. "Were these the same people who gave you their cards at Pops' funeral?"

"What?" Dad exploded from his chair. I didn't see it often, but he carried the same gene for the Donnely temper I did. "Someone came to Pops' funeral to talk to you about selling land?"

"Ken, sit down. No, they only gave me their business cards. And yes, Tom, it's the same young man. I think he's an island boy, but lives over in Seattle now. Really made a success of himself."

Bile rose in my throat. "What's his name, Gramma?"

"Oh, I don't remember, but I said no. I felt terrible about it after they made such a nice presentation with model homes and all their ideas for how the land could benefit the island. I'm not in a place right now to make any decisions. I told your cousins the same last week after we left."

Dad's neck went red with anger and his eyes bulged out, however his voice remained calm. "Mom, start from the beginning. Which cousins?" He began pacing the room.

"Bob set up the meeting."

Of course. Bob, the only Donnely in generations to serve time.

"Now, Ken, I don't want to start any trouble, not after losing Pops. We all need to stick together. I explained the estate was still in probate."

"It's a matter of respect, Mom. Pops hasn't been gone two months, and they're already sniffing around for an in. Like the miserable coyotes around here."

"Dinner's ready!" Amy announced cheerily from the hall. "Let's eat— Hey, what's going on in here? The Hawks losing?" Her eyes swept the room and landed on me. I gave a subtle shake of my head to say not now.

Mom entered the room, wiping her hand on an apron, her other hand still holding a glass of white wine. "What's going on?"

"I've got a phone call to make. Start without me." Dad stomped off toward his office.

"Not now, let's have dinner," I whispered to Mom, gesturing to the dining room.

Gramma fretted under her breath to Mom as they walked ahead of us.

I lagged behind to fill in Amy on the dirty dealings of our favorite cousin. I had to cover her mouth to keep her cursing from being overheard in the dining room.

"I think I know who's behind this," she said once I removed my hand.

"Go on."

"Kurt Jones," she whispered like it was a bad word and we were kids.

"Jones? The last name doesn't ring a bell. And I only know one—" *Shit.*

"Kurt. Hailey's ex."

"That little fuckwad." I spat out the words.

"I never liked him, but didn't think he would sink to trying to get a grieving widow to sell property when the grave is still fresh," Amy whispered.

"He gave her his card at the funeral. Shit. I saw him at the church. He stood near the door with a bunch of other guys I didn't recognize."

"He did not!" Her voice rose.

"Yep. I thought he must have been there to support Hailey, but I never saw him at the reception."

"They broke up months ago and she was more than clear she wanted nothing to do with him, so he wasn't there for her."

"Unbelievable."

She echoed me and then continued, "Hailey's going to die if she finds out he did this. I guess he was always talking about how underdeveloped the island was. He thought more subdivisions and fewer woods and farms would, to quote him, "bring you into the 21st century" as if we were some backward time warp." She huffed with the remembered insult.

"Well, he went after the wrong land and the wrong family."

"He picked on the wrong little old lady, that's for sure." She bumped shoulders with me as we made our way down the hall. "I can't say I don't want to kick his ass, though."

"Amy! You've never been in a fight in your life outside of tackling our sisters or whatever emotional warfare you waged on each other as teens."

She sighed. "I know, I know. But I love the idea of a good old-fashioned movie style ass kicking for Kurt. Come on, it would be awesome."

I blinked at her. "You know, I'm so going to bring this up when Sam gets in his first fight at school."

"That's different!"

"Uh huh. You're such a bruiser, Amy." I sat down and smiled at Mom, who appeared worried, and Gramma, who quietly ate her stew.

A few minutes later, Dad sat at the head of the table. "All settled. Where's my dinner?"

TWENTY-TWO

Confession:
Nothing surprises me when it comes to women.

P oor Kurt Jones. Born without a sense of humor, dumped
by his fiancée, and now, blacklisted on Whidbey. Mom may
have mentioned it to both Connie at the bank and Sandy at the
market. Living on the island meant word got around quickly
about Ellie Donnely being targeted at Pops' funeral. Wagons
circled and the big guns were brought out. No one messed with
the Donnely matriarch. As for Bob, he was off the Christmas
card list, permanently.

I didn't think how the island gossip would affect Hailey, the
former future Mrs. Jones. Or how easily someone could be
tarnished by association. The gossip in the break room at work,
which had once been around her legs, turned to greedy city
people coming to the island and trying to take advantage. It was
amazing to hear the things people said when they didn't realize I
stood in the room behind them.

"She probably used her family connections to get in sweet
with the Donnelys. I heard she's been friends with Ken's

youngest for years. Such a shame when islanders forget where they come from."

"She's always been a real stuck up bitch around here. She gets her coffee, but never eats in here with the rest of us."

"Didn't she call off the wedding?" Daryl asked, hope in his voice.

Geez, these guys were worse than my sisters with their gossip. Anyone who said men didn't gossip, hadn't hung around men very much. I cleared my throat from my place near the door.

"Hey, Donnely," Stu greeted me. "Sorry to hear about the business with Ellie."

With a shrug, I sat down. "Sounds like Ellie's not the only person being discussed."

A few of the guys at least appeared to be sheepish.

"From what I overheard, the bunch of you could give Connie's circle a run in terms of gossip. You all get vaginas for Christmas this year?"

"Fuck you," Jay said.

"This makes the second time you've stepped in to defend King. You sweet on her or something?" Stu asked.

"Maybe they like braiding each other's hair," some guy I didn't recognize added.

That didn't make sense. I shot him a look and he slunk lower in his chair. "This is why we can't have nice things. A woman works here and you numb-nuts spend your breaks talking about her."

"We don't talk about Bertha in the office."

A round of shudders made its way around the table like the Wave at Safeco Field.

Bertha had earned the unfortunate nickname of Bulldog around the yard. She didn't accept any bullshit from anyone, let alone the men around here. Her jowls and big eyes complimented her personality. I knew under her gruff exterior, she had a heart of gold. In her free time she knit afghans for soldiers and the senior center. You didn't piss her off if you could help it.

"Well, maybe you should pretend every woman is Bertha. Or your mother," I said, crossing my arms and tilting my chair.

"I'd never get laid again," Stu grumbled and drank from his mug.

"Again?" I joked. The tension dissipated into laughter. Talk moved to the Seahawks making the Super Bowl again, the price of diesel, and whether or not salmon season would be good this year.

"You think you'll take the Master Baiter up the Strait of Georgia?" Jay asked me.

"Masturbator? Who's that?" Daryl laughed.

"Besides you?" Stu snorted.

Conversation came to an abrupt halt. Not because of the inappropriate work conversation, but because Hailey stood at the counter, her empty mug dangling from her hand. Silence filled the space.

"Um, hi." She faked a smile at the group.

None of the guys responded, instead becoming interested in their finished lunches and the napkins crumpled on the table.

"Hi, King," I said, tossing my napkin at Stu's head.

"Hello, hey," he said.

Not awkward at all.

Hailey sighed and poured a cup of coffee. Pausing at the door, she said, "You know, I preferred it when you all talked about my legs instead of talking shit about my personal life."

Shit.

"Sorry you heard all that," Jay apologized.

"Nothing not being said all over the island." She shrugged and walked out.

My leg bounced, and I struggled not to jump up, and follow her. I counted to fifty and stood. "You're a bunch of assholes."

Daryl stared at his hands and remained quiet. Poor kid had it bad for Hailey.

"You better be fucking her with all this white-knighting she has you doing on her behalf, Donnely," Stu grumbled into his mug.

"They've got to be screwing," Jay added. "I've never seen him get all territorial about someone he wasn't related to before."

"I don't see any of your names on this building, Jay. Have some respect for the company. There are other boatyards that might be hiring." I threw away my lunch and stomped out of the room.

"Fucking assholes," I mumbled as they continued to talk shit.

I intended to head out to the boat, but instead found myself waving to Bertha as I passed through the front office. With two quick knocks, I announced my arrival at Hailey's door.

She glanced up, her mouth full of a bite of sandwich. A little dab of mayo lingered on her cheek as she chewed and swallowed. "Yeah? Not finished with the break room talk?"

I couldn't have a conversation with her with mayo on her face. I gestured to her cheek and she wiped it off, blushing.

"I'm really sorry you overheard a bunch of asshats gossiping."

She gestured for me to sit. Instead, I leaned against her filing cabinet.

"Honestly, it's nothing new. Trust me. Sandy gave me an earful when I bought groceries yesterday. She went on and on about my poor choice in men with a judgmental frown on her face. Everyone in the lines around us could hear her. No one seems to remember I called off the engagement."

"Why don't you remind them?"

"How? Put an ad in the local paper?" She threw the rest of her sandwich in the garbage.

"Might not be a bad idea."

"Stop giving me the dimples. They're not helping."

I froze my face into a serious expression. "You know the

island. Some other scandal will take the attention from your poor choice in men."

"Gee, thanks."

"Trust me. Some teen will get pregnant, or steal a car, some politician will do something corrupt, or any number of things will distract the locals. There are enough Donnelys around, someone else is bound to cross us soon."

She sighed. "I didn't do anything."

"I know."

"I stopped by and saw Ellie this weekend. She was so lovely, and told me she knew plenty of nice young men."

I smiled at my grandmother's kindness. "Did she mention me?"

"Oddly enough, no."

I pouted.

"She did say I needed to meet a nice young man like John Day. You know any guys like him?" She bit her lip to fight her grin.

"Oh, for fuck's sake. She did not." My pout turned sullen. "What does he have I don't?"

"A girlfriend and a dog?"

"What does Babe have to do with anything?"

"Shows loyalty and the ability to commit to something."

"I could get a dog. We had a dog growing up."

"Minnie? The schnauzer? I thought she hated you?"

"She did. Always peed in my room, but no one believed me. What about a fish?"

"Fish?"

"I could get a pet fish."

"Why?"

"To show I'm not a sociopath."

"People think you're a sociopath?"

"No, but my grandmother doesn't think I'm a nice young man."

She sighed. "Your grandmother loves you, and knows you well, apparently."

I twisted my mouth.

"Tigers don't change their stripes." She gave me a sympathetic smile.

"I did defend you back there."

"I heard. You don't have to come to my rescue. I think it might make things worse."

"How?"

"People will be suspicious, start asking questions about why you're taking my side, why you're so interested."

"So?"

"Isn't the first rule of Tom Cat never draw attention to yourself?"

"That isn't the first rule of Fight Club." My anger simmered. "I'm not the one who said we couldn't tell anyone. You're the one who worried about Lori finding out."

"You didn't object. Plus, that's over, isn't it? Back to being friends, right?" Her eyes were cold.

I nodded to placate her.

"Thanks for the knight in shining armor act, but I can handle things on my own."

"Fine." I pushed off the cabinet so hard it rocked.

"Fine," she echoed.

I stormed out of her office and right into the paunch of Al.

"Donnely. Everything okay in there?"

"It's *fine*." I emphasized the last word.

"I hope you aren't bringing your personal issues with King into work. Whatever happened between her fiancé and your grandmother should be resolved privately.

"Ex."

"Pardon?"

"He's her ex-fiancé. Ex. No one around this goddamn island seems to remember she broke up with him."

I shoved past him and out to my truck. Work wasn't over, but I was clocking out for the day.

My fists banged on the steering wheel while I decided what to do. Screw it. I'd drive and figure it out.

A short loop around Holmes Harbor cleared my head. This was exactly why I didn't get involved in other people's drama and bullshit. Anything happening to Hailey had nothing to do with me. As we'd both agreed multiple times, we were friends. That's it. Friends who had sex a few times. Now it was over.

I pulled into my yard and parked near the shop. Inside, I cranked up the classic rock station, fired up the wood-stove, and went to work on a new sculpture. Slicing through the wood with a buzzing chainsaw required all of my focus and I soon lost myself in drawing out the otter, which lay trapped in the log. Wood chips flew and fell to the ground, creating a blizzard around me.

I carved until my arms grew tired. Quieting the saw, I stepped away and observed my work.

Hailey's silver hood appeared through the trees and she slammed on the brakes a few feet from my truck.

"There you are," she shouted, stomping through puddles and mud to the shop's entrance.

I turned off the chainsaw and laid it on the bench before walking toward the doors to meet her. "What do you want, friend?"

"Stop butting into my business." Her voice screeched and her arms flailed.

"I don't know what you're talking about." I blocked her entrance to the shop by spreading my legs and putting my hands on my hips. "You're the crazy woman showing up at my house screaming at me."

"Al spoke to me after you took off. Something about not bringing personal drama into work and distracting the crew. Guess if your last name is Donnely, you can do no wrong at the boatyard." She poked me in the chest. It was annoying as hell.

I grabbed her finger and held her hand in mine. Her other hand gripped and clawed at my hand as she tried to free herself. "Let go." She pried my finger back, but I held fast.

"Stop hitting me."

"Let go," she whined.

"Are you going to stop acting like some crazed she-devil?"

"I can't make any promises." Scowling, she tugged her arm.

I shouldn't have done it, but the big brother in me saw the opportunity and took it. When she pulled far enough to be off balance, I let go of her hand, and she fell in a lump on the threshold in front of me.

"Damn you." She cursed out a string of expletives.

I laughed, closing my eyes. Next thing I knew, I was falling ass-over-elbows, tumbling on top of her, and landing with my head between her thighs, my weight on my forearms. I'd missed her foot coming up to swipe my legs out from under me.

"Get up!" She batted my head.

I smiled and bit her inner thigh through her jeans. Suddenly, this was the most ridiculous thing to happen to me in a long time.

"Ow!" Her thighs clamped tightly around my head, squeezing until I couldn't breathe. I used my knees and weight to shift forward to freedom and found myself eye level with her heaving boobs.

Angry or not, she was fucking hot. I hadn't had sex in a month. Hell, more than a month. Not since before Pops died.

"Remember the last time we were in here?" I let my mouth hover over her nipple, but raised my eyes to meet hers.

Her face was flushed. Behind her eyes a battle between lust and anger raged. The two emotions elicited similar physical responses, so I knew I was walking a thin line between sex and a knee to the balls. It was a risk I was willing to take. I held down her hands near her shoulders.

Giving into desire, I bit her breast through the thin material of her shirt and bra. It wasn't a gentle nip. I wanted to mark her, to inflict a moment of pain. I needed to see some evidence I affected her.

"Ahh," she whimpered, her hands struggling for freedom.

I released one of her hands, and she clawed at my bicep, her short nails digging into my skin. It hurt enough to make me pause, but not stop. I let my hand trail a path down her buttons until I reached the exposed skin above her pants while my nose skimmed her cleavage.

She held her breath, but didn't shove me away. I took that as enough encouragement and kissed her nipple with open lips. It rose to salute the familiarity of my mouth. Smiling, I bit it again, gently this time.

Her hands found their way into my hair and she pulled my face to hers. Our mouths clashed together in a collision of tongues and teeth, lips and breath. She bit my lip and tugged … hard. I expected to taste blood. Instead, she softly sucked away the pain.

She yanked my shirt over my head and then pushed off her jeans. I sat back to unbutton mine. My jeans ended up being shoved out of the way, but never taken off completely.

On the cold, concrete floor, covered in wood-chips and sawdust, I fought the demons of gossip and reputation the best way I knew how. My body silenced her arguments and anger. My tongue trailed over her skin, leaving behind desire. I worshipped her. She clawed, scraped, and dug into my skin, using my body to release weeks of frustration and shame. We weren't kind. This wasn't making love. This was claiming and owning one another on a purely physical level. This was passion. I held on as she thrashed and clenched, and then with a low moan, came inside her.

It was only after the haze of lust and orgasm faded did I remember the condom.

———

Shit.

I rolled off of her and sat up without a word.

"What?" She lay naked on the floor, where our bodies had created a bare spot in the sawdust, resembling a snow angel.

"Are you on the pill?" I tugged up my jeans, but didn't zip. I shot her a serious look.

"Why?" She sat up and rebuttoned her shirt, covering the mark of my teeth on her breast.

"Answer the question." *What if she's pregnant?*

"Thanks. That was great for me, I hope it was great for you, too." She stood and brushed wood-chips off her jeans. "Yes, I'm on the pill and have been since I was seventeen. Read into it what you want." Sawdust fell from her hair when she shook her head in disgust. She'd never looked more sexy to me. Or beautiful.

"Okay, good," I mumbled, distracted by the panic crushing my chest.

"Really? You honestly think I'd come over here and have unprotected sex with you? For what? Why? To get pregnant?" Hurt edged her words.

I shrugged. Coming from her mouth, I was instantly aware how wrong my words sounded. "Sorry." I was an arrogant prick to think she would try to trap me.

"Do I need to get tested?" She slid on her underwear.

It was my turn to be indignant. "Why?"

"No condom, remember?"

I muttered a string of expletives. "No. I always wear one and get tested. I'm not that big of a dipshit." I watched denim cover the legs which had taken over my fantasies.

"Good. Great." She stared at the floor as she ran her fingers through her hair.

"You started this." I gestured between us.

"Then I guess I'm finishing it, too. There's nothing to finish." She mimicked my gesture. "Listen, this has always been a casual thing. I knew from the first night what I was getting myself into. It's my own fault I didn't stop it before … when my feelings became involved," she whispered the last words. "But I didn't and that's on me."

I stood still, trying to absorb her words.

"Okay, then." She turned to go.

"Hey." I reached for her arm, but she moved it out of the way. "None of that came out the way I meant it to. I… freaked out." I studied her face.

"I …" Her words bounced around in my head, crowding out my own thoughts.

"I …" I started again, but whatever words I tried to find to express what was happening in my gut and how my chest hurt, not from panic, but from the idea of her leaving with hurt in her eyes, escaped me.

She exhaled, her cheeks pink from the cold and my beard, her hair still tangled and matted with wood shavings. "I need to go."

"Don't." My hand brushed her back as she walked away from me. Everything coming out of my mouth was wrong.

"I—" I didn't know what to say.

I tried again. "Don't go," I said with my eyes closed.

The slam of her car door answered me.

"Stay," I whispered to no one.

"Fuck!" I snarled, picking up the half-finished otter, and chucking it out into the yard. The soft bounce across the muddy grass didn't feel satisfying, so I swept all of the tools off my workbench. I kicked the saw across the shop, the blade scraping roughly across the cement. Nothing helped. I stormed out of the shop, then picked up the otter, and threw it into the woods.

TWENTY-THREE

Confession:
I'm a lover, not a fighter.

Taillights guided me north to Oak Harbor. If I focused on the car ahead of me, the rain and slick road faded away with the image of Hailey's sad face last week in the barn. I'd fucked up things with her and I didn't know how to fix it. At this point, I'd usually walk away and move on to the next woman. Yet lately I had zero desire to flirt or pursue anyone, and it freaked me out.

My wipers beat a loud swoosh-click-swoosh against the fogged windshield. I cracked my window to let in some fresh air, both to dissipate the mugginess and keep me alert. My wheels hit a deep puddle of water and the truck hydroplaned for a few feet before I felt the tires grip the road again. I exhaled. Being out on a night like this was crazy. Nothing good could come from hanging out in Oak Harbor tonight.

The streets of downtown were empty except for the parking spots in front of The Harbor Bar down near the water. Neon beer signs lit up the small windows of the nondescript corner building. A few men huddled under an awning, smoke creating clouds above their heads. This tavern wasn't a place I'd ever take a woman, but sometimes on dark, cold nights like tonight when I didn't want to be alone, I'd come here and have a drink, play pull-tabs, listen to Navy guys pick up local girls, and play old songs on the ancient jukebox in the corner. Dim lighting, a pool table, and three pinball machines completed the dive bar vibe. Best part was no one knew me here. South islanders typically didn't make the drive up here, and definitely not during a storm.

Ruby, the bartender, winked at me in acknowledgement. She chatted me up, but never asked questions. My guess was she had to be in her fifties, maybe sixties. I think she owned the place.

"What'll it be, sugar?" she asked, clearing some dirty glasses from the bar in the corner near the Keno machine.

"Something on tap. Surprise me."

She grabbed a pint glass and filled it with Kokanee. At least it wasn't a light beer.

"Thanks." I reached for my wallet in my jacket pocket.

"You want to open a tab?"

"Sure. And give me ten dollars in pull-tabs." I listed the games I wanted and put the bill on the bar.

She returned with a small pile of paper cards and wished me luck.

I removed my jacket and rolled up my sleeves. With a sip of the almost flat beer, I pulled the strips of paper with more force than needed to expose the combinations of symbols. Pull-tabs were the paper equivalent of a slot machine.

Rip.

Loser.

Rip.

Loser.

Rip.

Loser.

I drank more beer.

Rip.

Loser.

Rip.

Loser.

Apparently the universe agreed.

Loser.

The song *Brandy* came on the jukebox. The old guy a few empty stools down from me dedicated it to our bartender. She gave him a sympathetic smile and patted his arm where a blurry, blue-black tattoo vaguely resembling an anchor could be seen.

I let my eyes scan the bar and deduced most of the guys in here were Navy. The women wore clothes too small to be anything other than costumes used to seduce sailors. Lots of hair and lots of makeup mixed with a low level of desperation. Sex for companionship, a few hours of entertainment and a few free rounds of drinks. Some of the locals saw a military man as a means to get off this rock and see the world. Same story in every town near a military base.

A woman in a short skirt barely covering her ass slowly danced in front of the jukebox. With her arms over her head, she shimmied down and bent forward to shake her ass. All she needed was a pole. The nearby table of buzz-cut men whooped and cheered her on. She tossed her hair and wiggled on one of their laps. After seeing her face, I wondered if she was over twenty-one. She had the attitude of a teenager who'd snuck out on a school night.

None of my business, but I kept an eye on her.

I ordered another pint.

Rip.

Loser.

What was I doing here?

Trolling for a girl willing to sleep with a guy for a chance at a better life?

No way.

Being here didn't make me feel less alone. If anything, this place and these people reminded me of everything I didn't have because I didn't want it. Or told myself I didn't need.

I pulled another tab and smiled.

Winner.

I set it aside and drank my beer.

Loud male voices and the men they belonged to crashed through the door with a few curses and whoops. I glanced over at them as they took over a table. It was impossible to ignore them, and I suspected they demanded this kind of attention wherever they went.

I returned to my tabs and beer, attempting to tune out their sexist jokes about the bartender and other women in the place.

"How do you put up with all these men?" I asked Ruby.

"Oh, you get used to them. Sometimes I have to enlist Babe Ruth over there." She pointed above the bar where a baseball bat hung. "But the regulars keep an eye out for me. Have for thirty years." She smiled and pointed at my winning game. "Hey, you're a winner!"

She took the paper and handed me a twenty-dollar bill. "Things are looking up for you."

How wrong she was.

"Hey, I know you," a drunk voice slurred from the table of obnoxious guys. I didn't turn around because he couldn't have meant me, but the voice sounded familiar.

"Hey!" the voice called out again. "I'm talking to you."

Curiosity got the better of me and I spun around on my stool.

Kurt stood half out of his chair pointing at me.

Great. Exactly what this night needed—more asshole.

I gave him a head nod and turned away. I signaled for my tab and pulled my coat off of my chair to pay. The last thing I needed tonight would be talking to some asshat. Not with the mood I was in, and not with what I knew about him.

"You're not leaving, are you?" He blinked at me and frowned while he wove his way over to me.

"Hey, Kurt. How's it going?"

"You're an asshole." His stale beer and whiskey breath blew over my face from where he leaned on the back of the stool next to mine.

I jerked my head to escape his foul breath. I tried to stop the smile tugging at my lips.

"What are you smiling about?" He sneered at me and poked my shoulder.

"Nothing, man."

"You ain't nothing but a piece of island trash. You think you're the shit because you never left the island. Bunch of inbred stupid hicks with no sense, that's what your family is. You can't hold on to the land. Estate taxes are going to kill you. Your family really fucked up, my friend. And when you and your stupid family come begging me to buy it from you, I'm going to love paying you half the original offer."

It was the "my friend" part of his rant that raised my hackles. No way were we friends. I inhaled and counted: ten, nine, eight, seven, six …

"And don't think I don't know you're fucking Hailey. Hope you're enjoying my sloppy seconds. I swear she might've been a lesbian, so thanks for clarifying."

I faltered at five. "Listen, friend," I spat out the word, "you need to step back."

"Or what? You going to punch me? I've got five witnesses and two of them are lawyers."

I gave Ruby an apologetic smile, then stood up. I towered over him and he prattled on about "trying something". He blocked my way and puffed out his chest like the little rooster man he was.

The jukebox switched over to *Honky Tonk Women* and suddenly this whole scenario became an out of body experience. He took a swing with his right hand and attempted to grab my shirt with his left. I easily dodged both his hands. He came at me again and made contact with my arm.

"You hit like a little kid." I would have said like a girl, but I grew up with sisters, and they hit a lot harder than Kurt did. Laughing, I punched him in the nose. He didn't duck.

Chairs clattered to the floor and there was a rush of bodies in our direction. Kurt plowed into my stomach with his head and held me while he tried to hit my sides and back. I would've been fine had his friend not grabbed me around the neck. Two against one wasn't fair. I kneed Kurt and head butted his friend. A few stools went tumbling to the floor along with Kurt. The guys at the pool table stopped playing and watched. Buzzcuts in the corner yelled "fight" and some of them joined the brawl. I think a few were on my side.

Ruby blew a whistle. A wood bat thunked against the bar. "Not in my bar," she yelled. "Take it outside or I'm calling the cops."

Fists continued to fly and at one point I found myself up against a pinball machine. The guy had a scar above his eyebrow. I didn't recognize him from Kurt's group.

"Listen, the cops will be here any minute. I'm trying to save your ass. I saw him throw the first punch. I've got your back." He smiled and revealed a cut lip.

"Hey, thanks, but I'm good."

"You can head out the backdoor—"

"Okay, gentlemen. Let's break it up," a young cop shouted near the front.

I glanced around and saw men freeze. Most were standing around and watching the fight, but Kurt stood up from the floor, his nose bleeding and his shirt torn. He pointed at me and said, "He started it."

What an asswipe.

"You," the cop addressed me, "over here."

My new friend followed and tried to interrupt the cop, but the officer was having none of it. "Let's take a ride to the station and sort things out. Now apologize to Ruby for messing up her bar."

I gave Ruby an embarrassed look. She shook her head, but returned my smile.

"Can I get my coat?" I pointed to the floor by the bar. I pulled out my wallet and left her a fifty-dollar tip. The least I could do for brawling in her place.

Kurt and I sat in silence in the back of the patrol car during the ride to the police station. Another cruiser followed with three other guys who had been throwing punches. At the station, a list of charges were rattled off for fighting and busting up Ruby's place: drunk and disorderly conduct, public intoxication, property damage, and assault. After being processed, I was told to call someone to arrange bail and a ride home.

"My truck's at Ruby's. I only had two beers and can drive myself home. Ask Ruby herself," I argued.

Officer Olsen shook his head. "Buddy, your truck is spending the night in Oak Harbor whether you do or not. What part of drunk don't you understand?" His voice lost its friendly tone the longer he spoke.

I used my phone call to call John and got his voicemail.

"I'm in the Oak Harbor jail. Kurt started a fight," I said as explanation.

That was it. I knew he'd be here as soon as he could.

Nothing to do but wait. At least Officer Olsen put us in separate holding cells. If I had to hear one more time how Kurt was going to sue me, I'd probably end up punching him again.

Time crawled by as I lay on the metal bench staring at the ceiling. My knuckles had dried blood on them and I didn't know if it was mine, Kurt's, or someone else's. I gently poked around my right eye, which was swelling closed. Taking inventory of the rest of my body, I decide the extent of my injuries included some tenderness along my side. Not too bad.

At least Kurt had it worse.

I must have fallen asleep because the sound of my freedom woke me. "Donnely, your ride's here."

I blinked a few times in the bright fluorescent light and stretched before stumbling to my feet.

"You're a lucky guy," a mustached middle-aged officer said.

"Why?" I yawned as we walked down the hall to the front counter.

"All of the charges against you are being dropped. An off-duty officer came in and cleared you. Sounds like the other guy threw the first punch."

My anonymous friend by the pinball machine had saved my ass. "Is he still here? I'd like to say thanks."

"Nah, he left a while ago after giving his statement."

"Can I at least get his name?"

"King, Jesse King."

"No shit. He any relation to the Kings in Freeland?" *What were the odds?*

"Not sure, but I'll let him know you said thanks." He led me over to the counter where I collected my wallet and jacket. "Put a steak on your eye and maybe stay out of Oak Harbor for a while, Mr. Donnely."

I thanked him and said I'd follow his advice. Shoving my hands in my pockets, I felt like a complete tool. *Bar brawl? On a Tuesday?* I didn't know how I got to this point in my life, but things needed to change, and soon.

I checked my phone. No texts or updates from John. Escaping the judgmental stare of the officer at the front desk, I exited with a friendly wave, which was not reciprocated. The rain had stopped and fresh air would do me good. I rubbed my hands over my head and searched for John's truck. Tomorrow at work was going to suck. A shiner would be all the buzz in the break room. I dreaded the talk I knew would be coming from Al about being a Donnely and representing the company. Not to mention explaining a black eye to my family.

A parked car flashed its lights. Where was John? He hadn't

been in the lobby and his truck wasn't out front, yet the officer had said my ride was here.

Two short honks of the horn drew my attention to the curb.

The passenger window slowly slid down and a mop of brown hair leaned toward the opening.

"You going to stand there all night?"

TWENTY-FOUR

Confession:
I'm a man of my word.

I daho.

Hailey sat in her car and stared at me through the open window.

"I don't know what you're doing here, but I'm waiting for John."

"Fine." The window began to rise and her white reverse lights flashed as she shifted into gear.

Shit. I glanced around again, not seeing John, and it hit me she was my ride. My only ride.

"Stop!" I jogged up to the car. "At least give me a ride to my truck." I frowned and winced.

"Get in, Tom." The window closed in my face.

I slammed the door behind me and slunk low in the seat. "You shouldn't be here."

"You're welcome. And you really want to risk driving home after drinking and being in jail once tonight?"

"Fuck. You're right," I mumbled into my window. "Thank you. I owe you."

"When I said friends, I didn't expect it to extend to picking your sorry ass up from jail in the middle of the night, but that's what friends do for *friends*."

"Neither did I," I snarled.

"This is exactly how I wanted to begin Valentine's Day."

"Oh, shit." The night was getting better and better.

"Surprisingly, this isn't my worst Valentine's."

"I'm such a jerk. I didn't realize the date." So much for being a lover and not a fighter.

"It's no big deal. I swear. But let's agree you're a jerk."

I nodded and texted John. We drove along in silence until we hit Penn Cove.

"Do you know Jesse King?" The conversation had to start somewhere.

"He's my cousin."

"He saved my ass tonight."

"I know. He called me when you got hauled away. You're lucky he was there from what I hear. Sounds like a real old-fashioned bar brawl."

"It was insane. Men were throwing punches for no reason. I think a few pool cues got broken."

"Who started it?"

I really didn't want to tell her Kurt was involved.

"I didn't throw the first punch, if you're worried about me starting fights. In fact, I dodged a few before I was forced to defend myself."

"Forced to defend yourself?"

I sighed and hit my head against the glass a couple of times.

"Tom?" Her hand reached over the console and lingered above my thigh for a few seconds before she pulled away. I grabbed it and held it in the neutral territory between us.

"Don't be mad."

"I get a call at midnight from my cousin saying a friend of

mine is in jail for fighting in a bar, I think I passed mad around Greenbank."

"Okay. But it wasn't my fault."

"Tom—"

I cut her off. "Listen, I didn't start it, but I wasn't going to let him get away with being an asshole either. He was talking shit about me. Fine. Whatever. But when he started saying shit about my family (*and you, I thought*), what did he expect me to do? Sit there and take it? No one says shit about people I care about in front of me and walks away smiling."

"Who are you talking about?" Her eyes left the road and met mine for a second. Well, one of mine. I couldn't see out of my right eye at all.

"Jesse didn't tell you?"

"It was a short conversation. I hung up on him after he said Lori's brother was in jail."

"Kurt. It was Kurt."

She growled and cursed, "That ass-sandwich. I'm going to kick his ass."

"Ass-sandwich?" I laughed and raised my good eyebrow. "I've already done the ass-kicking part."

"What was he saying?"

No way would I repeat his words. "It's not important. It proved his lack of character. He doesn't deserve you."

"Please tell me."

"Why? It won't make anything better. I admit using my fists tonight was the wrong thing to do, but it's done. I think I made my point clear. He better keep his thoughts to himself about the Donnelys."

"I can't believe he was talking shit about your family."

"He's pissed because we won't sell to him. Like selling was ever an option. He may have gotten to the greedy cousins, but there's no way we'd let land be developed by him."

"He doesn't like losing." She sighed and squeezed my hand.

"Who does?" I wove my fingers with hers. I'd messed up

with her in ways I would never forgive myself for, yet here she was, driving my sorry self home.

"Please make me a promise?"

"Anything."

She started to laugh and caught herself. "Anything? Watch what you say, mister."

At this moment I would give her anything she asked for. Anything to make amends. Anything to have a fresh start with her. Anything except …

"This doesn't mean we're good," she whispered and put her hand on the steering wheel. "Please promise me you won't let Kurt get to you again. He's crazy and he'll use anything he can to get what he wants. I think the land is part of some sick revenge plot against me for breaking up with him. Promise me you won't be a pawn in his game." Her voice sounded worried and earnest; honest fear frayed the edges of it.

"I promise," I said to the window, resting my head against the cool glass. My eye throbbed and I needed to get ice on it soon.

Silently, I promised I would make this right. Whatever this was between us, making it right was my new goal.

When we arrived at my house, she put the car in park but didn't turn off the engine. The clock on the dash said one-thirty.

"Is it too much if I apologize again?"

"For waking me up?"

"That, but so much more. I —"

"It's late." She stared out the windshield into the dark woods. Illuminated by the car's lights, they appeared both ominous and magical.

"You're beautiful," I whispered, touching her cheek.

"Don't. Just don't." Her eyes sparkled with tears.

"Hailey—"

"Please. Let me keep a small shred of dignity and let me walk away."

I pulled her to me and encircled her with my arms. "I'm not meant to be a boyfriend," I whispered into her hair. "I don't want to hurt you."

She sniffled.

Oh, shit. Was she crying?

She pushed away, and rubbed her face on her sleeve. "It's fine. I guess I could use all the friends I can get right now."

"If you don't mind being friends with a known manwhore, and the potential gossip that comes with it, friends?" My smile brightened when her eyes crinkled in amusement.

"I suppose it might be worth the risk of promiscuous by association."

"People will assume we're having sex, just so you know."

"No more of ..." She pointed at our dust angel still untouched at the entrance to the shop.

Frowning, I scratched my chin. "I suppose. I'm open to a benefits plan."

"I don't doubt you are."

I shrugged. "You're the one who keeps attacking me."

"I'm sure I can find some self-control."

"Maybe see if you left it in the same place as your dignity."

She flipped me off.

"Stop with the dimples, Donncly!"

I held up my hands and got out of the car. "It's probably safer out here anyway."

With a wink and a smirk, I backed toward the house. She flipped me the bird again and drove off with me waving and laughing from the porch.

What the hell was all that? Did I agree to not have sex with her anymore? Ever? Maybe I had a concussion as well as a black eye, because I would never agree to it if I were in my right frame of mind.

TWENTY-FIVE

Confession:
I'm fine being a lone wolf.

Turned out, I would have spent the entire night in jail had I waited for John to come get me. The jerk went out of town with Diane. On Valentine's Day. And proposed.

Yeah, I called it last year.

Whipped.

I told him as much when we met to play pool a week later.

"You give her your mom's ring?" I asked though I knew the answer.

"Yeah," he said softly.

"You didn't hide it in her food or some dumb shit, did you? Because I'm not sure I can handle you turning into one of those guys from jewelry commercials with their balloons and bows, and no balls."

"No balloons or bows. I swear." He gave me a wide smile, revealing how ridiculously happy he felt.

"Good. Cause I can't be best friends with a pussy."

"Says the man whose nickname is Tom Cat?"

I dismissed his teasing with a tilt of my head. "I'm more like the catnip. All the pussies go wild for me."

He gagged.

"Can't help it if they can't resist my charms."

Olaf snorted from his spot at the bar.

"You got something to add, O?" I asked, lining up my next shot, but pausing to observe the opinionated old goat.

"Don't mind me. I'm proud of you, John. You found yourself a good woman and were smart enough to realize it," he said.

"Hey, what about me?" I took the shot, missed, and stood up to glare at O.

"You're an idiot." Olaf set down the pint glass he'd been drying.

John chuckled on the other side of the table, chalking his cue and studying the balls.

"Hey, now. I don't see a Mrs. Olaf around here. Us bachelors got to stick together."

"You want to wake up some day and be me? Tending bar and putting up with idiots like you?" He set down the glass with a thump.

John and I had joked over the years about taking over the Dog when Olaf retired or ever decided to sell. It didn't sound like such a bad idea.

"No offense, O, but I've always been more handsome than you."

I'd made him laugh and he muttered under his breath, "Stupid, cocky bastard. God cursed you with those good looks and not enough sense."

John was having himself a good old-fashioned giggle-fest as he made another shot and sunk his ball in the corner. I scowled at him, and he grinned at me.

"Whipped," I mouthed at him.

"So, how's the single life?" John asked.

"Eh." I fixed my eyes on the table.

"No hot new girl from over in town? No lonely, single lady on Valentine's Day?"

"The only woman I saw on V Day was Ruby in Oak Harbor." I lied by omission.

"When you called me from jail? What the hell were you doing all the way up there anyways?"

"Shh." I stared over his shoulder at Olaf. "Minding my own damn business."

"Defensive much? What's the story?"

I told him the short version: pull-tabs, bar brawl, jail, the phone call to his voicemail. I failed to mention Kurt or Hailey.

"You were in a full out brawl? Since when do you fight? First sign of trouble, you're out the door or walking in the other direction. What, or who, started it?"

"Some asshole," I muttered.

"He give you that black eye? Anyone we know?" He wasn't dropping it.

"No one you know."

He studied me. "You're being cagey. Why?"

I huffed and set my cue on the table. "And you're being fucking nosey."

"Did you get arrested?"

"No, no charges were pressed. I was more of a bystander." I rolled and cracked my neck.

"Don't pull any fighting bullshit around here," Olaf grumbled at me.

"When have you ever known me to fight?" I waited for a beat. "Ever?"

"I don't want to disrespect your grandfather's memory by calling the cops on you, Tom."

I threw up my arms. "For chrissakes! It was a one off thing. No arrest. No charges. It was only some assholes who thought they could run their mouths about shit."

I grabbed my jacket and reached in the pocket for my wallet. Pulling out a twenty, I tossed it next to our pitcher.

"How'd you get home?" John's words stopped me.

"Huh?"

"From jail. You called me, but since I wasn't around, who'd you get to pick you up?"

I closed my eyes and went with the truth. "Hailey's got a cousin on the force up there, and he gave her the head's up."

John pressed his lips together and nodded, but didn't say anything. I didn't have to say I'd fucked Hailey, but he'd probably come to the same conclusion on his own. "You definitely seem to have nine lives like a cat."

"Now she's a keeper, that King girl is. Talented artist, too. Came to her senses and didn't marry the wrong man," Olaf said, and then turned up the TV by the bar, ending this rare episode of giving his opinion.

I side-eyed O, and then met John's eyes. "This has been a most peculiar evening. I'm calling it a night."

"I drove your ass here, so unless you're walking, you better wait up," John called out to me at the door.

I closed my eyes and exhaled, long and slow, before stepping outside into the frosty night air. When John followed me out a few moments later, I laid some ground rules.

"Remember the conversation we had last year in this exact spot about relationships and women?"

He nodded.

"I think we're not due for another one of those for a while."

"Gotcha."

Those were the last words we spoke until he dropped me off at my house.

He was the best kind of friend a guy could have.

———

I waited for the fight to hit the island gossip circles, and the inevitable fallout from the family, but I never heard a word. Oddly enough, everyone seemed to buy my story about a chunk of wood hitting my goggles. The more time passed, the more the bruise around my eye faded, and the stranger the whole situation felt. I didn't think John would say anything. Or Hailey. Kurt? I figured he and his buddies would have rushed to smear my name all over the island. Wasn't that the whole point of the attack?

Unless he was so much of a wuss that when the police refused to press charges, he slunk back to Seattle with his tiny, micro-tail between his legs. It was possible.

Once again, Hailey and I avoided each other at work. Although, Bertha caught me wandering through the front office more often than typical. I started bringing her a fresh cup of coffee, four sugars and extra cream, as a cover, and maybe as a bribe.

A month after the fight, the proverbial shit hit the fan.

I was working away, sparks flying, when movement from the corner of my eye caught my attention. I turned down my torch and lifted my mask to try to catch what Al was shouting.

"I'm coming down." I gestured and turned off my equipment, set my gloves and mask aside, and lowered myself to the ground.

When my feet hit the gravel, I could tell whatever he needed to say, it didn't make him happy.

"You've got a visitor in the office."

"Who?" I asked the obvious question. No one dropped by to visit me during work. I was a welder. Not like I had an office. Hell, I never paid attention to my phone when I was working.

"She wouldn't say."

She. Shit. Who would be bringing personal drama to the yard? "Is it something with my family?"

"Wouldn't say. Told me you had to come meet her, or she'd wait."

Some woman I'd never seen before—yes, I was positive—stood in the office reception area wearing a lady suit with a skirt and blazer.

She turned at the sound of us walking through the door. "Tom Donnely?"

"Yeah?" I kept the counter between us.

"Tom Donnely, you've been served." She handed me an envelope. "Have a nice day."

Kurt had decided to sue me for his medical expenses and damages to his professional reputation.

Broken nose was probably my doing. Sullied professional reputation? He did it to himself.

My feet led me straight to Hailey's office. Completely focused on her computer, she didn't acknowledge me in the doorway until I rapped my fingers on the frame.

Her gaze flicked to mine before returning to the screen.

I waited and knocked again.

This time when her eyes landed on me she jumped in surprise. "Hi!"

I shut the door behind me and sat down.

"Have a seat?" she said with a question on her face. "What's up and why is the door closed?"

"Kurt is suing me."

"What?" She pushed back her chair, slamming into the wall behind her. "That's ridiculous."

I held up the envelope to show her the physical proof.

"I'm going to kill him."

"Better not. He might sue you, too."

"I told you he wasn't done."

"Well, it's not an issue. I'll call the family lawyer, and he'll take care of it."

"I hope it's so easy. He's on a rampage lately."

I tapped the envelope on my knee. "What did he do?" My temper reared its head.

"He kicked me out of my studio over in town."

"Studio?" My tapping paused.

"For welding. He owns a warehouse building in SoDo as an investment. He let me turn the ground floor into my studio. When we broke up," she paused, "when I called off the wedding and we broke up, he said he'd let me stay for a year and I could pay a quarter of market rate."

"Let me guess, after last month, he raised your rent to full price."

Her eyes crinkled in amusement. "No, double the going rate and denied ever saying I had a lease, so it's month to month."

"Didn't you sign anything?"

She ducked her chin and glanced to the side. "I trusted him."

I pursed my lips and my right hand balled into a fist.

"I know, I know. It's really not a big deal. I have to move all my stuff out of there and into another studio soon."

"By when?" I asked.

She sighed. "This weekend."

"Or what?"

"He'll padlock the door."

"Did you find a space?"

"I haven't really had time. Work's been crazy and leads from U-Dub friends keep falling through. I'll probably get storage space and shove everything inside."

Without thinking, I made her an offer. "We can move your stuff into the shop. There's plenty of room on the other side of my work space. Or upstairs in the loft."

"You don't know how much stuff I have. You've seen my work. It's all huge and ridiculously heavy."

"Not a problem. You need a moving truck? I have a cousin who rents them over in Lynnwood. We can enlist John and a bunch of the guys. Move you out on Saturday and you'll be done."

"Why?"

"Why what?" I asked, confused.

"Why would you do all that?"

"Besides the fact the asshole thinks he's going to sue me? Because we're friends and this is what friends do. Guys move shit that needs moving. I think it's in the sacred book of being friends, especially in the men being friends with women chapter. On page forty-two: Have a penis? Thou shall move shit."

She smiled and I returned it.

"So give me the address and how big a truck you need. We can meet in Clinton and catch the ferry together."

"Wow. You're not messing around."

"I'm pissed off at your ex. It's good motivation. Plus, I told you I'd have your back and I'm going to prove it."

She nodded, appearing a bit stunned with her eyes wide and her lips parted. She looked like she was about to be kissed, or expected to be.

"I make art to leave my imprint. I want someone to see something I made, and even if they don't know it was me, they know someone tried to add more beauty to this world. Somehow each piece proves I existed."

Her words coiled around me. This was the answer to the question I'd asked months ago.

I carved for the same reason, to leave a mark, to make someone smile or pause in their day to observe something beautiful, something to make them smile. My body reacted and instinctively leaned forward before I caught myself. I nodded and shoved away from her. "Friends."

I needed the physical distance.

And maybe a cold shower.

TWENTY-SIX

Confession:
I never confuse friendship with romance.

L ori. I forgot about Lori.
Shit.

How could I forget about her? Not she existed or she was my little sister. No, I doubted I could ever forget those facts. I forgot she might get all super sleuth suspicious about me suddenly helping out her friend.

How would she know? My mistake was thinking I could organize and rally a group of men together to move the studio to my place and no one would ask why. My other error in judgment centered around once again trusting one of my cousins. That side of the family had an issue in their bloodline. Or all got dropped on their heads as babies.

Okay, I didn't explicitly say not to tell anyone, and maybe me renting a big truck for the weekend might have piqued some interest, but did Dale have to tell his mother? Grown man gossiping to his mother about a truck rental? *What was that about?*

Post move, we all sat around drinking beer and teasing

Hailey for owning a lot of shit most people would think of as garbage, or at least a tetanus shot waiting to happen. Not to mention the weight and sharp edges had us all nursing a few bruises and a cut finger or two after moving torches, welding supplies, metal scraps, shovel heads, pic-axes, a bunch of rusty nails, and dandelions made from said nails. The guys complained, and suggested she should take up quilting or knitting.

The late afternoon sun and the heavy lifting warmed us enough to sit on the tailgate of the truck, in chairs on the lawn, or on the ground nearby, drinking our beer and giving Hailey a hard time about her hoarding. I sat in one of the Adirondack chairs and watched her jean-covered legs swing over the tailgate of the empty truck.

"You know, you can get most of this stuff at Island Recycling anytime," John advised.

"Where do you think it all came from to begin with?" she responded. "There and any salvage yard between Seattle and Spokane."

"I think it's pretty cool," Carter said, smiling at Hailey. "I'd love for you to tell me all about your art sometime."

"So lame, bro," Erik snarked at his older brother. "Women like the direct approach. Watch." He stood and walked over to the tailgate. We all tensed, Hailey most of all. He stared into her eyes and lifted his chin. "Let's have dinner some time."

I scoffed, Hailey laughed, and John snorted. These two were hopeless. The Kelso brothers were like golden retriever puppies. In their late twenties, they hadn't grown into their hands and feet yet. Lanky and eager met overconfident and spoiled. Classic island boys. Erik worked at Useless Bay Coffee in Langley, while Carter did grounds work at the golf course on Holmes Harbor.

They reminded me a little of myself. And for that reason, I frowned at their attempts to flirt with Hailey. They were up to no good, and I knew exactly what their end-game would be. In her pants, or die trying. Luckily, their moves were as smooth as gravel.

The sound of tires had me craning my neck around the truck. Lori's minivan pulled to a stop a few feet away from the truck's front bumper.

"Hi, brother," she said and gave me a wave. Her smile, which only I could see, scared me a little. It was the exact smile Mom used on us as kids. Shit. She'd only given birth a few months ago and already had the scary mom face down perfectly.

"Hi, sister." I widened my eyes and made the "I'm innocent of whatever you think I'm guilty of" face.

She greeted John and the Kelsos, then turned to Hailey with faux surprise all over her face. "Hailey, what are you doing here?"

Hailey's eyes flashed to mine and I shrugged, letting her explain exactly what was going on here. Better for Lori to hear it from her than me. Plus, I had no idea what version to tell my sister. Or how much she already knew. Other than the lawyer, I hadn't told anyone yet about the lawsuit. After being assured it was completely frivolous, I wasn't sure if I'd bother to tell either of my parents.

Hailey explained her lease being canceled and needing a place to store her studio. The way she described my offer made the whole thing seem innocent and brotherly. Feeling like a saint, I rolled my shoulders. I could be the good guy sometimes.

Lori narrowed her eyes at me. "That's so … sweet of you, Tom. So … unlike you."

John spoke up. "Kind of surprised me, too. Until he explained how he always saw Hailey as a kid sister because you two were so close."

I had no memory of saying such a thing to him. Thinking about Hailey as one of my sisters turned my stomach. I finished my beer and stood up, waving the empty between my fingers. "Who needs a fresh one?"

"I'll take a beer." Lori walked ahead of me into the shop where I kept a beer fridge.

I slowly followed, dreading the inevitable lecture about something she didn't understand.

Lori jerked open the fridge so hard the bottles rattled in the door and on the shelves. Huffing, she pulled out a Woodchuck cider. The way she ripped off the bottle cap had me wanting to cup my balls. She was riled up.

I cut her off before she had the chance to begin. "I'm not sleeping with Hailey."

"Not yet, you mean?"

Not anymore, I thought.

"No. We're friends."

She choked on her first swallow, and cider fizzed over the top of the bottle and on to the floor. "Since when?"

I thought about it. November? December? When had we shifted from random sex to actually hanging out?

"Around Pops' funeral, I guess."

"And you didn't feel the need to tell me?" Her eyes flashed with anger.

"Why would I? Do you tell me about everyone you hang out with?"

"I have a baby. I don't hang out with anyone!" Her voice rose.

I lifted my hands in innocence. "Okay, okay. You know she's working down at the boat yard, right?"

She nodded and waved for me to continue.

"Well, we work together. What am I supposed to do? Ignore and shun her because she's your friend? That'd be rude, don't you think?"

"You can be polite and professional, but this," she flailed her arms around gesturing at all of the metal work crowding my shop, "this is not something you do. Since when are you friends with women?"

"Ashley and I have been friends for years."

She snorted so hard she burped. "Ashley has been in love with you for years. Only she's too stupid to tell you."

"You're crazy. She's not in love with me. We have an understanding. We hang out some times, and then we don't see each other for months. Doesn't sound like love to me."

"I'm not crazy. She's biding her time until you're ready to settle down. Trust me, women know these things."

"I know Ashley. She's no more interested in relationships than I am. Hell, I haven't hung out with her in months."

"So who are you 'hanging out' with lately? Hailey? And since when did you stop calling her Idaho? It's always been your obnoxious thing with her."

"Are you asking who I'm fucking right now? Really? You really want me to discuss my sex life with my sister? How about you and Nick? How's your sex life?"

"We're not talking about me. And yes, I am, if you plan to fuck my friend." She scowled at me.

I glowered at her, then opened the fridge to get a beer for myself and the rest of the guys. Before standing up, I gritted my teeth and said, "There's nothing between Hailey and me. You have nothing to worry about." I stood up and set the beers on the workbench.

"You swear? I will personally kick your ass, or have Nick do it, if you touch her."

"First, you're a helluva lot scarier than Nick could ever be. Second, I'm not swearing anything. If I say there's nothing going on between us, then as your brother, I deserve your respect to be taken at my word."

If this was one of those chick movies my sisters obsessed over while growing up, this would have been the moment of the big misunderstanding where Hailey would overhear me, misunderstand, feel hurt, and the whole thing would turn into major girl drama in front of my eyes.

Instead, she stood in the opening to the shop, laughing.

Lori stared at her like she'd lost her mind. "What's so funny?"

"Me and Tom." She continued laughing.

"Don't you mean Tom and I?" I asked, an edge lacing my words, making them sound harsher than I meant. What was so funny about us hanging out? We hung out.

Hailey stopped laughing and cocked her head and winked. "Come on, Lori, quit giving your brother a hard time. You know I'd never stoop so low to become one of his harem. Girl's got to have standards."

What the hell?

"Hey—" I verbally stomped my feet.

Lori was too busy laughing to notice the subtle shake of Hailey's head.

In the Land of Mixed Signals, Hailey was Queen. The wink, the insult ... the harem? I didn't have a harem. Certainly not recently. Or ever. Harem implied all at once. Maybe more of a stable. A small stable. *Wait, was I the horse? Or an ass? Donkey? What was a mule?*

"What's a mule?" I asked.

Both women stared at me.

"Out of the blue much?" Lori asked.

"Like the drink?" Hailey asked.

"The animal," I clarified.

Their eyes met and both women fell into laughter again.

"It's a donkey and a horse," Hailey explained. "Why are you thinking about mules?"

"Long story." I sipped my beer and gave Hailey a look I hoped conveyed 'we need to talk because what the hell was that harem bullshit you were saying and do you really think I have a harem, a stable, or a conclave of women?' as well as I thought she was hot in those jeans. It was quite the expression.

She responded simply with a raised eyebrow. Her gaze settled on the old recliner for a few beats before she met my eyes.

From Lori's comment about Ashley, to Hailey's mixed signals, my head spun. I needed fresh air and less estrogen. Outside, boisterous male voices greeted me when I settled into one of the chairs.

Hailey laughing over the thought of being with me pissed me off. What was so funny? I knew I had limited boyfriend experience, but I wasn't an ogre or a troll living in my parents' basement.

"Where's my beer?" Carter asked.

"Get your own beer," I said, sipping from my bottle. Given my bad mood, I wanted everyone to leave, and soon.

I got my wish an hour later. Mostly because the Kelsos finished the last of my beer and started talking about getting burgers up in Freeland. John decided to join them. Lori still loitered around, sticking close to Hailey's side. What did she think she would accomplish? I'd never throw a woman down and have my way with her in front of everyone, especially if we were a real thing.

I still had to return the rental to Lynnwood and pick up my truck. It could wait until morning, but Lori didn't know that.

"Gotta return the truck, Lori. Idaho, I'll give you a ride to your car at the dock," I stated, leaving no room for Lori to argue. Hailey and I needed to be on the same page and we needed to get there before the great inquisition.

Lori huffed and invited her over for dinner later, essentially cockblocking me with a casserole. Not that there was cock to block.

I had no idea what was going on anymore.

I needed to talk to Hailey.

I wanted to hide in my shop and carve wood.

Both desires fought valiantly, but the clear winner was talking, and it freaked me out more than anything.

TWENTY-SEVEN

Confession:
I know what I'm doing when it comes to women.

The drive to the ferry felt like a thousand miles and less than a minute long. We wasted precious time with repeated thanks and welcomes about the truck and move. I took the long way around to give myself enough time to grow the balls to ask for clarity. At the top of the hill down to the dock, I finally found my voice, which cracked and sounded like gravel when I asked the question weighing down my tongue.

"I …wanted to know … in the shop … was for Lori's benefit, right?" I felt like I was asking to touch a boob for the first time.

She leaned against the door. "The mule conversation?" Her lip lifted in amusement.

"No, the part that came before the mule."

"The ass?" She snickered. When I didn't join her, she explained, "The ass, or donkey, is a mule's father."

"Oh, that answers that question. Thanks."

"You're welcome."

Silence settled over us.

"Tom?"

"Yeah?"

"The part with Lori? I said it for our sake."

"Ours?" *Were we a we?*

"You've met Lori before, right? Her business is her business, but everyone else's business is her business, too."

"She likes to be in the know," I agreed.

"Understatement of the year."

"I was keeping our pledge under the stars," she said.

I remembered our whispered conversation during the meteor shower. "In front of God and the cosmos?"

She nodded. "Plus, didn't we recently agree to be platonic friends? No sex. No dimples."

I grinned. "Oops. Sorry."

"No you're not."

"But what if—"

She stopped fidgeting and seemed to hold her breath, waiting for me to continue.

"—what if it was different." I drummed the fingers of my left hand on the steering wheel.

"Different how?"

"I don't know. Just not all the hiding and lies." I swallowed. "I didn't lie to Lori about hanging out, but it's none of her business if we've had sex. I've never been one to kiss and talk, and I'm not going to start with you, but she asked and I lied."

"I appreciate you'd lie for me. She's going to grill me over dinner tonight. I better stop for wine on the way. I've never lied to her since we were kids, but you're right, it's none of her business. I guess I should've thought this through when I hunted you down in October and to quote you, 'attacked'. I really didn't think further than finally having sex with you. "

Shit. I really could be an asshole when it came to the things that came out of my mouth. I inhaled and counted … four … three … two …

"I like you. I, um, I wanted you to know it wasn't only about the sex."

She crinkled her nose and her mouth twitched between a frown and a smile. "Thanks for saying so. It's okay if it was."

My fingers quieted. "Was it for you? Only about the sex?" I wiped my palm on my jeans. We'd stopped at the light at the bottom of the hill. I had about two minutes to find my manhood before she'd be getting out of the truck.

"Honestly? It was. At the beginning."

The light flipped to green and I pulled forward to the toll booths. Out of time. Time to man up.

"Hey, you want to go grab a bite to eat some time?" I allowed myself to focus on her eyes. "Or a drink?"

Her eyes narrowed, but her lips lifted into a small smile. "Are you asking me out?"

I rubbed my jawline. "Yeah, I guess I am."

After paying, getting my change, and steering the truck into a lane to wait, she still hadn't answered. She sat there in the passenger seat with her small smile. The low bellow from the ferry arriving at the dock broke the silence. She opened her door, and with her hand on the handle, she jumped down.

"Yes," she said before the door slammed shut. With a wave over her shoulder, she strode toward the parking lot.

I sat in the idling truck, smiling like a fool.

———

My smile faded halfway through the short ferry crossing to Mukilteo.

I think I asked Hailey out on a date, which was a huge problem because I didn't date. Ever.

I had no idea what to do. This change stuff threw me upside down and sideways. Dating? Me?

Did I make a reservation? We'd eaten food together before. I knew she ate.

Of course she ate food.

Should I bring her something?

Flowers?

Candy?

I'd never seen either at her house.

I realized the perfect person to ask all the questions about courting a woman would be Clifford. As the smoothest flirt I knew he would have given me the classic tips without judgment. Missing him all over again, I realized I'd have to channel my inner Clifford.

What would Clifford do?

He'd probably show up doused in cologne and hair pomade. Maybe a cowboy hat, or a fedora, depending on the decade.

Okay, those weren't going to work on Hailey. Did Aqua Velva exist anymore? Or was it Old Spice he wore? I'd never even tried aftershave and hadn't worn cologne since a weird period in high school where I smelled like an artificial pine car freshener after Caroline told me she liked some cologne. Hailey would probably laugh.

Skip the pomade and aftershave.

Sweet talk and compliments. He always laid them both on thick. Again, she might laugh.

Flowers might work.

I'd have to go to Mukilteo.

Wait, no. I'd buy them here. And if anyone asked, who cared? This was new Tom. Dating Tom.

Right.

I set up a plan of action in my head.

By the time the ferry docked, I smiled again. I could do this. If I got nervous, I'd imagine her naked.

TWENTY-EIGHT

Confession:
I'm always confident I know how to please a woman.

My brilliant plan had a fatal flaw. I hadn't actually asked Hailey out on a specific date. Clearly, I sucked at dating *and* making plans. I think the last real date I'd been on had been prom. No way was I showing up with a corsage and a bow tie.

Dinner. I'd ask her to dinner. People who dated went to dinner. It was the classic first date. Maybe over in town and away from nosey islanders. I could make a reservation. Okay, I had this. I could be the guy who did dinner and dating.

All Sunday I debated whether to text her, call, or ask her at work. Texting seemed too much like a hook-up. Work had its own risks and potential opportunities for being overheard or interrupted. I could catch her in the parking lot after. Would it be considered stalking if I hung around her car waiting for her like Daryl?

Cross off parking lot lurking.

In the end, I didn't have to worry. The entire conversation

lasted five seconds when I ran into Hailey in the hallway on Wednesday.

"Friday work for you?" I asked as we approached each other, barely slowing down my pace.

"This Friday? Sure." She gave me a slight smile.

"Six?" I asked as we passed

"Six is good." Her fingers brushed mine.

"I'll pick you up." I tugged her sleeve.

"Looking forward to it," she said over her shoulder.

"Me too." I grinned to myself as I pushed open the door to the yard.

Done.

———

On the way home from work on Friday, I stopped in Bayview for flowers. I felt like a ninja when I pulled into the parking lot and studied the cars and plates to make sure no one I knew, including the gossip ladies, were there. Inside, I stuck to the perimeter of the shop where the fridges were located. Buckets of flowers, fancy arrangements, and a surprising number of baskets involving little ducks crowded the displays. No way would I be buying something with a duck stuck to it.

A middle-aged woman entered the space through a curtain leading to what I assumed to be a backroom. I wasn't the first lost man in her shop from the way she obviously took pity on me and offered to pick out something. I wanted simple, no animals, no roses, and none of those little white flowers which reminded me of corsages.

On the bottom of one fridge sat a bucket of big flowers in whites and pinks. One of the pinks was the exact same color as Hailey's nipples. The scent was light, nothing too old lady.

Decision made. Sweat dampened my neck by the time she wrapped my choice in cellophane. She gave me a card, telling me to call her next time I needed anything and she could take my information over the phone. Grateful, I thanked her profusely for all of her help. Better than flowers from the grocery store, which I'd considered until I determined it would be as inconspicuous as skywriting I had a date.

———

Friday night after jerking off in the shower and trimming my beard, I tried on two different shirts and spent five minutes debating whether or not to wear boots. I mentally slapped myself, threw on a deep blue shirt, dark jeans, and my favorite boots, reminding myself the entire time this was a date, not a job interview, and I was a man, not a teenage girl.

When Hailey opened the door wearing a deep green dress and high boots, I was happy I hadn't shown up like a schlump in an old flannel and T-shirt.

"These are for you." I held out the bouquet of pink flowers. "They reminded me of your skin when you blush." Smooth. I could do this.

A rose color spread along her cheeks. I softly skimmed the heated skin. "There. Exactly like that."

Still touching her cheek, I whispered, "I think they're peonies."

"They are. Thanks." She took the bunch in her arms and I realized it was huge. "There are so many of them."

"I might have gotten carried away." When the flower lady asked me my budget, I hadn't wanted to appear cheap.

"A little, but it's been ages since anyone has given me flowers."

She put them in water while I waited near the door.

"Ready?" she asked when she returned. With a quick peck to my cheek, she wiggled her arm under mine. "If you're nervous, don't be." With a little squeeze of her hand, she tugged me out the door.

To calm myself, I checked out her ass and long legs in those boots. Of course she caught me.

"You look good, too." She waited by the passenger door for me to open it.

I jogged to my side of the truck and got in, then sat there waiting.

"Tom?" Her hand rested on my thigh.

"Yeah?" I covered her hand with mine.

"Are we having this date in the truck?"

"Oh, right!" I started the engine. "Sorry." I gave her a sheepish smile.

"You're a mess." She dissolved into laughter.

I closed my eyes and inhaled.

"Seriously. When was the last time you were on a date?"

"A first date?"

"Is that what this is?"

"It sure as hell feels like it."

"Then you should know I never put out on the first date. It's some stupid girl rule, separating the good girls from the sluts. Or something. I've always sucked at knowing the rules."

"Is this the third date rule?"

"You're familiar with the girl rules?" she asked. "Don't let anyone know! It's all very top secret. If men know, then how will we ever entrap you with our womanly wiles?"

"Sisters. I learned a lot." I shuddered for effect.

"Too much insider info ruin the fun?"

From the corner of my eye I saw her studying me. "Oh, the fun wasn't ruined. Not by a long shot, sweetheart."

"You know, you're a lot different than I thought you would be."

"Based on what?" I braced for her to bring up my reputation.

"On growing up around you, mostly. Girls talk, and over the years I heard what a player you'd become. I imagined a cocky guy with really terrible pick-up lines."

"Which part wasn't true?" I winked, knowing I'd been guilty of both.

"Neither. You're cocky and have the worst lines, but you've surprised me. Under everything, you're a good guy, a really good guy."

Not sure I could still do it, I felt my cheeks heat.

"Are you blushing?" She grinned. "Well, now I've seen it all. Who'd have ever imagined? What's next?"

I glanced behind me to change lanes. "The night is young."

We chatted, teased, and flirted all the way into Seattle. Despite asking me every five minutes where we were going like a kid, I refused to tell her. She threatened to tickle me until I threatened to drive us off the road into the ditch.

Once we exited I-5 in downtown, she threw out names of places and activities. I drove us around Seattle Center and through the city to listen to her ideas.

"EMP!"

"No."

"Pike Place."

"No."

"Belltown?" she asked as we headed north along the water. "Are you a secret hipster?" Her eyes lingered on my beard.

"No, and no."

"You do have a tattoo on your arm. Hipsters have tattoos and beards, so are you sure you aren't one?"

I didn't realize she'd paid attention to the line of numbers above my bicep representing the latitude and longitude of the farm on Whidbey.

"47.973N, −122.542W is the location of the farm, not some sort of cool guy code."

"More like nerd guy code." She traced my shoulder near the tattoo. "That's pretty cool. Much better than a pin-up girl or some chick's name."

"I'm not stupid. I've thought about getting a chainsaw on my back."

"That's a little creepy." She scrunched up her face.

"Yeah, I already regret the butterfly on my ass I got as a dare." I waited for her reaction.

"You don't have a butterfly on your ass."

"Good to know you've paid attention." I winked and parked the truck.

"You brought me to Ray's? This place is an institution." Her face softened and she pulled me closer by the neck. "Thank you."

I brushed my lips across hers. "You're welcome."

Inside, we were seated near a huge window overlooking the water. When she suggested a dozen oysters to start, I held in my smile.

"What?" she asked.

I leaned over the table and gestured her closer with my finger before whispering near her ear, "You know what. Remember our first night together? I'm still a sure bet."

She fell back into her seat and her lips parted.

I slurped an oyster and licked my lips. Salty, a little briny with a touch of sweetness, it tasted like heaven. The best thing I'd had on my tongue in ages. I moaned, deep and guttural, in my throat.

"I've never seen anything more perverted in my life than you eating those oysters." Hailey fanned herself with her hand and downed her glass of prosecco. "Is the moaning really necessary?"

I blinked and replayed the last minute or two. I'd done nothing intentionally perverse. Shaking my head, I sipped my beer.

Two more courses followed the oysters, both featuring local seafood. We fought over the crab, but I knew I'd let her win because I was on my best behavior, and it wasn't gentlemanly to wrestle a woman to the ground over a crab leg. Our laughter grew boisterous and a few fellow diners shot us sidelong glances, but nothing could break our bubble.

Over dessert, she confessed, "This is the best date I've ever had. I've never laughed this much."

"Really?" I felt stunned. "Surely you've been swept off your feet in grand gestures with roses and limos. Or whatever girls swoon about."

"I think you just described the final scene in *Pretty Woman*. You know she was a hooker, right?"

I snorted.

"Are you implying I'm a hooker?" The volume of her voice caused an older couple at the next table to gawk at us.

"She's not a hooker," I told them. "Really. Not even an escort or call girl."

The woman blinked and touched her pearl necklace before moving her chair further away from us as if those precious inches could untaint her night from the mention of sex for money.

"She's a very nice girl," I explained to the still gawking husband.

Hailey's hand touched my arm. "I think you've made your point."

"You don't look like a prostitute at all. You're way more classy."

She sipped her drink. "This is turning into a drinking game. Every time you mention sex for money, I have to drink."

Chuckling, I finished my water. "What was my point?"

"Other than your idea of romantic gestures comes from the movies?"

"Right." I rubbed my hands on my thighs. "I'm kind of inexperienced." I met her eyes. "Wow, that felt weird to say."

"Don't worry, for the right price, I'll make you a man."

A fork clattered against china at the table next to us.

I had to give her props. She maintained her serious expression the entire time it took me to call for the check and pay.

"I only have forty-dollars left after our meal." I stood and placed my hand on her lower back.

"Forty will get you a handjob in the parking lot," she said, staring at the man in his tweed jacket.

"I never!" his companion sputtered into her chowder.

We laughed all the way to the truck.

"I never!" She did a perfect imitation of the offended woman. "I bet she hasn't. No handjobs from her. Ever." Out of breath and giggling, she stole my breath with her beauty. My chest thrummed with the quick beats of my heart.

I opened the door for her and instead of immediately closing it once she got in, I leaned into the space and cupped her cheek. Our eyes met and her laughter quieted. Her hand came up to my neck, but she didn't tug or pull me closer. Instead, her fingers drew lines along my skin, sending shivers through my body from my spine to my toes. I ducked my head, breaking our eye contact. Her fingers lifted my chin again and her breath collided with mine.

"I really like you." My confession lingered in the air for a few quick beats of my heart until I pressed my lips against hers.

I opened my mouth to say more, and her tongue erased my words when it found mine. Leaning further into her, my hands struggled to find a place to settle. I couldn't decide where on her body I needed to touch most in the moment. She shifted to face me and one black boot rested on my ass, anchoring me. Her arms wrapped around my shoulders and she tilted backward. My balance shifted and what had been a heated, but perfectly respectable, albeit passionate, parking lot kiss turned into full-blown making out with the door open for all to see.

"Get a room!" an older man called out over the beep-beep of a car unlocking.

She fell against the bench seat and I rested my head on her thighs, both of us silently laughing.

"That'll be forty-dollars," she whisper-laughed.

"No way. You didn't touch my dick." I lifted myself off her and straightened my shirt.

One leather-clad toe skimmed up my thigh and toward my hip before brushing along my erection. "There."

"Kinky shoe fetishes have never been my thing."

"How did this date go from oysters and romance to parking lot negotiations to fetishes?"

"I have no idea, but I'm pretty sure those last things were your doing." I jogged to my side of the cab. "Now, unless you're giving me road head on the drive home, you might want to sit up."

Her upside-down eyes met mine. "Is that really a thing? You squealed like a girl when I mentioned tickling earlier. How do you think you could possibly manage my mouth sucking you while driving?" She blinked at me a few times before an evil smile spread across her face.

My eyes widened at her words and the images of her lips around my dick. Sadly, she sat up and buckled her seatbelt, ending the discussion.

"Maybe another time?" I suggested, hope squeaking around the edge of my voice.

"I think somewhere between dates three, seven, and never." She innocently went to kiss my cheek, but I caught her lips with mine.

"So there'll be more of these dates?" I stroked my finger over the smooth skin of her cheek, dipping below her jaw to follow the line of her neck down to the shadow between her collarbones.

"You couldn't quit me if you tried." Her breath sounded ragged and tightly controlled as my fingers skimmed over the small swell of her breast.

I raised my eyes to hers, letting my finger trace the outline of her nipple. "Does the third date rule still stand?"

Her kiss-swollen lips parted to speak, but she only nodded when I rolled her nipple between my fingers.

"Okay, then how about breakfast tomorrow morning and dinner tomorrow night?"

Her eyes closed and she hummed in pleasure.

"Or we could combine the two with brunch and call it good." I smiled when one hand clamped over my mouth, silencing me, and the other yanked me closer.

"Okay, brunch it is," I mumbled against her hand.

———

Hailey kept her word and told me to go home after making out in her driveway until my control frayed, unraveled, and disintegrated into dust. I was about thirty seconds from begging when she broke our kiss, pulled her hand from my pants, tucked herself in her bra and called time on our date. From her dilated pupils, flushed cheeks, beard burn and panting, she was in almost as much pain as I was.

"Be here at eleven. Sharp." She stumbled out of the truck and backed her way to the front door where she reached for her purse, but was empty handed.

I spied it on the floor of the truck. Hopping out, I stalked my way over to her.

She held up her hands in defense. "You. Step away. Set the purse down and no one will get hurt."

"Maybe you forgot your purse on purpose." I stood within a foot of her, watching, breathing, waiting.

"That would be ridiculous."

I pinned her to the door with my hips and lifted her hands above her head with one of mine. I ran my nose up her neck to her ear and whispered, "You know what's ridiculous?"

She slowly shook her head.

"Denying ourselves the pleasure of being together for even another day. Another hour. Another minute." I wrapped my lips around her earlobe and sucked.

Her breath hitched and her hips met mine.

"Thought so."

In a flash she grabbed her purse and found the keys. Soon

we were stumbling over shoes and feet into the house as fingers and hands unbuttoned and flung clothing off and away. It didn't matter we hadn't turned on the lights or checked the door was locked behind us; what mattered, the only thing that mattered in the moment, was skin touching skin. Lips, hands, arms, torsos, legs making contact. She tripped on the stairs and I landed on my hands above her. My boxers disappeared, leaving us both naked and eager.

I shadowed her movements while attempting to keep kissing her as our bodies bounced against each other. At the top she gave up the fight. I let my weight cover her, settling between her hips. Her fingers wove into my hair and tugged to the point of pain. I squeezed and stroked her curves, the need to consume her overwhelming me.

After making out with her in the truck twice already tonight, prolonged foreplay seemed redundant. I'd been ready to go since I first saw her earlier. I suspected I wasn't the only one more than ready. My fingers confirmed this when I dipped between her legs.

Never breaking eye contact, I aligned our bodies before thrusting inside of her. We'd had sex once before without a condom, but I'd been too out of my head to pay attention to the new sensation. This time it engulfed me. I gently rocked further into her. Pleasure sparked and spiked over my body, and the brink loomed too close already. I shifted my weight on one forearm so I could touch her, strengthening the connection between us while I stopped the tide threatening to pull me under.

"You feel amazing," I whispered reverently.

"So do you." She shifted and rolled her hips, encouraging me to move.

"Give me a moment, or this will be over sooner than I'd like." I hated to admit I was an inch from losing it like a teen on prom night.

"I love how out of control I make you." Her hands squeeze my ass, encouraging me.

It wasn't the hands on my ass, or the way she felt without a barrier between us which pushed me over the line in a loud roar of pleasure.

It was the words I, love, and you scattered in her sentence.

———

"Stay," she whispered.

So I did.

TWENTY-NINE

Confession:
I don't like to loiter.

Our brunch consisted of bowls of cereal eaten bundled under blankets on her deck. Saturday's sun blazed with the promise of future warm days and summer heat. It wouldn't last and the week's forecast threatened daily rain, so we happily stayed outside despite the chill. She sat on my lap, holding her coffee. My arms encircled her waist under the layers of blankets.

I eyed the hot tub cover. "You ever use it?"

She followed my stare. "Not really. Although the owner always comes by to make sure the chemicals are balanced."

"Ever had sex in it?"

"No!" She squirmed on my thighs. "Have you?"

"In that one? No."

"I meant in general."

I stared at her.

"On second thought, I don't want to know." She grimaced.

"Hey, I have a history. So do you. Doesn't change the fact we're together now. Or make it less."

She lightly kissed my lips. "Are we?"

"Are we what? Going to have sex in the hot tub? Sure, if you want." I braced my hands on the wide arms of the chair and leaned forward.

"Not about the sex. Are we together?" Her voice softened into a whisper, but her green eyes held my gaze.

"Will my answer confirm or negate the potential for hot tub sex?" I arched an eyebrow, buying myself some time.

"Quit stalling." She rose to stand up and I tugged her closer.

"You're the only woman I've had sex with since November." Until I said the words, it hadn't occurred to me we'd pretty much been exclusive since the first time together.

"Really?" The shock of my confession colored the word. "No one else? Not even—"

I cut her off, knowing what she was going to say. "Not even Ashley. Whatever you think you saw, or more likely what she wanted you to think you saw, nothing's happened with her since that party last fall."

"Which party?"

Time to go big or go home.

"She took me to a swingers' party."

"Ohmygod. You went to an orgy?" She struggled to get off my lap, but I held her close.

"First, stop struggling. Second, it wasn't an orgy. Third, it wasn't sexy and you're going to laugh." I told her the briefest story possible about the party, including the weird ferret cage in the corner and my parting words about delicious dip.

She bounced with laughter, throwing her head back. "What's up with the dip?"

I used my thumbs to wipe the tears gathered in the corners of her eyes. "It was really good dip. I should've asked for the recipe."

She regained her composure, only the infrequent giggle bubbling to the surface. "Okay, since we're confessing things, I have a confession, too."

"You want to have sex in the hot tub?" I kissed the side of her head. "Say the word."

"Seriously. Let it go."

"I can't. It would be so warm and you'd be naked. I'd be naked, too." I licked my bottom lip.

"If we get naked, we'll have sex."

"And?"

"I'm enjoying the talking."

"We can talk when we're naked, warm, and I'm inside of you."

"You think you can carry on an entire conversation and have sex at the same time?" Disbelief crinkled her forehead.

"I'd be willing to give it the Tom Cat try."

———

Sitting in the bubbling water, the faint scent of chlorine rising in the steam around us, I learned I could have sex and talk at the same time, but not for very long. Also, sex in a hot tub was less than I'd imagined. The water, despite being wet, created a weird friction. Giving up the fantasy, we sat on opposite sides of the jacuzzi, our legs entwined, and talked.

"Why don't you sculpt in metal?" she asked, her finger trailing along the bubbles on the surface of the water.

"I like wood." I smirked. "Why do you?"

"I like how tough it is. It takes a lot of effort to change its shape or transform it into something new. I love how it can withstand the elements, yet slowly shows its scars and wear with prolonged exposure. Despite slowly breaking down, it exists and is ever changing. Rust is beautiful."

"Says the artist. To shipbuilders, rust isn't considered a good thing."

"Why do you still work as a welder at the yard? You've been doing the same thing pretty much since high school."

"I don't like change?"

"Am I supposed to answer for you?"

"I don't know. I like welding. I'm good at it. I make good money. Why change?"

"It explains a lot." Her foot made a slow path along my shin, heading north toward my thigh.

"Like what? I like my job?"

"No." She gave a subtle shake of her head, water droplets falling off the wet tips of her hair.

"What?"

"You don't like change in general."

I started to protest, and stopped myself. I opened my mouth to deny it, and paused. Truth weighed heavy on my chest, and taking a deep breath required effort.

"I'm right and you know it."

Realization and acceptance crept up my spine. Feeling too hot, I sat up and shoved out of the water. The cool morning air tingled on my skin.

"Where are you going?" She scrambled to sit up in the bubbling water.

"I … inside." I strode across the deck.

"What is it with you parading around naked outside my house?" She swung her legs over the side and gathered up our clothes.

"No one can see us." To prove my point, I lifted my arms above my head and did two jumping jacks. "Look!" I yelled. "I'm naked!"

"Ack! My eyes! My eyes!" Lori screamed from the door behind me.

———

At Lori's screaming, Hailey had hidden her important stuff with our wadded up clothing while I was once again standing in the breeze with my pecker out. Shoving past me while my sister muttered about brain bleach, Hailey had made a mad dash upstairs to put on her clothes. I'd loved the view of her ass bouncing up the stairs.

"I knew it! I knew you were fucking each other." Lori paced inside the kitchen. She was on her third lap around the island.

Sitting at the table, I laughed and sipped my coffee. Luckily, Hailey had thrown my jeans at me before running away.

"Did you stalk us?" I asked, smirking over the memory of standing with my hands on my hips like Superman without a cape. If she wanted to sneak up on us, she would get an eyeful.

"No. I was at Payless Foods. Connie and Sandy were there chatting."

Dread settled in my stomach.

"Imagine my surprise when Sandy shared she saw the two of you kissing in your truck on the ferry late last night."

Fucking gossips.

She made another lap around the kitchen. "So I decided to stop by and see Hailey on my way home."

"And saw my truck in the driveway."

"Yep." She stopped her pacing and hopped on the counter. "Busted."

"Quit glowering at me. You'll get wrinkles."

"I can't believe of all the women on this island, Everett, Seattle, the whole western part of the state, you had to go after my best friend."

"I didn't—"

"Stop." She held up her hand. "I don't want to hear your excuses. I've always defended you and not judged."

I snorted. Where was Hailey? Hiding out upstairs? How long did it take to get dressed? The sound of the shower turning on answered me. Great. Left alone for the inquisition.

"You've judged."

She flipped me off. "You're my big brother. When we were kids you were my idol and my nemesis. Then you discovered girls and your power over them, and my life became a night-mare. All my friends, all of them, except Hailey, had the hots for you. *Ooh, Tom's so cute. Do you think he likes me?* Yuck." She added a gagging sound to emphasize her disgust.

Ah, the memories. I'd been terrible flirting with her friends, encouraging their crushes while knowing I'd never cross the line. "I love you, but this has nothing to do with you."

"It has everything to do with me." Her feet thumped against the lower cabinets. "She's my friend, my best friend. How awkward is this going to be when you break her heart?"

With my arms crossed, I stared down my sister. "It's none of your business. Wait, who said anything about breaking hearts?"

"It's what you do. You leave a trail of women crying over not being able to keep you."

"I never lead women on. Okay, maybe in high school, and those few years in my twenties, but I've grown up. I'm straight with them. Hell, Hailey came on to me."

Her mouth opened and closed. "No she didn't."

"Yes, she did. We're adults."

"She doesn't do one-night stands. She was engaged. To be married this year."

"Maybe you don't know her as well as you think."

"Still, I know you. Gah. Don't do it, Tom. Don't break her heart. She's been through enough."

I set my cup on the table. The coffee had gone cold. "Listen, if I tell you something, something to make you feel better and leave me alone, can you keep it to yourself?"

This was risky, but I needed Lori to shut up and stop with the judgmental bullshit.

"I'd love to hear this." She rolled her eyes and sighed.

"You have to swear it stays between us. No telling Cara or Amy. Or mom."

"Swear." She held up her pinky.

"And no teasing or laughing?"

"Oh, for fuck's sake, I swear."

"I like Hailey. *Really* like her. It scares me, but I haven't so much as glanced at another woman, let alone touched one, all year." In my mind, kissing on New Year's Eve didn't count.

"Like *like* her?" Lori said as if we were two girls in middle school.

I nodded.

Amusement sparkled in her eyes. "Do you love her? Like Tom and Hailey sitting in a tree …" Her voice sing-songed the familiar words.

Had I been paying attention, I would have heard the shower being turned off and footsteps on the stairs. But I was too busy being annoyed and amused by my little sister in a way only an older brother could be.

"Yes. I think I do."

A moment too late I saw Hailey at the foot of the stairs, a mix of shock, horror, delight, and confusion flashing across her features.

"Oops." Spying her too, Lori giggled. "Looks like the cat's out of the bag." She hopped off the counter. "Nothing for me to see here. Gotta go." She continued to ramble as she opened the door. "Ice cream melting in the car. You kids have fun." Halfway to out the door she called out something sounding like "Toodle-loo."

The entire time she babbled, Hailey stood and I sat, frozen in place by my flippant confession.

"Nothing awkward about that encounter," she finally said. "I told you running around naked out there was a bad idea."

"You assumed you have spying neighbors, not a nosey best friend who sneaks into your house unannounced. Serves her right. And it's nothing she hasn't seen before. Four kids, one bathroom, stuff gets seen and can't be unseen."

"The naked part was pretty funny."

"Yeah. A riot."

Her voice dropped lower. "What about the other stuff?"

"That wasn't for you to hear. Not yet."

"No, I imagine not."

"I said it because it's true, but I'm not ready to say it again. Not that it's not true, but this isn't how or why I ..." Again, I reverted to being a tongue tied boy around her.

"I know. I mean, I didn't know. I'm happy to know, but yeah, it's too soon and not the right time, or something." She toyed with the hem of her flannel shirt, which resembled one of mine.

"Did you steal my shirt?"

She studied the fabric held in her fingers. "Yeah, I guess I did. You can't have it back."

Whatever possible moment had presented itself passed into another reality. It was too soon to have serious feelings for her. That much I knew.

What I felt was a whole other thing.

THIRTY

Confession:
I don't like change.

The following Thursday found me sitting around the Dog House's pool table with John. A few random twenty-somethings drank at the bar, asking Olaf questions about the good old days, whatever those were. My dear friend and his bride-to-be were fully, disgustingly entrenched in wedding planning.

John racked up the balls and then took stripes.

"How'd the wedding planning go? You get your balls monogrammed yet?" I teased.

John ignored me and took his shot.

"I'm taking your silence as a yes. I can't believe in a year you've gone from bachelor to married."

"We're not married yet." He scowled at me.

"Having cold feet?" If he was, I'd have to kick my best friend's ass.

"Not at all. I would've kept driving to Idaho and gotten

married at the Hitching Post if she'd said yes. It's the wedding I'm not excited about. All the fuss."

"Hey, didn't you get free cake out of the deal last weekend? Can I fake being engaged and go get free shit?" Why hadn't I thought of this scheme before?

He missed the side pocket. "Trust me, you'd never survive the process. Tom Cats can't be domesticated."

I frowned. "You never know."

"That'll be the day." He laughed. When I didn't joke back, he raised his eyebrows at me, but I lined up my shot and refused to pay attention to him. I frowned at the clock, watching the minutes tick pass. I hadn't seen Hailey since Saturday. Lori's surprise visit and my half-assed declaration had freaked us both out. I'd spent Sunday carving and then had dinner with the family.

———

On Friday, I dropped off a fresh cup of coffee for Bertha, asking about her new grandchild and complimenting her on the lovely framed photo of the sea-monkey on her desk before strolling down the hall to Hailey's office.

Standing in the door was none other than Daryl. He chuckled and posed with his forearm resting on the door jamb above his head like he was right at home. I stopped a few yards away and observed his moves.

He got a few points for his confidence.

Lost a couple on his pose. It was too over the top.

A few more points for laughing at whatever Hailey said.

Ah, and the hand near his mouth, drawing attention to his lips. Yep. I'd used that one often. Another point.

Now his hand was in his front pocket and he rocked forward. I bet he wanted to see if her eyes drifted south.

Not the smoothest move, but effective.

"You like Chinese food?" he asked.

Her response was muffled.

"Yeah, me too. We should get a bite sometime. I know a great place in Seattle. Best dumplings I've ever had."

Asking her out on a date at work took nerve, so he got a point for balls.

"What are you doing on Saturday?"

Nope.

We were done here.

I strode to the door and shoulder bumped him out of the way. "Darryl, does Ms. King have something in her office that needs welding?" I sat down in the chair opposite hers, crossed my ankle over my knee, and made myself at home.

"No, we were only chatting." Hailey smiled at me.

"You taking an unscheduled break? I'm sure Ms. King has plenty of work she needs to get done without you interrupting."

He focused on her, ignoring me. "So let me know if you're free this weekend."

Now he annoyed me. "I don't think she'll be free this weekend. Or any weekend in the future for dumplings with you."

Hailey's pen dropped on her desk blotter. Our eyes met and she mouthed, "What are you doing?"

I shrugged and beamed at her.

Her gaze rested over my shoulder at the door where Daryl still stood.

"Daryl?" I turned around.

He broke away from staring at Hailey. "What?"

"Get back to work." I dismissed him and focused on my woman.

Yep, mine.

He huffed and stomped away.

"What the hell was that about?" she asked, pushing away from her desk, and further from me.

"I don't like him sniffing around you all the time like a dog."

"A dog? That's not nice. Is he peeing on me or are you?"

"Trust me."

"Why?"

"He's me at the same age. With the smug cockiness and the same end game."

"Which is?"

"Sex. It's always sex."

"I don't think that's true for every guy in his twenties," she scoffed.

I snorted. "Darlin', have you ever been a guy before?"

She blinked at me.

"Exactly. We're either thinking about it, planning for it, or remembering it."

"Which one are you right now?"

I gave her a slow, lazy smile. "All three." I turned to her door. "Does your door have a lock?"

"Tom!"

"That's not an answer." I stood to check out the lock situation.

"We're not having sex in my office," she whispered.

I frowned. "No? Too bad. I told Al we're dating and we're all clear there. Thought we could celebrate."

"With work sex?" She frowned, but her lips fought a smile.

"Seemed like a great idea to me. So, what are you doing for lunch?"

"Eating at my desk like usual. Why?"

"Ever had a nooner? We could probably make it to your place and back with time to spare."

A rosy blush crept over her cheeks and neck. "Stop."

"What?"

"Teasing."

"Who said I'm teasing?"

She stared at me.

"Fine. What are you doing this weekend? Or more specifically, come over tonight and spend the weekend with me."

"The whole weekend?"

"Why not? You have plans?

She spun her pen on her desk. "One condition."

"Only one?" I ran my finger over my top lip.

"We spend some of the weekend not naked and in the shop. I want to play."

"We could be naked then, too."

"Around a chainsaw and molten metal?"

I reflexively crossed my legs and put my hands in my lap. "Right. Bad idea. Okay. I'd love to watch you weld."

Her smile was shy and small, but said everything. "Deal."

———

The Allman Brothers blasted from the wireless speakers in the shop. Her choice. I wasn't sure she liked any music of this century. I cut into a cedar log outside while Hailey worked on a smaller project inside involving pic-axes she was turning into a fish skeleton for one of my clients. It was her first commissioned work in years. I'd convinced her to make a collection of smaller pieces for the arts festival in Langley in July. We could split a booth. Already, a row of tiny metal dandelions lined a shelf above my smaller wood pieces.

Occasionally, we'd catch the other staring, but didn't act on it. Seeing her in goggles and an apron affected me more than it should have. I thanked the patron saint of welders she wasn't on my gang at work. I'd never get anything done and probably end up burned, blistered, and blind from not paying attention.

Last night I'd stripped her out of her clothes in the living room and refused to return them until this morning. She padded around in one of my T-shirts barely covering her ass, which was fine with me. I'd locked the doors and set the dead-bolt in case anyone decided to stop by unannounced.

Finishing the feathers on my eagle, I checked out the symmetry of my work. Nodding in approval, I cut the engine. In the relative quiet, I could hear my phone ringing on the bench.

"Hi, Dad," I answered.

"Good, I caught you. You home?"

"Working in the shop."

"I'll be over in five." He hung up. Never one to chit-chat, Dad, like Pops, was a man of few words.

I waved to catch Hailey's attention and she killed her flame. "Dad's coming over."

"Want me to go?" She turned off the gas on her acetylene torch.

"No way. Nothing to hide here. Plus, we're both fully dressed, much to my dismay." I kissed her softly on the lips, once, twice. Despite her safety-goggles, she was gorgeous.

A few minutes later Dad walked into the shop.

"Hi, Hailey, didn't expect you," he greeted her with a hug and a quizzical expression aimed at me.

"Hailey's been working here. We moved her stuff over from town. Figured Lori would have told you," I explained.

"That's awfully nice of you. Never knew you to share your *space* with anyone before." The emphasis on 'space' meant a whole other conversation for another time.

"It sure was," she said, removing her goggles. "Either of you want a beer?"

"You don't have to leave on my account. In fact, this might be of interest to you too, since it involves Kurt."

She paused near the door. "In that case, let me grab the whiskey." She smiled and walked across the lawn to the house.

Dad raised his eyebrow at me and leaned against a workbench. "Your sister know about this?"

"She does. The whole naked truth."

"Which would be?"

"We're seeing each other."

"Casual thing?"

"Not so much, no. Pretty exclusive as a matter of fact."

Dad nodded once. "Your mother gets wind of this and she'll start planning your wedding." He slapped a hand down on my shoulder. "Proceed with caution."

I bit my top lip and reflected on his warning. "Probably shouldn't tell Ellie either."

"You know how the two of them are."

She returned with three beers, but no whiskey. Her worried eyes met mine.

Dad took a big sip and swallowed. "I spoke with Mitchell."

"He's our family lawyer," I explained to Hailey, standing next to her and linking our fingers.

"Right. He got Kurt to drop the suit. It'll all go away like it never happened."

"Wow, that was quick."

"Mitchell gave Kurt a list of eye-witnesses who said he started the fight." Dad's eyes flashed to her. "Also, he presented some things Kurt didn't want to go public."

"What kind of things?" My eyes flicked between the two of them.

"Hailey?" Dad asked.

Her gaze rested on the ceiling for a few beats. "Let's just say there might have been a few permit issues on a couple of his projects."

Dad chuckled. "That's putting it mildly. The biggest issue was the eagle's nest found on a high bluff property he bought here to build his house."

"Get out." I set my bottle down on the wood a little too hard and it wobbled precariously before I caught it. "Eagle's nest?"

She dropped my hand and scratched her cheek. "He moved, and probably destroyed, a nest."

"Holy shit," I said. "You knew about this? Does Fish and Wildlife know?"

"I'm the one who spotted it on the property before he bought it. He kept telling me it wasn't a bald eagle's nest, and wouldn't be an issue. Then one day, gone." She frowned.

"What an asshole," I growled.

"I know. It's a long list of many questionable things he did. When you told me he was suing you, I got in touch with Mitchell, hoping with the witnesses and other stuff, I had enough to scare Kurt away for good." She sounded hopeful, but I wasn't so sure.

"Appears you did," Dad said, smiling. "I have more good news."

"What's that?" I put my arm around her shoulders and kissed the top of her head before whispering, "Thank you."

"It appears the property is recently home to a mated pair of eagles. Guess they rebuilt." Dad studied his fingernails.

"He won't be able to build there." A smile crept across my face.

"Not in the near future. Shame really. The good news is Mitchell convinced him a reputable but anonymous buyer would be happy to take the property off his hands, for a fraction of what he paid, given the nest and all." Dad's eyes twinkled with triumph. He loved nothing more than sticking it to the big guys who wanted to turn Whidbey into another Seattle suburb.

"Oh, really?" I matched his smug grin. "Anyone we know?"

Dad clinked his bottle against ours. "I'm sure you do. It's a small island."

"All's well that ends well." A weight lifted from my shoulders.

"Next time let me know when you get sued. I don't like hearing these things from Mitchell."

"I love that you think there'll be a next time." I pouted out my bottom lip.

"There's a reason we keep a lawyer on retainer. You never know. If not Kurt, there'll be someone else who wants to develop more land, ours or someone else's. For the right price, most people would sell." He frowned, knowing preserving the island he loved against development was an uphill battle.

"Hey, Dad?" I stepped away from Hailey's side. "I'm sorry. I should have told you about the fight and the stupid suit. I was too embarrassed. I mean, hell, I sat in jail for hours. Pops would've killed me."

Dad cupped my shoulder. "Nah, he would've done the same

thing if he were a younger man. Bad enough to talk smack about a man's family, but to insult a lady? No way would Pops have stood for any sort of disrespect."

The last bit was news to Hailey from her soft gasp. I grimaced and ducked my head.

"You got in a fight over me," she whispered, embarrassment coloring her cheeks.

"Um, yeah." I lifted my eyes to hers.

"Really?"

"Don't cry. It wasn't a big deal." I swiped my thumbs under her lashes to catch the gathering tears.

With a quick hop, she jumped into my arms. Her elbows rested on my shoulders and she stared in my eyes for a beat or two before I couldn't stand it anymore and kissed her. I lifted her and rested her on the bench, kissing her as if everything depended upon it.

"Well, I should be going," Dad laughed.

"Ohmygod, I jumped you in front of your father," she whispered against my lips, trying to hide her face on the other side of mine.

"You totally did. I told you, quit attacking me."

She tried to slide down, but I held her in place.

"Nothing to worry about, sweetheart. Tom's mother used to do the same thing to me all the time when we were dating."

I groaned and instinctively stepped away from Hailey, who made her escape, laughing at my horrified expression.

"Thanks for the visual," I said to my amused father.

"No problem. You kids should come to Sunday dinner when you're ready. Hailey, we've always liked you."

Family dinner was the ultimate Donnely blessing. If we were homesteaders back in the day, I think Sunday dinner and Dad's blessing counted as matrimony.

I waited for the panic attack at the thought of getting married. Anxiety scuttled around in my chest and then dissipated. I felt neither a fight nor a flight urge. Instead, laughter bubbled up and I let it escape. Happy, I felt happy.

Both Dad and Hailey stared at me curiously.

"He'll be okay," Dad said. "I was the same. When I fell for Teri, I laughed all the time like I was on the funny gas at the dentist." He gave me a slap to my shoulder, and walked out the door. "Don't let your mother hear about this from Connie. She'll be madder than the Sibley's bull if you don't tell yourself." With a laugh and a wave he was gone.

THIRTY-ONE

Confession:
I'd rather hang out with the guys.

After surviving another couple of weeks of wedding planning, John declared he needed a guys' camping trip to the San Juans. We planned to take my boat because it was the biggest to hold all of us and a bunch of camping supplies. We'd fish and sit around shooting the shit, maybe play some poker, and not talk about anything to do with weddings, brides, or showers.

Sounded like heaven.

We took off early Friday afternoon from work and met at the marina where my thirty-foot cruiser, aka the *Master Baiter,* sat docked, ready to go. Thirty feet for my thirtieth birthday Pops had joked when he gave me the boat. Not sure he ever approved of the name, but he'd smiled and shook his head.

John's brother Jim lived in Arizona and couldn't make it, so he invited Nick and the Kelso brothers, along with Dan the pizza man, to make it an even six.

The late afternoon sun bounced off the water when we

motored into Friday Harbor for supplies. We'd booked a camp-site over on Orcas Island at Moran State Park for Saturday, but Friday Harbor was a good stopover for the night. We could get a real meal, drinks, and sleep on the boat. It would be crowded, but the weather was good enough for some to sleep on the deck.

Carter and Erik jogged up the dock to stake out a place for beers and food. Dan knew a guy who ran a pizza place he wanted to see. We joked about a pizza guy mafia. Dan didn't laugh, which kind of worried me there was a pizza mafia, and I'd gotten myself banned. Life without pizza wasn't worth living. Unless it was the pineapple and jalapeño shit John and Hailey ate.

The guys found a big table at Herb's and ordered a pitcher. They'd made the decision based on a random selection of bras hanging off of a bicycle above the bar. I knew from experience, Herb's had great burgers, so I didn't complain about their criteria. Summer season was a few months away, and with it the main flood of tourists, which meant the bar was mostly empty. Men sat around a couple of tables talking about Blackmouth and the upcoming Coho season. A few waitresses worked the room and used their trays to deflect any wandering hands.

I held my phone in my lap and checked to see if I had any bars or service. A text from Hector caught my eye.

Miss you. Want me to send nudey pics?

I chuckled, and John raised an eyebrow. I still hadn't told the guys about my new domesticated status.

I quickly texted, ***Of you or random naked people? I need more info before confirming.***

I set my phone on my thigh and drank from the glass of beer in front of me. My phone vibrated with an alert and fell to the floor when I tried to grab it.

"Who are you texting?" Erik asked, picking up my phone from the floor. He studied the screen. "Who's Hector and why is he offering you naked pics?" He tossed the phone on the table like it bit him.

"Shut up." I stuffed the phone in my shirt pocket. "None of your business."

"Who's Hector?" John asked. "I can't remember you ever mentioning him."

"And why is he texting you dick pics?" Erik asked.

I flipped him off and drank my beer. Might as well fess up now and get it out of the way before the weekend. "Hector is a code name, not an actual dude."

"Ooh, secret lover," Carter said in a falsetto.

"Is it Ashley?" Erik asked.

I shook my head. "No."

"Are you going to tell us? Because this game of Twenty Questions is fascinating," John huffed. "You're not going to make us list every possible woman in your black book who'd need a code name …" His voice faded away.

I shot him a 'don't you dare' expression. "Dude."

"Holy shit. It all makes sense now."

"What makes sense? What? Who is it?" Carter and Erik said almost simultaneously.

"It's Hailey King," John confirmed, no doubt in his voice.

I nodded.

"Shit! Does Lori know?" Nick asked. "She's going to kill you."

"She knows."

"And you're still breathing?" John joked.

"She caught us in the hot tub."

"Were you doing it?" Erik asked, excitement for details raising his voice.

"No, and if we were, I wouldn't tell you. I was standing on the deck when Lori decided to stop by."

"Dude, you were naked in front of your sister?" Carter gagged. "That's messed up. So wrong."

"Shut up, Kelso."

John leaned into his chair. "So you and King, huh?"

I nodded, a smile spreading across my face. "Yeah."

He appraised me for a minute and then his beard twitched. "Cool. You plan to be good to her?"

"Swear on Pops' grave." I couldn't think of a more solemn vow.

He nodded again, knowing I was serious. "Well, I'll be damned. The Cat's been domesticated."

I ran my tongue over my teeth. "Pretty much."

"You know what I want to say, but I'll reserve it for another time." He raised his glass. "To the women who can put up with the likes of us."

He and I clinked glasses.

"I'm never settling down," Erik said. "I can't see the point. Where's the fun in that?"

"Way too much work," Carter agreed. "Hey, does this mean I can hook up with Ashley now? I've had my eye on her for ages. You know what they say about redheads?"

"They're crazy?" John said.

"True, but they're extra wild when it comes to sex." Carter smiled.

"Ashley's always done exactly what and who she wanted, so it's up to her, but you have my blessing." I chuckled knowing Carter couldn't handle her, but would go down in flames trying. Hell, stranger things had happened. Maybe they'd be perfect together.

Dan rejoined us and we ordered burgers.

Carter craned his neck to survey the bar filled with fisherman. "There are too many guys in this place, where are all of the chicks? Are we getting strippers tonight?"

"No, we are not getting strippers in Friday Harbor, but we can drop you off over on Shaw," I offered. "Pick you up on Sunday on our way home."

"What's on Shaw?" Erik asked.

Nick and Dan chuckled.

"Are there lots of strippers on Shaw?" His eyes widened. "I'll go. Better than sitting around in the rain with you smelly assholes."

"Yeah, lots of chicks and they're not used to young, hot guys being around. I'm sure you'd be really popular." I encouraged him.

"Really? Why aren't we going to Shaw already? Isn't this a bachelor's weekend?"

John was the first to crack. "How do you not know about the nuns of Shaw Island, doofus?"

"Nuns?" Carter and Erik's faces fell.

"Seriously? That's messed up. No way are they going to put out," Erik mumbled into his beer.

Locking eyes for a moment, John and I had a silent conversation. Tonight we passed the wingmen torch to the next generation. I finally understood what he had with Diane, and what was developing with Hailey was better than anything the Kelsos were going to find in a bar or random hookup.

In my head, I heard Pops' voice:

It's about damn time, knucklehead. Oh, and I told you so.

I raised my glass in tribute.

Old man knew what he was talking about.

THIRTY-TWO

Confession:
Sometimes I can be a Sasquatch.

Six showerless men, stinking of fish, campfire smoke, and general manliness arrived in Langley harbor early Sunday evening. We never did drop Carter on Shaw Island, despite his bragging he'd convert the nuns. I had images of him being smacked with a ruler and repeating a bunch of Hail Marys. Then again, he might get off on the punishment. Forty-eight hours was about my limit for guy time and I was grateful to load up the truck's bed with the remainder of our supplies.

"Say hi to Hailey for me," John yelled with a wave as he got in his own truck.

I hadn't said anything about seeing her tonight, but the bastard somehow knew I'd head over to her place. I flipped him off and started my engine.

I didn't bother texting on my way. I wanted to surprise her … if she didn't smell me coming first. I needed a shower. I contemplated how warm the lake might be in April. Much warmer than January, but still crazy cold for swimming. A plan solidified in my head as I turned off the road: me and Hailey in a hot shower.

An unfamiliar black car blocked my usual spot by the garage. In the few moments it took me to decide to back out of the driveway and call her from my house, the front door opened. Hailey exited with the older woman who had sat with her at the funeral.

Seeing my truck, Hailey gave me a big smile and waved. I grinned. I'd missed her. However, there was no way I was getting out of the truck to meet her mom smelling like a Sasquatch. I rolled down the window and said hello, not moving other than turning off the engine.

She said something to her mom and walked over to me, a strange smile plastered on her face. "Why aren't you getting out of the truck? Are you not wearing pants?" She leaned through the window to peek inside.

"Of course I'm wearing pants. What kind of guys' weekend do you think we had?"

She shrugged and the green of her eyes sparkled. "I've heard stories of men in the woods. Did you have a drum circle? Get naked and paint your faces with mud?"

"No one played any drums. Or painted their faces. We offered to drop off the boys on Shaw to visit the nuns."

She laughed and then wrinkled her nose. "What's that smell? Do you have a wet dog in there I didn't see?"

I pushed the button to raise the window. "It's me."

Her fingers pinched her nose closed. "Did you roll in dead fish?" she asked through the closed window.

"No. I should go."

"You can't. My mom's standing right over there and wants to say hello." She waved at her mom, who walked in our direction.

"You really want me to meet your mom after you said I smell like a wet dog?"

"Too late, we don't have a choice. Plus, you've met her plenty of times."

The woman with the same green eyes as her and short gray hair stood beside the truck with a sweet smile and a confused expression. She didn't have Hailey's height, but there was no mistaking the family connection.

I lowered the window again. "Hi, Mrs. King."

"Tom, it's so nice to see you. Why don't you come inside?" She smiled but her nose wrinkled slightly and she took a step away from the truck. "Or we could sit out on the deck with some coffee."

I begged her with my eyes to come up with some excuse as to why I had to suddenly leave without having coffee with her very nice mother.

Instead, she smiled and agreed coffee on the deck was a great idea.

The best I could hope for would to be downwind.

"You two go on ahead. I'll meet you out there."

"Smart, smart. Yes, probably wise not to let you inside of the house." Hailey inhaled before leaning through the window to kiss me with tightly closed lips, clearly holding her breath.

"Nice. Can I shower first? I promise to run through the house as fast as I can."

She picked something out of my beard and held it up for me to see. It was a twig.

"I'm debating which would be more awkward. Waiting around with my mom while you're naked in my shower doing who knows what. Or sitting near enough to you to have a conversation."

Something itched my scalp. I pulled a leaf out of my hair. "Maybe I should throw myself in the lake again."

"Yep, shower it is. No more naked family time." She laughed.

I opened the door to get out and she moved away. "Give me a two minute head start so I'm not breathing your stink trail."

"I missed you, too." I lunged after her, but she was too fast and dodged my grasping hands.

Screaming, she dashed inside of the house. I counted to thirty, and then followed.

"Excuse me, Mrs. King, I'm going to borrow Hailey's shower before joining you for coffee. I apologize for my appearance. I was camping with some friends in the San Juans this weekend." I used my most charming, parental-ass-kissing voice to charm her.

Both women gave me a pained smile and waved me upstairs. I waited at the top of the stairs to overhear how Hailey explained me in her shower.

"He's very handsome, but I hope he doesn't stink this much on a regular basis. We'll have to get you some of those plug-in room scents."

"Mom," she whined. "I swear this is a one-time thing."

"Well, as long as you're happy."

"I am, I really am."

My chest puffed up with pride and I wondered how long her mom planned to stay.

———

After my shower, I discovered one of my stolen shirts sitting on the bathroom counter. I didn't have clean jeans, but all in all I smelled human again.

Hailey met me in the kitchen with a non-parental appropriate kiss and ass grab.

"Thanks for the shirt."

"You're welcome. And so you know, I totally peeked at you naked in the shower."

"I figured. How could you resist?" I smirked. "Sorry about the dirty jeans."

"No problem, you won't be in them for long." She brushed her fingers along my fly.

The sensation fired up my blood and I had to move her hand before things escalated to the point I wouldn't be able to walk outside in front of her mom. "You know what's worse than being naked in front of my sister? Tenting my jeans in front of your mother." I held her grabby hands between mine, lifting them to my lips to kiss her knuckles.

"Fine. But just know the entire time she's here, I'll be imagining you naked." She walked to the slider with two cups of coffee. I raised my eyes to the ceiling and thought about anything but the sway of her hips or her ass in those jeans. Thinking about her long legs around me was the last thing I needed. I distracted myself by making a cup of coffee.

We sat on the deck, making small talk about our families for hours. Or at least twenty-minutes until her mother declared she had to get home to finish a pot roast. I think she said pot roast. Hailey had been rubbing her fingertips along the skin behind her ear, completely distracting me. I loved that spot. It smelled so strongly of her, and when I dragged my whiskers along the same line, she always shivered with pleasure.

"Tom?"

I snapped out of my fantasy. "Yes?"

"Mom's leaving."

"Oh, right. Nice to see you, Mrs. King."

"Call me Angela. You two should come to dinner soon. Do you golf, Tom? I can't remember."

Golfing? Dinner? "My golf game is mostly a round at Island Greens with old clubs."

"You'll be fine. Martin makes more divots than he does shots, but don't tell him I said so."

"Mom, Tom doesn't want to golf with Dad." She sighed. "Don't overwhelm him. He's skittish and might run away." She winked at me.

I wanted to wrap my arms around her from behind and bite the tender skin where her shoulder met the curve of her neck.

Instead, I smiled and aimed my charm at her mother. "I look forward to it. We'll make it a foursome."

Her mom's hand toyed with her necklace and a slight blush colored her skin. I bit the inside of my cheek to hold in my smug smile. Very few women were immune to my charms, and Angela King was not one of them.

The door closed softly behind her when she left. I locked it, and the slider too for good measure.

"Were you flirting with my mother?" She leaned against the couch. "I can't believe you were flirting with my mother." She shook her head with amusement.

I shrugged. "Every woman, no matter her age or marital status, likes to feel charming and beautiful. A little flirting is good for the soul." I stalked closer to her. "Now what were you saying earlier in the kitchen about getting me out of my jeans?"

———

I kept my promise to Dad and showed up for Sunday dinner a week later with Hailey.

We parked near the barn and stared at each other in the silent cab after I turned off the engine. I cupped both of her cheeks in my hands "Ready?" I searched her eyes for the same nervous energy I felt.

She nodded. I gave her the softest kiss, but didn't push for more. Instead, I rested my forehead against hers and shared her breath.

"You?" she whispered.

I rubbed my skin against hers when I nodded yes. "Give me a minute to enjoy this peace before everything changes."

"Everything?"

I retreated far enough so I could meet her eyes. "I don't want to share you. Or this."

Her lips brushed against mine. "You'll be fine." With a squeeze to my hand she reached for her door handle. "Rip the bandaid? One, two, three ..." She jumped out of the truck and jogged toward the front door.

I quickly caught up with her before she could knock. "You're crazy."

"Why?" she asked, slightly breathless. I imagined other ways I'd like to make her lose her breath involving fewer clothes and being horizontal.

"Knocking only makes it awkward." I opened the door. "Mom, Dad? We're here." I grabbed her hand and wove our fingers together.

We discovered Mom in the kitchen. At first she was confused and explained Lori hadn't told her she'd be bringing an extra person.

"Mom, she's my guest."

Mom blinked at me as the cogs in her brain ground against each other, falling into place when she saw our intertwined fingers. Her bachelor son had finally brought home a date.

"Oh, well, then, well, we'll use the nice china." Her hands fluttered around the counter, straightening spoons and spatulas, stirring pots that didn't need to be stirred, and opening the oven door twice despite nothing being inside.

"Teri, it's only me. I've been over to this house a million times since I was a kid," Hailey reassured her.

"Of course you have. No reason to be awkward now." Mom poured herself a large glass of White Zinfandel and added two ice cubes. "Who wants wine?"

I ducked out of the room to find the men folk. The Mariners had an afternoon game. Frankly, I couldn't be around Mom anymore and keep a straight face. Plus, I was honestly worried she'd start talking weddings, or worse, kids.

"Your mom knows now?" Dad greeted me.

"Yep."

"You left Hailey in there with her?" He nodded toward the kitchen.

"Uh-huh."

"Probably for the best."

We watched the game and talked about new players, the young pitcher, and chances for a World Series' run until dinner was ready. When we pulled out our chairs at the table, I noticed Hailey had her own glass of white wine, complete with ice cubes. Cara and Amy each gave me a thumbs-up while Ellie spent the entire meal chatting with Hailey about her family. Over dessert, Lori handed me Noah, who squirmed in my arms, tugged at my beard with his sticky fingers, and spit up on my shirt all within three minutes. Gross.

"Better get used to it," Lori said, full of smugness. "Hailey always said she wanted a bunch of kids."

"Kids and I don't get along." I passed Noah to Hailey, who smiled at her, showing off his Donnely dimple. Little man was making the moves on my woman and he couldn't walk yet. Had to hand it to him; he would be a charmer like his uncle. After wiping the vomit off of my shirt, I held up my hand for a fist bump.

"What are you doing?" Hailey asked.

"I taught him this trick a few weeks ago."

Sure enough he bumped his hand against my knuckles. "See? Taught him everything he knows."

My sisters groaned in unison, but Hailey's eyes softened as she sniffed Noah's ginger curls.

"Did you huff the baby?" I asked in a low whisper.

"Smell him." She tipped him closer to me.

"No thanks, he already puked on me once. We're better off at a distance. Plus, sniffing babies is weird."

"You sniff me."

"That's different." I leaned closer and rubbed my nose near her ear. "Pheromones and all," I whispered, my hand traveling up her thigh and resting close to her hip. Her lips were inches from mine, so I closed the gap to kiss her.

"Not in front of the baby," Lori scoffed, taking Noah.

"Honey, that's exactly how babies get made." Nick draped his arm over her shoulder.

I scooted away from Hailey faster than a bullet, and nearly fell out of my chair.

Everyone laughed at me, including Gramma. "This family needs more grand babies."

"Time to go." I stood and tugged Hailey up with me.

Dad gave me a sympathetic look. "Escape while you can, son."

Female giggling and chatter about combinations of hair and eyes followed us down the hall. I couldn't get outside fast enough.

In the bright light from the moon, she stood and laughed at me. "You should have seen your face inside. You can't let their teasing get to you so easily. Never show weakness. Ninja rule number one."

I scrunched up my brow. "What are you talking about?"

"Your family was giving you a hard time in there. I don't think any of them seriously want us to start having kids tomorrow."

"Even Ellie?" My own grandmother was in on this?

"She probably instigated it. Seriously, you about passed out when you were holding Noah and Lori started in about babies."

"I did not."

She stepped into me and encircled my waist with her arms. "You did. It was cute."

"And the head sniffing? That part of it, too?"

"No, I really do like the way babies smell. It's like laundry fresh out of the dryer."

"Only the dryer is a vagina."

"Gross." She slapped my chest.

"You have to give me a break. I've spent my entire sexual life avoiding getting someone pregnant. Hard to shift gears."

She leaned into my arms. "I really am not ready to have a baby. Lori was teasing about me wanting a ton of kids. Or if she wasn't, she was referring to my Nick Carter phase which coincided with *7th Heaven*."

"You wanted to have kids with a Backstreet Boy?" I tapped her nose with my finger. "That is the most ridiculous thing ever. You shouldn't have told me."

"Why?"

"That's golden material for teasing. So I'm a second choice to Nick?"

"Not at all. Well, not anymore."

I chuckled, and leaned down to suck on her full lip. I gave it a little nip before whispering, "You're a weirdo."

"Yes, but I'm your weirdo." Her hands lifted to my neck and she arched into me.

"I'm the luckiest guy in the world." I picked her up and spun us once.

"My Nick Carter loving teen girl heart thanks you for saying so." She sighed. "But don't tell Nick. He'd be devastated."

"I won't ever mention we had a conversation involving the Backstreet Boys this evening. Trust me."

"Deal."

"Let's go home." I carried her to the truck. "I meant my house, by the way."

"I know. Although, since I have all of my studio supplies there, I consider the shop half mine."

"For some strange reason that doesn't bother me at all." I kissed her forehead. "Weird?"

"Not weird at all. You *like* me." The way she spoke the word caused me to snort.

"I do, especially when you revert to being a teenage girl."

Her eyes widened.

"Wait, that didn't come out right at all."

Her laughter joined my own as we drove the short distance to my house.

THIRTY-THREE

Confession:
I let women down easy. They're satisfied. I'm satisfied. Everything's good.

One evening Hailey and I sat sprawled in the chairs on my porch, watching a warm spring rain drip off the eaves. Each day further trapped me in the web she wove around my heart. I couldn't remember a reason why I'd resisted this. She never made demands and I didn't feel the urge to run or deflect. I fell into dating Hailey like falling off a boat: panicked and fighting at the beginning but floating on the surface with little effort once I accepted I was in the water.

My fingers traced a random pattern on her arm, and she rested her feet across my lap.

Over the past two months, we'd survived going public with parents and siblings, work, and friends. It had all gone well, better than I imagined. No one screamed or tore their clothes when they learned I was off the market. There had been shock, disbelief, and laughter over the idea of me settling down, but all in all, uneventful.

With the exception of Ashley. I hadn't seen or heard from

her. Her silence worried me. I hadn't expected her congratulations, I wasn't that egotistical. Or delusional. I anticipated some reaction from her, especially after Lori's insight.

Then again, no one expects a package of hamburger meat to the head.

I ran into Ashley while grocery shopping. I had been standing in the meat section when the sound of stomping feet approached. I glanced up and got a package of ground beef straight in the face.

"What the hell?" I asked.

"You, Tom Donnely, are an asshole." Her hands rested on her hips and she glared at me.

I picked up the cellophane enclosed tray and set it in the case. "I'm sure many would agree with you, but can you give me the reason this time?" I knew the answer, but I figured she would feel better getting it off her chest in person, in front of the butcher, Connie, Sally, and Sandy, who all conveniently stood off to the side.

"You ladies need some popcorn for the show?" I called over to them.

"No, we're good," Sandy said. "Carry on."

I closed my eyes and shook my head. "Can we do this somewhere less public?"

"Oh, no, this is perfect." Ashley showed her teeth.

"Great," I muttered to myself and braced for the floor show.

"You. You and I were alike. No strings, no commitments, no dating. I got you. I never asked for anything more. I waited. I bided my time."

"We were friends, Ashley. For years."

She snorted. "Right. Friends."

"What else would you call it? We hung out, we enjoyed each other's company and had fun." I kept my voice low. It didn't matter with our attentive audience gathered around us. I thought I saw Connie with her phone pointed in our direction. Sandy's fingers flew across the screen of her own phone. Great.

One of them was probably live Tweeting this entire conversation.

"Ashley, please don't. You're better than a big dramatic scene using meat as a weapon. You're a cool girl. I'm not the right guy."

"You weren't the right guy for anyone. You're not the boyfriend type!" Her voice rose to screech level. "What does Hailey have that I don't? A magical vagina?"

Soft gasps came from the peanut gallery. I stared at the ceiling, my nose flaring as I tried to count.

"I'm not doing this here." I set my basket on the floor and marched toward the entrance.

"And another thing?" Ashley called from behind me.

"What?" I paused and turned, waiting for another round of crazy-woman.

"You're banned from the coffee huts. Don't come around asking for your morning hit or afternoon pick-me-up anymore." She spun on her heel and stomped past me, knocking over a display of paper towels on the way out of the store.

Someone clapped at the end of the aisle. I needed to get out of here.

"So it's official with you and Hailey King?" Connie's voice dripped with sweetness. "We're so happy to hear the good news."

What did I say? Thanks? I rubbed my ear and shook my head. "Okay then, I'll let her know you send your congratulations," I responded politely, slowly backing away until I reached the far end of the aisle.

Outside, I inhaled fresh air and stood in the misty rain for a moment before I texted Hailey the short version.

You missed a great new performance of This is Tom's Life at Payless Foods, starring Ashley as the angry woman. Chorus played by the Island Gossips.

I heard it was amazing and people applauded at the end.

What?

Connie sent me the video. You're very handsome in that flannel. Come over and I'll give you an afternoon pick-me-up.

*Oops. Forgot the ;) *

I smiled despite the ridiculous situation. Damnit, I loved her.

My breath caught in my throat.

I loved her.

The new truth washed over me.

I was in love.

THIRTY-FOUR

Confession:
I think romance is for suckers.

For thirty-three years, I shared my birthday with Pops on May 18th. Hence the middle name and our close bond. To honor him, I decided to go fishing since we never got another season out on the water together. However, Hailey had other plans for the weekend. Plans she enlisted John and my family to execute. They were all in cahoots together, plotting to take me down, rejoicing in my demise, and reveling in my comeuppance.

Instead of John and my dad meeting me at the marina Friday afternoon, Hailey stood at my slip when I walked down the dock. Gorgeous in some sort of flowing, non-boat appropriate dress, she could have been one of those old ship prow figureheads.

"Surprise!"

I hated surprises.

"I'm kidnapping you for the weekend."

"With my own boat?" I asked warily, stopping a few yards away.

"Don't find flaws in my plot." She closed the distance between us and gave me a soft kiss.

"Okay. Where are you forcing me to take you?" I dropped my bag and pulled her against me.

She stuck out her tongue. "I'm not telling you."

"How will we get there?" I kissed her and sucked her tongue into my mouth.

"It's a need to know basis. Right now, all you need to know is to head north up Saratoga Passage."

"Okay, that doesn't really limit our options."

"Maybe I'm taking you to China."

"We'll never make it to work on Monday."

"Fine. Not China."

"Canada?"

"Nope. Quit stalling. This will be fun. The MB is all stocked thanks to your dad."

"Then what are we waiting for?" I swept my arm in front of her. "After you."

———

Clouds blocked the sun before we hit Oak Harbor and the wind created white-caps on the water. After crawling into the queen size berth, Hailey changed into jeans and a down jacket. She handed me a vest and my knit hat. The calendar said mid-May, but this felt like an early spring storm brewing.

I checked the tide chart and determined we'd miss the slack water when we hit Deception Pass. I hated going through the pass with its eddies, rip currents, and the stray logs swirling through the racing, choppy water. At least the tide would be against us. More work, but more control meant an easier passage.

Flanked by steep, rocky cliffs dotted with pines, we passed under the twin arched spans of the bridge. I steered us closer to the southern shore and slowed, wondering if she remembered the last time we were at the park. I know I'd never forget our picnic table.

"Having happy memories?" she asked, stepping close enough so I could wrap an arm around her.

I squeezed her closer. "I am. One of the best motorcycle rides of my life."

"I'd hope so. Do most of them have head at the halfway point?"

"Only the best ones." I dragged my teeth over the line of her jaw. "Speaking of, even though my birthday isn't until tomorrow, when do I get my birthday blow job?"

She snorted in response. "Is that a thing?"

"It isn't now, but I think it should be a new tradition."

Her fingers traced my growing wood, its outline clear through my jeans. "Where did you have in mind?"

I blinked at her, not understanding the question. "The usual place. In your mouth."

"No, I meant on the boat or later."

I steered us around the small islands to the north and into the calm water of Rosario Bay before dropping anchor. "Here works fine."

I kissed her while turning to face her in the small aisle between the captain's chair and the dinette. With the poor weather, we were the only boat in the bay, giving us all of the privacy in the world. I gave her a devilish grin and lightly pushed on her shoulders until she caught on and knelt in front of me.

Sexist, chauvinistic, whatever some people might call it, there was something so hot about seeing a woman on her knees in front of me. Unless she was standing and bending at the waist, nothing beat this view.

She pulled down my zipper and kissed me through my boxers before her warm breath brushed against me. Once again her hot mouth contrasted with the cool air as she licked and sucked. Her eyes fixed on mine for a few seconds and I almost lost it. Unexpected emotions crashed over me. I touched her cheek and fought the urge to tell her how I felt. Her hand stroked my base, adding to the sensation of her mouth. She hummed and I felt it vibrate deep under my skin. In this position, I couldn't touch enough of her. Other than her head and face, the rest of her was too far out of reach.

A brilliant idea popped into my head.

"Stop," I whispered.

She obeyed and sat on her heels, with her hand still around my shaft. "What?" She released me.

"I have a better idea." I held out my hand to help her stand, then pulled her into the berth with me. Struggling out of my jeans, I unbuttoned her shirt at the same time. My multi-tasking resulted in a tangle of limbs and clothes, and was completely unproductive.

"Take off your jeans," I said, attempting to remove my boots.

"It's cold." She pouted, but complied.

"I'll warm you up."

Once naked, I pulled her on top of me. She rubbed herself against me while we kissed, but I had other plans. "Flip around," I said with a small slap to her ass.

She paused in nipping and biting my neck.

"Flip around," I said, again, this time with a slightly harder slap.

She wiggled her ass, but didn't move.

I pinched her nipple and she yelped, but scrambled to change her position. Her mouth found my dick again and I trailed my tongue between her thighs, using my hands to open her to me.

Inside our small cocoon, only the sound of water splashing the sides of the boat and rain falling on the deck above us, we licked, sucked, and kissed our way to simultaneous orgasms. I was certain our moans carried over the water and anyone on the shore could have heard us, but in the moment it felt like we were the only two people in the world.

———

The storm delayed us in the bay for an hour until finally letting up enough to let a weak sun break the clouds. Under the covers inside of the cabin, we watched the light brighten through the hatch above our heads. She lay across me, and I drew lazy circles on her arms and down her spine.

"So far this is the best birthday of my life."

"Didn't you get this boat for one of your birthdays?" she asked without lifting her head.

"I did. Still this one beats it."

"And didn't you get your land when you turned twenty-five?"

"Yep. This one's still my favorite."

"Spending it in Rosario Bay in a storm?"

I paused my movements until she turned her head to focus on me. "I'm spending it with you."

A slow, blinding smile lit up her face. "Better than the best birthday cake?"

I nodded and licked the corner of my mouth. "Sweeter, too."

The blush I loved spread across her cheeks.

"We could stay here," she suggested. "Although, I'm not sure we have any real food, but there's wine."

"Where are we going, by the way? Have I mentioned I hate surprises?"

"You seem to like this one so far." Her hand trailed over my navel and further south, teasing me until I stirred.

I gripped her fingers. "Okay, I'm liking this surprise, but you need to tell me where we're going so I can get us there."

A shy smile tugged at her mouth. "Oh, some place up in the San Juans." She shifted so she could kiss me.

I opened my lips and my tongue brushed hers, the kiss escalating quickly. She climbed over me and lifted my hands to my shoulders, lacing her fingers with mine, and trapping me between her thighs. I could have escaped if I wanted, but I wasn't a fool.

"Where in the San Juans? Friday Harbor?" I asked.

"No," she whispered against my lips.

"Visiting the nuns on Shaw?" I rolled my hips into her.

"So wrong to bring up the good Sisters while naked and grinding yourself into me." She met my thrusts. "Don't you think?"

With the right angle I could slip inside of her, if she lifted her hips a little. Reading my mind, she did. I moaned and her breath caught in her throat when I thrust deep within her.

She sat up, but held my hands. Her cheeks were flushed and her nipples peaked.

"You're beautiful," I said because it was true.

Her full lips were swollen from my mouth.

"I love your mouth," I said.

She smiled.

"I love your boobs."

She pursed her lips.

"I love there is a flower the exact shade of your nipples."

She blushed.

"I love being naked with you, but I love when you're clothed, too."

She leaned forward to kiss my lips, lifting our hands to her boobs and releasing mine. I held her soft weight and gently squeezed.

Still moving above me, but not racing toward her release, she stared into my eyes. In the swirls of green and gold, I saw her heart, and my future.

"I love all of you." I closed my eyes because I hadn't wanted to say those words for the first time during sex. What an asshole move. I had plans. Big, elaborate, cheesy plans involving candles and a fancy dinner, and maybe flowers and music. Feeling like a noob, I opened my eyes and my mouth to apologize.

"I love you, Tom." Her words shattered me.

"I love you," I repeated.

"I love you," she echoed.

"I love you." I traced my finger over her cheek, tucking a strand of hair behind her ear.

"I love—"

Her finger silenced me. "Show me."

I rolled us over and took control, loving her with every thrust and touch. My lips brushed her cheek near the corner of her mouth. "I love you."

"*A chuisle mo chroí,*" I whispered.

A happy sigh escaped her lips. "I know."

———

Close to midnight, we arrived at the Roche Harbor Resort, the most romantic location in the San Juans. I didn't balk when she told me. I wanted her naked and all to myself for the weekend, and couldn't think of any reason to complain. Lights illuminated quiet buildings and empty pathways, continuing the feeling we were alone in the world. The constant sense of loneliness I'd fought for years had disappeared. Her hand warmed mine as we walked to our cabin.

Inside were two bedrooms on the lower level and upstairs a living room with a fireplace shared the open space with a kitchen. I immediately made plans to have sex in every room. We had the weekend. Easily accomplished. The wrought iron headboard could prove interesting, too.

Everything had closed at midnight, leaving us to feast on wine and the snacks Hailey had packed. The fire I built warmed the room as we ate.

I yawned and leaned against the leather couch. "Thank you."

"For what?" Sitting on the floor, she rested her head on her hands near my hip.

"For everything." Content, sleepy and warm, my eyes grew heavy.

"Come on, sleepy. Let's go to bed." She stood and pulled my hand.

"I can't believe the following words are about to leave my mouth, but can we go to sleep? I could cuddle, but I'm too tired for sex. Rain check?" I opened one eye to gauge her reaction to find her yawning, too.

"I'd probably fall asleep on you and crush your delicate man-ego. I better take the rain check."

I padded down the stairs to our room. "Idaho, you've laughed with your face inches away from my most prize possession. My ego was crushed months ago."

She managed to pull off an expression which might have been considered sheepish if it weren't for the amusement in her eyes. "Sorry about that."

"No, you're not." I fell face first on the big, soft white bed.

When she didn't respond, I turned my head.

"I think your ego will make it."

"It might need resuscitation in the morning." I lifted my arms to reach in her general direction. "Come to bed, so I may spoon you."

Laughing, she did a slow, sleepy intimate and beyond sexy strip of her clothes. Yawning, she climbed under the covers next to me and rolled to her side.

I pulled her curved body against mine, sliding my knees behind hers, and wrapping my arm around her waist to cup her breast.

"I love you," I whispered.

"I know."

"Why do you keep saying you know?" I frowned and moved closer so our skin touched in as many places as possible.

"Because you've shown me for months how you feel." She

rolled to face me, resting her thigh on top of my hip. "With your body, your words, and your actions."

"I have?"

She nodded, and in the moonlight, I could see the truth in her eyes. "I love you. Maybe I always have."

"I know." I kissed her softly, but deeply.

Despite saying I was too tired for sex, my body craved hers. She responded to my kiss and guided me to her. Facing each other on our sides, we found a slow rhythm, allowing us to keep kissing while I rocked inside of her. Each movement brought us closer, our breaths slowed and synched. My heart raced, and holding my hand against her chest, I felt hers keeping the same rhythm. I reached between us to stroke her, bringing her closer to a place of pleasure where her mouth would open and a low moan would gather in her throat before being exhaled. I loved that sound, and the feeling of her tightening around me as I moved. When she got there, I followed, not crashing or raging, but with a quiet explosion.

As I drifted into sleep, I listened to the wind tapping branches against the windows. Moonlight spilled over the bed, casting the rest of the room in shadow. Her breathing deepened and slowed as she fell asleep. Peace enveloped me. This was now my life.

EPILOGUE

The last time I wore a suit had been Pops' funeral. I tugged at my shirt cuffs under my jacket and stared at Hailey's reflection through the mirror. She wore a pale blue, short strapless dress and her curled hair skimmed her shoulders.

"You're beautiful."

"I know." She grinned and twirled for my benefit, revealing a peek of lace under her full skirt.

The small glimpse of lace turned me on more than it probably should have. "I feel like we're going to prom." I attempted to adjust my tie, a Douglas tartan in honor of John's mom.

"I know what you mean by that, and no, I'm not having sex with you at the reception." She stood in front of me and loosened my tie so she could retie it properly.

"How about after? I know what weddings do to you women. Turns you into hellcats." I smirked and tried to kiss her.

She dodged my pursed lips and patted my now straight tie. "Hellcat?"

I held her in front of me by her hips. "Completely wild and out of control. I can't wait."

"You're ridiculous." She gave me a quick peck to the lips and then ducked under my arms to escape.

"I know." Those two words had become our code for saying I love you as often as possible. We still said those three words, but in public or at work, "I know" worked better. Every time she said it, I smiled, knowing without a doubt, she meant it.

I'd marry this girl someday, but not today.

Today, I played the role of best man to my wingman, my best friend and brother. Two years ago we catted around, acting like boys who would always be boys, and having what we thought were the best years of our lives. This last year proved how very wrong we'd been about the last part. I'd envied him and chided him in equal measure until Hailey crashed into my world … again. I finally understood what Pops had been telling me.

"Ready?" I asked.

Her eyes met mine, searching and seeing straight to my soul. Answering my yet to be asked question, she replied, "Yes."

———

I couldn't prove we were set-up, but the odds of Hailey catching the bouquet in a crowd of thirty, with only two other single women, were ridiculously high. I had offered to take Diane's garter and save John the trouble of throwing it to me. He'd scowled. Diane laughed when she told me she didn't have one.

I loved Diane like a fourth sister and said as much in my toast.

"So despite my best efforts to charm Diane with offers to hunt geoducks, she fell for John. I suspect it was love at first sight, despite taking them months to figure out the obvious." I let my eyes wander to Hailey. "To my best friend, the second luckiest man in the world, and the woman who loves him." I raised my glass to complete the toast.

When I sat down, Hailey leaned over to whisper in my ear, "Second luckiest?"

"A very distant second." I circled my arm around her, resting my fingers on the hidden words curving around her ribs. "*A chuisle mo chroí.*"

———

So there you go. A year in the life of Tom Cat Donnely. A birth, a death, a bar fight, and a wedding. I can't wait to see what life brings me next. Marriage? Definitely. Kids? Thinking about it. Spending the rest of my life loving a girl named Idaho? I'm the luckiest guy in the world.

NOTE FROM DAISY

Thank you for reading this Wingmen novel. I hope you enjoyed Tom's story. I had the best time writing his downfall, I mean, about him falling in love. Thanks for all of your support for these characters and this series.

Keep reading for the first chapter of the next Wingmen book, *Anything but Love*.

Be sure to subscribe to my mailing list to receive updates, new release alerts and an exclusive ebook as a thank you!

SNEAK PEEK

ANYTHING BUT LOVE

You know what's awesome? Sunshine, the beach, and a cold beer. The only thing that improves on that trifecta is being naked.

———

Sitting around the resort's pool, Carter and I start a drinking game. Every time we see a dude in a man bun, we drink.

Bad decision.

Really stupid game.

We're seriously buzzed in an hour.

Too many hipsters and wannabes from LA around this over-priced hotel.

This place is crawling with them like a horde of fedora wearing zombies.

An all-inclusive resort isn't typically our speed. As two regular guys from Whidbey we kind of stick out, but passing on the deal we got would have been stupider than most of the outfits on the hipsters. Our beards help us blend in a little bit. Not sure that's a good thing or not.

Getting off the island for a long weekend of beers, sun, and boobs is exactly what I need. Since I quit Useless Bay Coffee to start my own roasting business, I've been working hundred-plus-hour weeks.

When our mom found the deal for cheap through her travel agency, Carter and I jumped at it. Actually, he jumped and booked it, then told me he'd drag my sorry, pale ass onto the plane to Cabo if he had to.

I should be nicer about the hipsters. My business partner, Jonah, looks kind of like these guys with his tats, stretched earlobes, and undercut. Somehow on Jonah, the look is authentic. Like he could kick ass at a punk show, but also has mastered the art of creating perfectly foamed milk.

I suggest another drinking game: real or fake. With all the minuscule bikinis, it's not hard to tell who is au natural and who could be on a reality show about plastic surgery.

Not that I'm complaining.

Boobs are boobs.

Buzzed and a little bored, I suggest we go paddleboarding or some other water sport.

Carter lowers his sunglasses and thumbs to the other side of the pool where two women in thong bikinis lie on their stomachs. "Nah, I'm happy with the view here. Catch you later."

"Suit yourself."

I tromp over the hot sand down to the water, cursing that my shoes are sitting next to my abandoned lounge chair. Nodding at Pedro in the equipment rental kiosk, I grab a board and paddle.

I'm not saying I'm into water sports, not the kind that immediately comes to mind if you've ever watched porn, but there's something about being out on the water that speaks to me. Could be growing up on an island.

Maybe it was all the time we spent as kids on our dad's boats.

When we were young, Dad bought a twenty-nine foot

wooden sailboat from the seventies that he restored with Gramps. As his construction business took off, the boats got newer, bigger, and nicer. Until his business partner turned out to be an asshole and embezzled all but a thousand dollars out of the business accounts, then disappeared. Ten years later, we're still picking up pieces after everything crumbled.

Dad still has the wooden sailboat. Unless Carter or I take it around the island, or up to the San Juans, it sits on a trailer surrounded by weeds behind my parents' house.

I balance up on the board, bending my knees as I ride over the small waves crashing toward the beach. Past the shore, the swells gently roll, leaving smooth water in between sets. Nothing but clear skies and blue water through the lens of my Ray-Bans.

To the right a tall cliff, more an outcropping of rocks, juts into the water, isolating our hotel from the Pacific Ocean. My curiosity piqued, I head in that direction. I've heard there's a place called Lover's Beach near here. Sounds like it's a nude beach, or at least topless.

Sadly, the only breasts I spy are on a bunch of pelicans perched on the rocky cliffs. More sun-bleached cliffs extend farther west heading toward the famous natural arch. I paddle by the arch and pivot to return to the resort when a splash off one of the rock islands catches my attention.

A whoop follows another splash.

What look like seal heads bob in the water.

As I approach, I see a body fall from the cliff.

No, not fall, dive.

People are diving from a giant rock in the water. By choice.

I drift on the water, not getting too close to where the divers are hitting the surface. A small group of boats and kayakers crowd the surrounding cover. People on the beach stand and watch as well.

The guys in the water confidently swim near the sharp rocks, their strokes guiding them away from the undertow that would crash them into the jagged edges. Timing their exit, they wait until the water is high enough to allow a handhold on the rock wall. With ease, they pull themselves up the face. At the top, hollers and back slaps greet them.

Someone from above yells down to me to try it out. I smile and wave them off. Not right now. All this sun and the gentle rocking of the water against my board have amplified the beer from earlier, clouding my judgment.

Maybe on our last day tomorrow.

————

After dinner we decide to leave the resort and explore town. "Explore" is code for going on the prowl. The resort is great, but in terms of hooking up, it's been a lot of nothing. Sadly, all-inclusive doesn't include hook-ups. Too many couples and too many hipsters.

Loud music pulses from the bars lining the main street off the beach. Almost all the places have open windows that take up most of the exterior walls. People in various states of inebriation loiter around and line the sidewalks. I brush past two girls leaning over the window-counter of a club blasting Katy Perry. They're grabbing anyone who walks by to kiss their friend wearing a white veil.

As we pass, I feel a thwack to my head and turn.

One of the women is holding a long, pink, inflated penis, and telling by her sloppy grin, she's the one who hit me in the head with an inflatable dick.

Carter is laughing too hard to speak, but slurs out, "You're a legitimate dickhead now, bro."

A thump to his head with another inflatable super-dick stops his laughter. "That hurt!"

"Sorry. I'll buy you a shot to make up for it." A sunburned blonde rests her boobs on the windowsill. "Or I can rub it and make it all better."

Carter stops short and leans towards the cleavage as if

pulled by a magnet. "Can I choose what you rub it with?"

The girl's mouth opens, but it's her friend who comes back with a reply. "You touched my dick, I'll return the favor and touch yours."

I about choke and shove him into the bar ahead of me. "If he doesn't take you up on that offer, I will."

We shoulder our way through the crowd to their spot at the window.

"Ooh, are you two identical twins? Like those guys who redo houses on TV? I've always liked blond guys." A redhead with a gleam in her eyes begins petting my shoulder. She reminds me of Ashley back home. "That's hot."

Carter's eyes are focused on the purple lace peeking out from her shirt.

"It's hot that an egg splits in two at conception?" How is that more appealing?

Her mouth hangs open a little as her eyes try to focus on my face. "What?"

"Nothing." Carter shoves my shoulder. "My brother is trying to be funny. It's his attempt to make up for being the ugly twin. Right, Erik?"

"We're not even twins." I elbow him.

Ginger girl's face falls. "Oh, that's too bad. I've always wanted to be with twins."

Carter and I stare at her, then both shudder. No way. No. We step away from each other at the same time.

I scratch above my ear. "I'm too sober. I need a drink."

"Let's do shots!" the veiled woman shouts.

"Tequila!" they all scream and clap their hands.

I volunteer to go to the bar for shots and beers.

Two of the inflatable-dick-wielding girls squeal about their favorite song playing, and drag me by my hands to the dance floor. They sandwich me between them as they screech out their love for the pop singer, the guy in the lyrics, and each other.

I spin the one in front of me, trying to reclaim a little bit of personal space. She follows my lead, allowing me to step out of the girl-sandwich before she slams back into her friend. Both go off balance and tilt into me, causing me to grab the hips of a woman in a backless green dress to steady myself.

Rather than shoving me away, she keeps dancing. My hands rest on her swaying hips.

Okay, this works. I move closer, not like a typical club asshole or a dude in a body spray commercial, but close enough I can feel her body heat.

The purple tips of her long hair brush against my arms as she moves in front of me, her body inches from touching mine. The floral scent of her shampoo mixes with something beachy and tropical on her skin. She smells like vacation sex. Blood begins to rush toward my cock and I still haven't seen her face.

Two pairs of arms wrap around my middle from both sides. Now I'm the meat in a triple-decker sandwich.

"We thought we lost you!" one of the blondes screeches.

"We're thirsty." The other one pouts. Somehow her thirst requires her to shove her breasts at me.

Distracted, it takes me a moment to realize purple-tip girl has disappeared into the crowd.

"I'll get us some shots." I wiggle myself out of their grip.

At the end of the bar, I find a spot to stand.

Next to me a guy shouts at the person on the other side of him. He's tall, but shorter than I am by a couple inches, and I can see where his hair is thinning on top. Given he's not that broad in the shoulders, the recipient of his anger must be petite because I can only see her bare arm behind him. By the tone in his voice, she must be a wife or a girlfriend. No guy trying to pick up a woman would ever use that tone. Unless he is a complete asshole and being an asshole is what gets him laid.

Her voice carries over the music. "Stop being a jealous prick. I wasn't dancing with that guy."

"He was behind you, with his hands all over your ass. Trust me, you made it perfectly clear you were interested." He steps closer to her and mutters something about never forgetting who's paying for this trip.

When she moves out of his shadow, I catch a glimpse of dark hair with purple tips. "Damien, stop being an asshole. Maybe if you ever decide to dance with me, I won't have to dance by myself."

The bartender stops in front of me, and I order tequila shots for the army of bridesmaids currently being entertained by my brother.

"You want to flirt with every guy in here all night, fine. I'm not going to stand around and watch. If I want to waste money on trashy women, I'll go to one of the strip clubs down the road."

"Did you just compare me to a stripper?" Her voice rises, nearing an octave only dolphins can appreciate.

"If you dance like one, you might as well be one."

I let my gaze travel down her body. She's not even showing any cleavage in her green dress. Hell, most of her thigh is covered, too.

"I hate it when you drink too much and get like this." When she turns, I let my focus rest on the small dimples at the very bottom of her back, right above the curve of her ass. She's not skinny and I'm not sure if there's a right angle on her body. Her waist narrows about the roundness of her bottom. How had I missed the perfection of it on the dance floor?

A sharp jolt to my shoulder brings my focus back up. "Quit checking out my fiancée, asshole."

Whoa.

"I'm not your fiancée! Do you see a ring on this finger?" She shoves her left hand in his face before tucking all but her middle finger down. "Or this one?"

Two beers and a tray of tequila shots appear before me on the bar. I motion for two more tequilas and hand the bartender a bunch of pesos.

He pours the additional shots. I take one, down it, and flip the glass on the bar. No lime or salt needed. The burn hits the back of my mouth as I shake my head. I lift the other shot and meet the green eyes of the woman staring at me.

"Here." I hand her the glass. "Sounds like you need this."

"What does that mean?" the jerk asks, puffing out his chest as he attempts to appear bigger.

She takes the shot and tipping her head back, swallows it. Her face contorts for a second before she licks her lips and gives me a grin. "Thank you."

"Now you're letting strange men buy you shots? I can't even believe this. Who are you?" He slaps his hand down on the bar.

"I doubt he had time to roofie me, given that we've been standing here next to him the whole time. In case you were worried about my safety." Her tone is dry and the smile is gone.

Lifting another shot, I nod. She takes it and downs it like the other one, fast and smooth. Like a champ.

"You get drunk and puke, I'm not holding your hair." Now he's full out scowling. His hands grip his biceps as he puffs out his chest like a rooster in some sort of exaggerated macho posturing.

I've had enough. The last thing this night needs is for me to be in the middle of some lame-ass lovers' quarrel. But I can't stop myself from one, final parting shot.

I lean into her space. Even though the entire bar smells like the bottom of a tequila bottle, her scent of sun and coconut surrounds me. I don't whisper. Nah, I want him to hear me. "His penis better be enormous."

Keeping my focus on her, I slowly lean away and reach for the tray of shots.

A fist makes contact with my jaw. Shock more than pain sends me reeling back a step.

ACKNOWLEDGMENTS

A big thank you to everyone who takes the time to read this book and leave a review. I know your time is precious and there are so many good books being published these days that it's impossible to keep up with TBRs and new releases. The fact that you made time to read my book means the world to me.

Readers bring my stories to life. Without you, these books would just be words on a page or computer. Thank you.

Huge thanks to my husband and family for continuing to support this crazy writing life.

A big thank you to Heather for giving CoaRTC a thorough (and often tear-inducing funny) read-through. Thank you to Ashley, Dianne, Traci, and Kelly for reading early and very messy drafts—your feedback is always invaluable. Penny Reid, thank you for being brutal. The book is better for it.

Thank you to Melissa Ringsted for correcting my sins against grammar and Marla Esposito for her eagle-eye proofing. (Any remaining errors are my own.) Thank you to Julianne Burke at Heart to Cover for a gorgeous cover and to Jennifer Beach for the updated interior design.

Many thanks to early readers and bloggers, who shared their

enthusiasm and love for this book, including: Mandy, MJ, Tara, Laurie, Lisa, Tiffany, Beth, Lynsey, Kiersten, Debbie, Charleen, Lori, Daiana, Margie, Margaret, Charlene, Erika, Teresa, Jiff and Stacy.

Special thank you to my agent, Meire Dias at Bookcase Literary, for believing in my work and wanting to bring it to the rest of the world.

Thanks in advance for writing a review, telling a friend about Tom Cat, or reaching out to let me know you enjoyed this or any of my other books. Hearing from readers is the best part of publishing.

Happy Reading!

xo

Daisy

OTHER BOOKS BY DAISY

Wingmen

Ready to Fall

Confessions of a Reformed Tom Cat

Anything but Love

Better Love

Small Town Scandal

Wingmen Babypalooza

The Last Wingman

———

Love with Altitude

Next to You

Crazy Over you

Wild for You

Up to You

———

Modern Love Stories

We Were Here (prequel to Geoducks)

Geoducks Are for Lovers

Wanderlust

———

Bewitched Series

Bewitched

Spellbound

Enchanted

Charmed

———

Wicked Society

Get Witch Quick

Someday my Witch Will Come

Four Witches and a Funeral

———

Stand Alones

Tinfoil Heart

———

Want a reading list?

www.daisyprescott.com/books/

To keep up with my latest news and upcoming releases, sign up for my mailing list.

www.daisyprescott.com/mailing-list/

ABOUT DAISY

Daisy Prescott is a USA Today bestselling author of small town romantic comedies. Series include Modern Love Stories, Wingmen, Love with Altitude, as well as the Bewitched and Wicked Society series of magical novellas. Tinfoil Heart is a romantic comedy standalone set in Roswell, New Mexico.

Daisy currently lives in a real life Stars Hollow in the Boston suburbs with her husband, their rescue dog Mulder, and an indeterminate number of imaginary house goats. When not writing, she can be found in the garden, traveling to satiate her wanderlust, lost in a good book, or on social media, usually talking about books, bearded men, and sloths.

Mailing list
www.daisyprescott.com

f facebook.com/daisyprescottauthorpage

🐦 twitter.com/Daisy_Prescott

📷 instagram.com/daisyprescott

BB bookbub.com/authors/daisy-prescott